Nonsensibility

Nonsensibility

Or Finding Love, Freindship, Pride, Sensibility, Persuasion, Dilemma, and Creative Spelling in Mansfield Abbey

A Comical Mash-up of the Classic Jane Austen Novels

Valerie Estelle Frankel

Other Works by Valerie Estelle Frankel

Henry Potty and the Pet Rock: A Harry Potter Parody

Henry Potty and the Deathly Paper Shortage: A Harry Potter Parody

Buffy and the Heroine's Journey

From Girl to Goddess: The Heroine's Journey in Myth and Legend

Katniss the Cattail: The Unauthorized Guide to Name and Symbols

The Many Faces of Katniss Everdeen: The Heroine of The Hunger Games

Harry Potter, Still Recruiting: A Look at Harry Potter Fandom

Teaching with Harry Potter

An Unexpected Parody: The Spoof of The Hobbit Movie

Teaching with Harry Potter

Myths and Motifs in The Mortal Instruments

Winning the Game of Thrones: The Host of Characters & their Agendas

Winter is Coming: Symbols & Portents in A Game of Thrones

Bloodsuckers on the Bayou: The Myths and Tales Behind HBO's True Blood

The Girl's Guide to the Heroine's Journey

Choosing to be Insurgent or Allegiant: Symbols, Themes & Analysis of the Divergent Trilogy

Doctor Who and the Hero's Journey: The Doctor and Companions as Chosen Ones

Doctor Who: The What Where and How

Sherlock: Every Canon Reference You May Have Missed in BBC's Series

Symbols in Game of Thrones

How Game of Thrones Will End

Joss Whedon's Names

Pop Culture in the Whedonverse

Women in Game of Thrones: Power, Conformity, and Resistance

History, Homages and the Highlands: An Outlander Guide

The Catch-Up Guide to Doctor Who

Remember All Their Faces: A Deeper Look at Character, Gender and the Prison World of Orange Is The New Black

Everything I Learned in Life I Know from Joss Whedon

Empowered: Symbolism, Feminism, and Superheroism of Wonder Woman

The Avengers Face their Dark Sides

The Comics of Joss Whedon: Critical Essays

Mythology in Game of Thrones

We're Home: Fandom, Fun, and Hidden Homages in Star Wars: The Force Awakens

A Rey of Hope: Feminism, Symbolism and Hidden Gems in Star Wars: The Force Awakens

Contents

This book is an unauthorized guide and commentary on the Jane Austen books. None of the individuals or companies associated with the books, films, or any merchandise based on this series has in any way sponsored, approved, endorsed, or authorized this book.

ISBN-13: 978-0692619933 (LitCrit Press)
ISBN-10: 0692619933

With thanks to the Whensday Group for all their suggestions

Introduction

In the tradition of fractured fairytales everywhere, this book investigates what happens when characters from all six Austen novels are thrown together to flirt and fall into scandal. As a fan of *Reduced Shakespeare*, *The Five Minute Iliad*, and other shortened tightened spins on the classics, my first thought was, why not? Catherine and Marianne Dashwood are much of a type, given to filtering life through the fantasies of their novels, possibly to compensate for their unexciting lives. Anne Elliot and Fanny are both the practical, put-upon ones, subsuming their own needs to deal with their flighty relations, much as Elinor Dashwood does in her own book. All the balls and picnics easily join up, with perhaps a modern-day spin on the books' classic "teazing" and rivalries. And who wouldn't leap at the chance to punish Wickham, toy with Mr Collins, give Fanny someone better that Edmund the oblivious prig? If this seems blasphemous, do consider it an homage, a chance to play with the characters who are so beloved. Nods to Austen's smaller works, namely *Love and Freindship*, *Lesley Castle*, *The Watsons*, and *Sanditon*, also appear, along with a few of her independent *Emma*-style "charades."

These novels have been through almost uncountable adaptations, from BBC and theater movies to the many zombie mashups, to an unforgettable scene on *Red Dwarf*, with a World War Two tank invading the girls' countryside walk. There are countless sequels, and other adaptors retell *Pride and Prejudice* from Darcy's point of view or the servants'.

NONSENSIBILITY

Carrie Bebris's beloved mysteries have Mr and Mrs Darcy visit Highbury, Lyme, and Sandition, solving crimes all the while. This comedy of manners, in such a formalized society, is oddly easy to parody (though those who write parodies regularly will confess that terribly serious works like *Wuthering Heights* are easier to parody than works that are already satiric and ridiculous). So here's the book, attempting to be lighthearted, whimsical and witty as it explores how to recombine six books that all sprang from one delightful mind.

Chapter 1: The Arrival

It is a truth universally acknowledged, that a single man in possession of a good fortune must be in want of a wife. Or preferably six.

However little known the feelings or views of such a man may be on his first entering a neighbourhood, this truth is so well fixed in the minds of the surrounding families, that he is considered as the rightful property of some one or other of their daughters. In the Fussbudget household of Longbore, with six girls in need of marrying off, the odds were certainly in their favour.

"My dear Mr Fussbudget," said his lady to him one day, "have you heard that Netherbum Park is let at last?"

Mr Fussbudget replied that he had not.

"But it is," returned she; "for Mrs Moneygrubber has just been here, and she told me all about it."

Mr Fussbudget made no answer, consumed as he was with setting his newest acquisition, a golden filigree shoe buckle among its many fellows in his golden shoe buckle collection.

"Do not you want to know who has taken it?" cried his wife impatiently.

"*You* want to tell me, and I have no objection to hearing it."

This was invitation enough.

"Why, my dear, you must know, Mrs Exposition says that Netherbum is taken by a young man of large fortune from the north of England; that he came down on Monday in a gold-plated chaise and four to see the place, and was so much delighted with it that he agreed with Mr Morris immediately; that he is to take possession before Michaelmas, or at the least Mardis Gras."

"What is his name?"

"Wentworth."

Their niece, Fanny Anne, jumped at this exchange, but the Fussbudget couple were too settled into their usual routine to notice.

"Is he married or single?"

"Oh! single, my dear, to be sure! A single man of large fortune; four or five thousand a year. I hear his wealth derived from luxury hotels in the West Indies built entirely of bananas. What a fine thing for our girls!"

"How so? how can it affect them? Are they monkeys? Or will they be visiting these hotels with the makings for coconut upside down cake?"

"My dear Mr Fussbudget," replied his wife, "how can you be so tiresome! You must know that I am thinking of his marrying one of them. Just think of it!" Netherbum boasted fifty or eighty bedrooms, in comparison with their penurious eight, and thus would be quite an acquisition. "My dear, you must indeed go and see Captain Wentworth when he comes into the neighbourhood."

"It is more than I engage for, I assure you."

"But consider your daughters. Only think what an establishment it would be for one of them. They have no fortunes of their own, and no relative has been obliging enough to die suddenly and leave them one. Sir William and Lady Moneygrubber are determined to go, merely to get their own brood married off on the spot. Indeed you must go, for it will be impossible for us to visit him, if you do not. Mrs Notapenny next door *also* has five daughters who will also be setting their caps for the gentleman. Oh how I *wish* they would marry that family of five nearly penniless brothers who so coincidentally lives down the lane."

"What, all of them?"

"Oh, you know they're so evenly matched." There were other young people in the village, but those who were married were of course of no consequence and might visit as much as they pleased. In fact, all of Marrytown was remarkable for its lack of children and average folk, with only quality young people, their foible-filled parents, and a few near-invisible servants in residence. Her daughters' lack of any female friends was quite proper, as all other young women were merely competition in the only game that mattered.

Mrs Fussbudget sat heavily on the sofa to punctuate her point, so heavily in fact that all of the embroidered cushions and antimacassars six stifled young women can produce leapt in all directions. "If you do not go visit him, I will have to contrive an acquaintance by having our girls throw themselves in front of his carriage."

"You are over-scrupulous, surely. I dare say Captain Wentworth will be very glad to see you; and I will send a few lines by you to assure him of my hearty consent to his marrying which ever he chooses of the girls; though I must throw in a good word for my precious Dilemma. She's the eldest, after all, and so excellent around the house."

"I desire you will do no such thing. Dilemma is not a bit better than the others; and I am sure she is not half so handsome as our sweet, flighty Marianne Catherine, nor half so good humoured and expressive as Lydia Louisa. And then there's our other daughter, er, how-d'you-call-her." For the fourth daughter of the family, Jane Harriet, was quite forgettable in her quiet amiability. The third daughter, Scary, was also conspicuously skipped. "But you are always giving *Dilemma* the preference. Besides, she *will* say she's not looking for a match for herself, only those she can bring about in others." This last had long been a source of vexation.

"They have none of them much to recommend them," replied he; "they are all silly and ignorant like other girls; but Dilemma has something more of quickness than her sisters.

As soon as she sees a person, she knows at once all their business and all she might do to arrange their lives more agreeably." Finishing with the shoe buckle, he moved on to his collection of antique suspender clips, which likewise needed polishing. "And you know the young gentlemen usually will find and court the silliest lady with the deepest bonnet in all of town. Best have the girls sew on additional ruffles and otherwise fret no more."

"Mr Fussbudget, how can you abuse your own children in such way? You take delight in vexing me. You have no compassion on my poor nerves."

"You mistake me, my dear. I have a high respect for your nerves. They are my old friends. I have heard you mention them with consideration these twenty years at least." He began assiduously polishing the nearest clip, as if to remind his wife of his own consuming interests over those decades.

"Ah! you do not know what I suffer."

"But I hope you will get over it, and live to see many young men of four thousand a year come into the neighbourhood."

"It will be no use to us if twenty such should come, since you will not visit them."

"Depend upon it, my dear, that when there are twenty I will visit them all."

Mr Fussbudget was so odd a mixture of quick parts, sarcastic humour, occasional ill-planned bouts of juggling, and obsession with trifles, that the experience of three and twenty years had been insufficient to make his wife understand his character. *Her* mind was less difficult to develop. She was a woman of mean understanding, little information, random descents into pantomime, and uncertain temper. When she was discontented, she fancied herself nervous. The business of her life was to get her daughters married; its solace was visiting and news. She considered her husband a madman, for his obsession with his frivolous collections and his utter indifference to the demands of family life. And he in turn resolved to blow her brains out the next time she described her nervous complaints in detail.

Fanny Anne, who had been a most attentive listener to the whole, left the room, to seek the comfort of cool air for her flushed cheeks; and as she walked along a favourite grove of horse chestnuts, enjoying the gentle patter of the squirrels hurling them at her, said, with a gentle sigh, "A few months more, and he, perhaps, may be walking here."

NONSENSIBILITY

Chapter 2: Fanny Anne

The reason that Mrs Fussbudget, mother to five daughters, had in fact six girls to marry off was due to her astounding charity, for which she predicted a large recompense in the future.

Mr Fussbudget's brother had married, in the common phrase, to disoblige his family, and, upon his death, he left behind two small children (though not of course in that order). Upon this, his rather flighty tradesman's daughter of a wife (rather like Mrs Fussbudget herself) fixed on a Lieutenant of Marines named Collins, without education, fortune, or connexions. She could hardly have made a more untoward choice – the man had no interest in handkerchiefs, cravat tying, or even shoe buckles – all the minutiae of refinement.

Mr Fussbudget would have been glad to exert for the advantage of his brother's widow; but her new husband's profession was such as no interest could reach; and before he had time to devise any other method of assisting them, an absolute breach between him and his embittered wife had taken place. It was the natural result of the conduct of each party, and such as a very imprudent marriage based on affection rather than highly contracted financial settlements almost always produces. To save herself from useless remonstrance, Mrs Collins (as she must now be called) never wrote to her family on the subject till actually married. Mr Minor-Character, her brother-in-law, regarded matters with equanimity and sent her many gifts of jellied mutton and calf's foot soup in aspic each season.

However, Mrs Fussbudget had a spirit of activity, which could not be satisfied till she had written a long and angry letter to Frances, to point out the folly of her conduct, and threaten her with all its possible ill consequences. For she had hoped her husband's sister-in-law would marry splendidly, so much so that she might use her vast fortune to assist her own family. Mrs Collins, in her turn was injured and angry; and an answer which comprehended each woman in its bitterness, and bestowed such very disrespectfully accurate reflections on the silliness of Mr Fussbudget and his wife as put an end to all intercourse between them for a considerable period.

Their homes were so distant, at at least twenty miles off, and the circles in which they moved so distinct, as almost to preclude the means of ever hearing of each other's existence during the eleven following years. However, though Mrs Fussbudget had cut off communication, she was determined to maintain all connexions, even those which would likely produce no assistance to her family, and so she sent her sister-in-law long Christmas letters bragging about her daughters' many talents resulting from their superior upbringing. Occasionally, she lowered herself enough to send a package of embroidered wall hangings and or watercolour art, but this was more practicality than sense, thanks to her daughters' massive production scale. However, one painful thought worried at Mrs Fussbudget through all the years. Her husband's estate was entailed to the male line. So too were entailed the family dog, the milking stools, the horde of garden gnomes, and the antique furniture polish. The girls were left in a sad state – If she never produced a son (and with five young daughters, this seemed nearly certain) Mrs Collins' own son from the first marriage would inherit her own home of Longbore upon her husband's death. He was a total twit, but his XY chromosomes decided all. The girls should be left with nothing. Except the cat and their extensive piles of embroidery.

Vainly she importuned the solicitors and Mr Fussbudget

himself to find a way to save the estate. But such a thing was impossible. With no sons from Mrs Fussbudget, the very sister-in-law she loathed would provide their heir. This kept Mrs Fussbudget at a far greater state of fury and disdain toward her relations than she might otherwise have cultivated and she satisfied her feelings by satirizing them in many an elaborate pantomime show of her own devising.

By the end of over twenty years, however, Mrs Collins could no longer afford to cherish pride or resentment, or to lose one connexion that might possibly assist her. A pair of lively twins (one fortunately male, one significantly less fortunate in her choice of gender), a husband disabled for active service, but not the less equal to company and good liquor, and a very small income to supply their wants, made her eager to regain the friends she had so carelessly sacrificed; and she addressed Mrs Fussbudget in a letter which spoke so much contrition and despondence as could not but dispose them all to a reconciliation. Mrs Fussbudget proposed that they host the Collins twins for a time, and introduce them into better society than they might find so far in the country. That her own village of Marrytown was equally countrified bothered her not a whit. In truth, she may have been harbouring deeper plans, for a woman with five daughters to settle cannot afford to disdain a male cousin who is destined to inherit her own house. An alliance between him and one of her daughters would provide them all with security and comfort for the future, as well as an imprudently-matched sister-in-law who might benefit from more than twenty years of neglected advice.

Mr Fussbudget hesitated to have two more young people in his already-crowded house. He was the sort of person who was most happy ensconced in his study and freed from all parental obligations, and as such shuddered at the burden of more needing care.

Mrs Fussbudget was eager to offer her own opinion: "Introduce the girl properly into the world, and ten to one but she has the means of settling well, without farther expense to any body. A niece of our's, Mr Fussbudget, I may say, or, at least of *your's*, would not enter this neighbourhood without many advantages's's.

"Are you sure you quite pronounced that right?"

"Oh stuff!" was her only reply. As she continued, "I don't say she would be so handsome as her cousins. I dare say she would not; but she would be introduced into the society of this county under such very favourable circumstances as, in all human probability, would get her a creditable establishment. When she was not scrubbing our floors and providing some relief for the maid of all work, of course. More to the point, she will come to regard our own girls as sisters, and will deal kindly with them when the time comes when you are cold in the ground, with your treasured collections sold to pay our maintenance."

And so, Fanny Anne Collins arrived, accompanied by her twin to whom the estate was entailed. William Collins was a minister, and thus was apt to sermonize his cousins when they took too little care to avoid him. His greatest passion was books – particularly the ones that might bore listeners into states of utter despair or at the least, listless apathy. Despite their pleas for mercy, however, he continued to share these with the family on every occasion and considered himself well rewarded with their piteous groans. For, as he liked to remark, if he did not sermonize them at every occasion, he was convinced no one else would.

For Fanny Anne, Longbore was bewildering and occasionally terrifying. There were too many forks at dinner, too many sighs of longing disappointment, and too many doilies on every surface. Her cousin's rooms were a flurry of gowns, petticoats, spencers, pelisses, entire baskets of complex undergarments, and bonnets on every surface. All the downstairs rooms seemed crowded with painted china cups and end tables, shellwork, scrollwork, stencils, and all the girls had ever produced so that an inch of blank wall or table could not be found. Upstairs, the halls echoed with shrieks as Lydia and Marianne debated ownership of a shawl, or Scary banged away at the pianoforte. There were benefits, too, of course, as their cottage bulged with more clothes in her size than her male twin had ever provided. Fanny had her own tiny dark garret room, with goosedown pillows so luxurious they were still attached to the geese. Still, much remained foreign.

One day, as Fanny Anne was regrouting the tiles in the kitchen ("Oh, Fanny, be a dear and do this little chore," her aunt had said), her cousins came in chattering such strange nonsense that Fanny Anne was tempted to grout her ears to prevent being subjected to more of it.

"Oh it has been so long since we've seen our cousins the Edmunds," cried Marianne Catherine. "How do you suppose their estate at dear dear Snoreland must look?"

"Dear, dear Snoreland," said Dilemma, "probably looks much as it always does at this time of the year. The woods and walks thickly covered with dead leaves, and vagrants of uncertain parentage camped under the trees. I wonder our cousins should let such inferior persons roam about."

"I know many vagrants, and some are quite good people," Fanny Anne felt herself protesting. "My brother is kind enough to read them sermons sometimes, when he is not making rounds among the farmers."

"Oh, them," said Dilemma. "The yeomanry are precisely the order of people with whom I feel I can have nothing to do. A degree or two lower, and a creditable appearance might interest me; I might hope to be useful to their families in some way or other. But a farmer can need none of my help, and is, therefore, in one sense, as much above my notice as in every other he is below it."

"Oh," cried Marianne, still on about the leaves. "with what transporting sensation have I formerly seen them fall! How have I delighted, as I walked, to see them driven in showers about me by the wind! What feelings have they, the season, the air altogether inspired! Now there is no one to regard them. They are seen only as a nuisance, swept hastily off, and driven as much as possible from the sight."

Scary, the middle sister, blinked. "Do remember, dear sister, that opium is not wholly appropriate for ladies, and can lead to ruin and degradation."

As Marianne stared at her in fury, Lydia Louisa giggled. "Imagine if the officers started dispensing the drugs from their medical stocks. How many young ladies, confined at home to embroider all day, would quickly become their friends." As she spoke, she traced the low neckline of her dress with a finger, as if daydreaming about far more than friendship. Jane Harriet wordlessly took her hand and led her upstairs, and their sisters quickly followed.

"What is wrong with my cousins?" Fanny Anne cried to her aunt.

With a sniff, her aunt carefully moved away from the trowel in Fanny's hand. "Oh, they are rather gullible girls and think their storybooks reflect real life. Each has a particular volume she cherishes, so much so that she lives as though she's a character in it."

Suddenly, the girls' ludicrous behaviour made sense. "Scary enjoys tracts of sermons and ladies' guides to proper behaviour. Marianne, tragic romances and ballads, along with the gothic novels of Mrs Radcliffe. Dilemma, happy romances where everyone ends up wed in neat couples, or perhaps the *Peerage*, which boasts so of the same. And Lydia…" Fanny Anne hesitated over how to say it.

"Filthy magazines," the girls' mother finished. "I believe my dears spend their days trying to work out what sort of a story they're in. So charming of them? So full of sensibility!"

But hardly of sense. "That seems…" Fanny Anne struggled for words. She finally settled on "rather oblivious to reality."

Her aunt raised her eyebrows. "Our friends the Miss Brontes do not think so. And is that a terribly well-worn copy of *Cinderella* I see in your pocket?"

"I withdraw my observation," Fanny Anne said quickly. "I haven't seen much of Jane Harriet."

"That's because you haven't gone walking out," her aunt

explained. "Every family needs a young lady who will make the perfect companion – who will walk out when a lady desires company and vanish expediently when a tête-à-tête is needed for the exchanging of confidences. That is her purpose in this family, and she fills it well."

"And what does she read?"

"Read? You know, I am scarcely made aware of her existence, unless we all go out walking, you know. Perhaps because she reads so little. Indeed, what do you think of her?"

It was hardly possible to think anything of a girl with so much niceness of character and so little of desires or even personality. Jane Harriet was a very pretty girl, and her beauty happened to be of a sort which was particularly admired. She was short, plump, and fair, with a fine bloom, blue eyes, light hair, regular features, and a look of great sweetness. She had never had an unkind thought of anyone, or at least never spoken an unkind word. Jane Harriet certainly was not clever, but she had a sweet, docile, grateful disposition, was totally free from conceit, and only desiring to be guided by any one she looked up to. As her sisters knew, she was exceptionally gullible and prone to believe whatever she was told. Her early attachment to her whole family was very amiable; and her inclination for good company, and power of appreciating what was elegant and clever, shewed that there was no want of taste, though strength of understanding must not be expected.

After a moment, Fanny Anne noted, "She is a pretty little creature, and I am inclined to think very well of her disposition. Her character depends upon those she is with; but in good hands she will turn out a valuable woman."

"Yes, indeed! Now pour me a glass of wine, and let us see to your education."

"May I remind you, ma'am, it's only nine in the morning," Fanny Anne noted meekly.

"Oh, yes? Yes of course. Best make it brandy then." As she held out a large tea mug, the pouring went on for quite some time.

Over the next weeks, the place became less strange, and the people less formidable; and if there were some amongst them over whom Fanny Anne could not cease to puzzle, she began at least to know their ways, and to catch the best manner of conforming to them. The little rusticities and awkwardnesses which had at first made grievous inroads on the tranquillity of all, and not least of herself, necessarily wore away, and she was no longer materially concerned about her fussy uncle, nor did her aunt's shrill screeches make her start very much.

As her appearance and spirits improved, Mr and Mrs Fussbudget thought with greater satisfaction of their benevolent plan; and it was pretty soon decided between them that, though far from clever, she showed a tractable disposition, and seemed likely to give them little trouble. A mean opinion of her abilities was not confined to them. Fanny Anne could read, work, and write, and do perfectly useless things like set a bone, make cheese, and quilt, but she had been taught nothing more; and as her cousins found her ignorant of many things with which they had been long familiar, they thought her prodigiously stupid, and for the first two or three weeks were continually bringing some fresh report of it into the drawing-room. "Dear mama, only think, my cousin cannot put the map of Europe together – or my cousin cannot tell the principal rivers in Russia – or, she never heard of Asia Minor – or she does not know the difference between water-colours and crayons! – How strange! – Did you ever hear anything so stupid?"

"Very true indeed, my dears, but you are blessed with wonderful memories, and your poor cousin has probably none at all. There is a vast deal of difference in memories, as well as in everything else, and therefore you must make allowance for your cousin, and pity her deficiency. And remember that, if you are ever so forward and clever yourselves, you should always be modest; for, much as you know already, there is a great deal more for you to learn."

Lydia nodded assiduously. "Yes, I know there is, till I am

seventeen. Then I can marry and forget it all. But I must tell you another thing of Fanny Anne, so odd and so stupid. Do you know, she says she does not want to learn either music or drawing."

"To be sure, my dear, that is very stupid indeed, and shows a great want of genius and emulation. But, all things considered, I do not know whether it is not as well that it should be so, for it is not at all necessary that she should be as accomplished as you are; – on the contrary, it is much more desirable that there should be a difference."

Such were the counsels by which Mrs Fussbudget assisted to form her daughters' minds; and it is not very wonderful that, with all their promising talents and early information, they should be entirely deficient in the less common acquirements of self-knowledge, generosity and humility. In everything but disposition they were admirably taught. Mr Fussbudget did not know what was wanting, because, though a truly anxious father, he was not outwardly affectionate, and was far too caught up in his work of collecting monographs on Roman teakettles.

The Fussbudget girls indeed spent their days training at being accomplished. They played the piano. They sang duets and trios, and occasionally all as a group. They learned to draw, paint, and sew. They embroidered long, fantastical borders on cushions and wall hangings until the room itself seemed to be a multicoloured spider web of thread. Each day pots and pots of fresh tea were ordered, with spun sugar meringues and slices of cake studded with currents, all to greet the visitors who never arrived. The ladies spent much of their time studying walking with simpering grace and praising one another for their perceived elegance. They sat in the parlour for hours, listlessly awaiting a gentleman who might come and propose marriage to one of them. And they learnt languages: French, Italian, and even German though they had no conceit of ever meeting a person from any of those places.

Dilemma, the eldest, decided to make Fanny her special project, noting with great pomposity, "Beware, my Fanny.

Beware of the insipid Vanities and idle Dissipations of the Metropolis of England; Beware of the unmeaning Luxuries of Bath and of the stinking fish of Southampton."

"Alas! (exclaimed Fanny) how am I to avoid those evils I shall never be exposed to? What probability is there of my ever tasting the Dissipations of London, the Luxuries of Bath, or the stinking Fish of Southampton? I who am doomed to waste my Days of Youth and Beauty in an humble Cottage in Marrytown." The more dramatic and bombastic her cousin became, the more pitiful and romantic it seemed her own dialogue would trend. Marrytown itself seemed to bring it out in people. "Was that all right?"

"Very pitiful and romantic indeed," Dilemma assured her. "Dearest Fanny Anne, the misfortune of your birth and country upbringing ought to make you particularly careful as to your associates. There can be no doubt of your being a gentleman's relation, and you must support your claim to that station by every thing within your own power, or there will be plenty of people who would take pleasure in degrading you."

This attention was an honour Fanny hesitated to accept. "I can never be important to any one," she modestly assured her cousin. For indeed, the geography and languages would not sort themselves out, especially from the arm's length she kept.

"What is to prevent you?"

"Everything. My situation, my foolishness and awkwardness."

"As to your foolishness and awkwardness, my dear Fanny, believe me, you never have a shadow of either, but in using the words so improperly. There is no reason in the world why you should not be important where you are known. You have good sense, and a sweet temper, and a wonderful talent at getting the stains out of muslin. I am sure you have a grateful heart, that could never receive kindness without wishing to return it. I do not know any better qualifications for a friend and companion. You need only giggle uproariously at the men's feeble witticisms, and jump for joy when one wins at cards, and you shall soon be as charming as the rest of us."

Indeed, Dilemma had hit on it — she indeed lacked a certain something her cousins all possessed. In the country, Fanny Anne was accustomed to look after her friends' brothers and sisters, who could usually be found helping in the garden or running through the woods, boys and girls together. This stilted indoor pastime, however, of decorating bonnets and painting tables that no one would see seemed to Fanny Anne nonsensical. None here had ever washed so much as a teacup, and regarded such suggestions with horror. On one day they reached a new height of foolishness, when, having finished making over their own gowns, and being too old for dolls, they proceeded to dress up the family pets.

The dog, now actually wearing a cravat, gazed at his mistresses with a look that suggested he should rather they skip the twenty paces gentlemen would normally take, and proceed directly to shoot him.

"Oh, he looks so sweet," Jane Harriet said. "Lydia, get the cat." Mittens had begun sleeping in the oven, possibly as a reaction to the girls' new sewing projects. Jane Harriet began briskly brushing the dog's fluffy head in such a manner that at least it wasn't able to see itself.

Dilemma considered. "I like it, but I do not *love* it. Perhaps if we add a bonnet…"

"Have they nothing better to do?" Fanny Anne burst out, as soon as she'd left the room.

"Than practice at sewing and being accomplished? No indeed. And their time could be no better spent, if they wish to catch husbands," her aunt explained.

"And be wed for their abilities to paint?" Fanny Anne asked, shuddering. Only embroidery was worse.

"With no chance of profession, ladies must focus on the social, moral, and intellectual challenges of matrimony."

"And they are enough to sustain you?" With servants to tend to the household and the girls old enough to manage their own embroidery, Mrs Fussbudget seemed to have plenty of leisure time to matchmake and complain of her nerves.

"Well, it must be admitted that some married ladies go around the bend into paranoia, hypochondria, or suicidal depression, but many find that a good dose of laudanum will straighten them out. The opium within is quite soothing…or so I hear," the redoubtable lady quickly added.

Her cousins were eager to add to her list of novels, though each had her own fixations (even Jane Harriet lent her a book of pastoral drawings). Though Dilemma seemed to have given her up as a lost cause, Marianne Catherine was the most eager to supplement her reading habits. She said one day, "It is so odd to me, that you should never have read *Udolpho* before; but I suppose Mr Collins objects to novels."

"No, he does not. He very often reads *A Gentleman Who Never Has Adventures At All*; but new books do not fall in our way."

"*A Gentleman Who Never Has Adventures At All!* That is an amazing horrid book, is it not? All everyday people in run-of-the mill situations. I do not recall anyone dying tragically at all."

"It is not like *Udolpho* at all; but yet I think it is very entertaining."

"Do you indeed! You surprise me; I thought it had not been readable. Why, there is not a single murderer or damsel in distress. Oh my!" Caught up in her protests, Marianne appeared one of those very damsels in truth.

Lydia burst in, giggling like a hyena. Joined by her sister, they laughed and laughed. "How much fun we all have! But enough of this room," Lydia concluded. "Let us go and laugh and be merry in a corridor."

A short conversation between Lydia and Fanny revolving only around flirting with the entire newly arrived regiment had already increased Fanny's dislike of her, and convinced her that her Heart was no more formed for the soft ties of Love than for the endearing intercourse of Freindship. Or so her thoughts tended when she had stayed indoors too long.

And so Fanny Anne settled down to becoming

accomplished, whiling away her hours learning subjects that were useless except for their ability to fill time and nodding along when her cousins confided in her about beaux she had never met. Her time in, as she thought, a house of mad-women, would build her character and teach her steadiness through adversity. And though the hated embroidery and fervent floor scrubbing kept her hands busy, it left her mind distressingly idle, with far too much time to contemplate her past.

Captain Frederick Wentworth, who being made commander in consequence of the action off St. Domingo, and not immediately employed, had come into Somersetshire, in the summer of 1806. He was, at that time, a remarkably fine young man, with a great deal of intelligence, spirit and brilliancy; and Fanny Anne an extremely pretty girl, with gentleness, modesty, taste, and feeling. – Half the sum of attraction, on either side, might have been enough, for he had nothing to do, and she (though devoted to her cheese-making) had hardly anybody to love; but the encounter of such lavish recommendations could not fail. They were gradually acquainted, and when acquainted, rapidly and deeply in love. It would be difficult to say which had seen highest perfection in the other, or which had been the happiest; she, in receiving his declarations and proposals, or he in having them accepted.

A short period of exquisite felicity followed, and but a short one. – Troubles soon arose. Fanny Anne's father thought it a very degrading alliance; and her mother, though with more tempered and pardonable pride, received it as a most unfortunate one. Both had hoped that Fanny Anne would marry their childhood friend, who was in all things wealthy and respectable, save in his habit of making all his visitors recite off-colour limericks, at which he would laugh with great hilarity. Still, in a wealthy gentleman, these habits must merely be considered eccentric, rather than mad, and the connexion was in all other ways a fortunate one.

Fanny Anne, with all her claims of birth, beauty, and

mind, to throw herself away at nineteen; involve herself at nineteen in an engagement with a young man, who had nothing but himself to recommend him, and no hopes of attaining affluence, but in the chances of a most uncertain profession, and no connexions to secure even his farther rise in the profession; would be, indeed, a throwing away, which she grieved to think of! True, Captain Wentworth was hoping to distinguish himself by inventing a pistol that didn't take ten minutes per shot to load and fire, but so far his efforts had proved unsuccessful. His plans to hurl coconuts at the enemy in tropical waters (and if his experiments of loading them into the cannons were successful, the ships could substantially decrease the weight they carried) also carried much of his hopes.

Fanny Anne, so young; known to so few, to be snatched off by a stranger without alliance or fortune; or rather sunk by him into a state of most wearing, anxious, youth-killing dependence! It must not be! Such opposition, as these feelings produced, was more than she could combat. Young and gentle as she was, it might yet have been possible to withstand her father's ill-will, though unsoftened by one kind word or look on the part of her pompous brother; – but her mother, could not, with such steadiness of opinion, and such tenderness of manner, be continually advising her in vain. She was persuaded to believe the engagement a wrong thing – indiscreet, improper, hardly capable of success, and not deserving it. But it was not a merely selfish caution, under which she acted, in putting an end to it. Had she not imagined herself consulting his good, even more than her own, she could hardly have given him up. – The belief of being prudent, and self-denying principally for *his* advantage, was her chief consolation. She condemned herself to a life of misery deliberately, knowing she was pleasing her family in the task and so might live out her days as a martyr, succumbing to sadness for the greater good. Under the total misery of a parting – a final parting, every consolation was required, for she had to encounter all the additional pain of opinions, on his side, totally unconvinced and unbending, and of his feeling himself ill-used by so forced a relinquishment. – He had left the country in consequence.

A few months had seen the beginning and the end of their acquaintance; but, not with a few months ended Fanny Anne's share of suffering from it. Her attachment and regrets had, for a long time, clouded every enjoyment of youth; and an early loss of bloom and spirits had been their lasting effect.

Now Captain Wentworth had indeed made his fortune. With all these circumstances, recollections and feelings, she could not hear that Captain Wentworth was likely to live at Netherbum Park without a revival of former pain; and many a stroll and many a sigh were necessary to dispel the agitation of the idea. Still, her feelings continued to churn, as she knew they would until she was forced to meet Captain Wentworth in person. Such an event arrived sooner than she had expected.

NONSENSIBILITY

Chapter 3: The Assembly

For some time, an assembly had been planned at the home of the Fussbudgets' friends, the Moneygrubbers. Captain Wentworth had been invited, and it was thought he would bring several of his friends. In the end, however, he only brought one, a tall, proud gentleman whose sideburns were even longer than his own. Like the captain, he was unattached and must, as these stories go, be seeking a wife. All wondered who he could be, and once again, the ladies began to converge. This gentleman, Admiral Haughtyton, soon drew the attention of the room by his fine, handsome features, noble mien; and the report which, was in general circulation within five minutes after his entrance, of his having ten thousand a year. This figure made *his* figure all the more attractive in comparison with his friend the captain, until he dribbled soup from his chin during dinner and broke into an hour of wheezing that threatened to drown out the music.

Despite this display, or perhaps because of it (such a man assuredly did not have long to live, after all), a veritable crowd of young ladies swarmed him with delicate little giggles and flirtations as each strove to present herself in the best light, all amid the room's crush and overwhelming noise. Admiral Haughtyton gestured briefly, and a pair of armed escorts complete with uniforms and sabres firmly escorted the young ladies across the room. This did nothing, however, to deter their mamas, who were willing to brave far more than a few sabres to see their daughters well matched. Now they converged on Admiral Haughtyton, who was quite prepared to topple over under the invitations to teas and dinners amidst a positive sea of babble. Then he took command of himself and fixed all the ladies with a single glare. So formidable was this ponderous state that even the most determined ladies felt themselves quite unequaled and backed away trembling.

The rumor soon circulated that he was a powerful man with a *dark past* who had even killed a man (not the snail-eating Frenchies or the myriad of people around the world who had the bad taste to not be white or wear complicated corsetry) but an actual British man. This was true, several times over, but boring one's acquaintances to death was not yet a crime on English soil.

And so Admiral Haughtyton was left to his own company at the assembly, which was as he preferred it. He was quite a haughty fellow who sneered at all he saw. This was likely difficult for the gentleman, as he was elderly enough to be bent nearly double over his cane. As such, he had to twist a great deal to sneer *up* at anyone. But sneer he did, a great deal, especially after Scary Fussbudget, the middle sister, seated herself at the piano.

Scary, who having, in consequence of being the only plain one in the family, worked hard for knowledge and accomplishments, was always impatient for display. Scary had neither genius nor taste; and though vanity had given her application, it had given her likewise a pedantic air and conceited manner, which would have injured a higher degree of excellence than she had reached. She reached for her piano keys, lifted her head, and proceeded to liven the room with a cheerful air:

> *A dog starved at his master's gate*
> *Predicts the ruin of the state.*
> *A horse misused upon the road*

Calls to heaven for human blood.
Each outcry of the hunted hare
A fibre from the brain does tear.
A skylark wounded in the wing,
A cherubim does cease to sing.
The game-cock clipped and armed for fight
Does the rising sun affright.
Every wolf's and lion's howl
Raises from hell a human soul

Everyone cringed and squirmed as the song went on in this vein for quite some time. Scary, at the end of her long elegy, was glad to purchase praise and gratitude by Scotch and Irish airs and a brief bagpipe solo, at the request of her younger sisters, who, with some of the Moneygrubbers and two or three officers, joined eagerly in dancing at one end of the room.

After this, Jane Harriet, who had been collecting many of the small riddles called charades, shared a short one with those assembled:

You may lie on my first on the side of a stream,
And my second compose to the nymph you adore,
But if, when you've none of my whole, her esteem
And affection diminish – think of her no more!

The multitude were quick to get "bank," and a little slower to achieve "note," rather than poem or letter. But these combined and added to the last two lines revolted the party, at the all-too-true, but only whispered of, fact that one who lacked banknotes would hardly find a match. Poor Jane was scorned the rest of the night.

Mr Tightly-Wound, who before these men's entrance had been the most recently arrived and therefore most exciting prospect in their small village, was looking miffed. He had been trying to approach the eldest Miss Fussbudget for a dance but the wall of gawking young ladies was quite preventing him. While she had always found his mouldering black coat highly attractive, and his extra-starched cravat the latest word in men's fashions, it seemed he would have to look elsewhere for a partner.

But the attention of every lady was soon caught by a young man, whom they had never seen before, of most gentlemanlike appearance, who entered the room at the side of Lydia's handsome friend, Sergeant Denny. As the newest visitor to town by at least a quarter of an hour, he was soon the figure of the most attention. Lydia, determined if possible to find out his identity first, led her sister Jane Harriet at a run toward the door, under pretence of needing the light of the hallway to tie her shoe. Upon seeing her, Mr Denny entreated permission to introduce his friend, Mr Willoughby Wickham, who had returned with him the day before from town, and he was happy to say, had accepted a commission in their corps. This was exactly as it should be; for the young man wanted only regimentals to make him completely charming. His appearance was greatly in his favour; he had all the best part of beauty – a fine countenance, a good figure, an extra waxed moustache, and very pleasing address. His sideburns, remarked Lydia, must be a full half-inch longer even than the admiral's.

Moments later, the other young ladies converged on the scene, eager to get his name and yearly income statement. The new gentleman smiled, charming them all in a moment with his easy graces. "Ladies, I hear Mr Darcy has newly come to town, and has just been bathing in the river. If you make haste, you may indeed catch him in such a state of dishabille that he boasts a rather *wet shirt*.

"Oooh!" shrieked all the young ladies, and for the moment, at least the hall was nearly empty as the ladies veritably stampeded down to the river in manner more hasty than becoming. Thus Mr Wickham was free to make the further acquaintance of Lydia and her sisters. The introduction was followed up on his side by a happy readiness of conversation – a readiness at the same time perfectly correct and unassuming; and the whole party were still standing and talking together very agreeably, when the sound of gnashing teeth drew their notice. Indeed, from across the room, Admiral Haughtyton was staring and his teeth were indeed grinding so loudly that all in the room could hear them. Mr Wickham, after a few moments, touched his hat – a salutation which the admiral just deigned to return, as it was insupportable not to bow or tip one's hat when offered the same, even by someone one wished to stab through the heart and spit upon the remains. What could be the meaning of it? – It was impossible to imagine; it was impossible not to long to know.

For his own part, Mr Wickham approached Captain Wentworth and bowed. "I am always honoured to meet one of my naval brethren in arms."

Captain Wentworth, with a glance at his friend, drew himself up stiffly. "Indeed. I am a veteran of thirty sea battles aboard the HMS Take That, Frenchies! with my companions bayoneted, blown to bits, and burned alive in front of me. I have navigated through tempests and typhoons. It is only through providence that I managed to survive. And you... you march around the land in gleaming red uniforms, flirting with tavern wenches and attending balls. Many of us, born with nothing, *earned* our places capturing French ships and selling our prizes of runny French cheeses and powdered wigs on the black market."

"As we have earned..." here Mr Wickham hesitated "our commissions," he finished with a weak smile. Clearly feeling this was not sufficient, he added, "We go where we are sent, after all."

"Oh yes? And why are you stationed in a backwater country town? To protect it from Napoleon's armies in case the French try to steal our sheep?"

"They are quite excellent sheep, sir," Mr Wickham managed. "And likely in need of defending."

"Cowardly Lobsterback!"

"Uncultured Limey!"

The men glanced about, and suddenly realized that the company were watching them. "That is to say," Captain Wentworth managed, gaining at least a slight mastery over himself. "I doubt very much if your services have been needed to protect the sheep, unless of course, some of your officers have been tempted to carry them off to Gretna Green and elope with them." Several of the young ladies gasped at such effrontery and not a few chaperones glared.

"Indeed. Thank you for voicing your opinion," Wickham replied. "I might add that I shall be ready, with my sword, to meet you in those very sheep fields, perhaps tomorrow, where we might terrify those very sheep with a sight of your decapitated body."

"Or, indeed, yours," said Wentworth, who appeared in perfect accord with Wickham. His face, scarred with powder burns and carved on the cheekbone with a dirty French word, had turned bright red and a vein throbbed visibly in his forehead.

"Come, gentlemen," Sir Moneygrubber quickly interceded. That was his sheep pasture after all. "Do not spoil our fine gathering with death threats, but be merry and come celebrate with us all."

Denny asked Lydia to dance, and the moment passed as Scary struck up the wretched bagpipes louder than before.

As Fanny Anne crept behind a group of ladies to avoid accidentally making eye contact with Captain Wentworth, or indeed, any of her acquaintance, she beheld Dilemma speaking to Mr Collins in the hallway. Though Dilemma was endeavouring to lower her voice, she was in fact quite loud, and Fanny Anne caught the words, "...indeed, you *must* wed Scary. If you are determined to take one of our family, it should be the one that no one – that is, she's so steady and practical. I am sure she will be a fine choice of partner."

Mr Collins stiffened. "Scary? The one who resembles – that is, the one with such a fine...personality? I fear I could not possibly. In fact, my affections tend toward a rather closer source...I feel prepared to burst with my feelings and you must allow me to exclaim them. What a discerning lady you are, with such a fine sense of class distinction!" He trembled with strong emotion, or so it might appear. Fanny, who knew him intimately, understood that the effort of keeping his gut sucked in was clearly proving quite strenuous.

Fanny listened to Dilemma stammer something uncomfortable and considered intervening, but of course, her brother would never forgive her such a thing. In fact, Fanny Anne doubted her "sense of class distinction" was truly what her brother admired in comparison with the generous contents of Miss Fussbudget's stays. As her brother continued to wheedle and flatter by turns, Fanny Anne made a hasty escape. Jane Harriet was fortunate that she only appeared when someone needed a walking companion, as it likely saved her from being the next contestant in this game of marriage-market-hot-potato.

Across the room, Captain Wentworth, though a quiet, serious sort who had seen most of his friends blown to bits at sea and was now surrounded by gaggles of frivolous laughing young people, managed to comport himself politely after the incident with Mr Wickham. What a contrast between him and his friend! Admiral Haughtyton danced not at all, declined being introduced to any lady, and spent the evening in walking about the room silently, clattering his cane. His character was decided. He was the proudest, most disagreeable man in the world, and every body hoped that he would never come there again. Worse yet, there was a rumour Captain Wentworth had an understanding with Admiral Haughtyton's daughter (who was to have 30,000 pounds on the event of her marriage!) and this was the source of their friendship, a grievous blow indeed for all the hopeful ladies of Marrytown. Amongst the most violent against him was Mrs Fussbudget, whose dislike of his general behaviour was sharpened into particular resentment by his having slighted all of her daughters.

"Come, Haughtyton," said Captain Wentworth, "I must

have you dance. I hate to see you standing about by yourself in this stupid manner. You had much better dance. At least doing a jig in the centre of the room will help you fit in, here in the country, and be far more dignified than simply standing there."

"I certainly shall not. You know how I detest it, unless I am particularly acquainted with my partner. At such an assembly as this, it would be insupportable. There is not a woman in the room whom it would not be a punishment to me to stand up with."

"I would not be so fastidious as you are," cried Wentworth, "for a kingdom! Upon my honour I never met with so many terribly silly girls. But it is not their fault, as they have never been to war or had their limbs blown off, and they have no reason not to take joy in life. Besides, there are several of them, you see, who are uncommonly pretty. And they seem quite taken with wounds incurred in defending our shores." Here he presented his left side, where his ear had been bitten off by a savage Frenchman in the heat of battle. Still this did not unbalance his face, as he'd lost the other at sword practice (this was only embarrassing as he'd been practicing solo).

"*You* are dancing with the only handsome girl in the room," said Admiral Haughtyton, looking at Miss Marianne Fussbudget, who had been quite won over by the romance of the Captain's wounds. He and Marianne Catherine each had discovered in the other a sympathetic figure, as she was drawn to figures of tragedy and romance, and he, most fortunately, had lost his left leg while cleaning his rifle. His wooden leg clattered on the floor in quite a loud counterpoint to the music, but an enchanted Marianne didn't seem to have observed.

"Oh! she is a terribly pretty creature! But she has several sisters sitting down just behind you, who are very pretty, and I dare say very agreeable. Do let me ask my partner to introduce you."

"Which do you mean?" and turning round, he looked for

a moment at the sisters. Lydia had started giggling, fervently enough that she was starting to mimic a hyena's raving yowls. Scary, now finished with the piano and bagpipes, sat reading a book in the midst of the party. Jane Harriet had vanished somewhere, as no one seemed to need anyone to go walking with. And Fanny Anne was so avoiding Captain Wentworth's gaze that she'd placed a handkerchief over her face so that she need not glance upon him accidentally. Behind them, Dilemma was engaged in a whispering contest with a respectable widower she seemed to have designated for one of her sisters (though there was no determining for which, if a specific sister had indeed been put forward).

Admiral Haughtyton winced. "I am in no humour at present to give consequence to young ladies who are slighted by other men, especially such indescribably silly ones. You had better return to your partner and enjoy her smiles, for you are wasting your time with me." He shook his head. The silly girls and romantic longings that filled Marrytown to overflowing had clearly caught up with his friend, and there would be no saving him for a sensible conversation ever again.

Captain Wentworth began to follow his advice. However, Marianne had overheard this bit of callous dismissal, and was suddenly, irrepressibly, head-over-heels in love. For indeed, such disdain must always conceal a deep affection and sensibility, or so it went in all her novels. Marianne instantly attached herself to Admiral Haughtyton; though he took no notice of her, she could not be pried loose for the whole of the evening.

NONSENSIBILITY

Chapter 4: Marianne Catherine

No one who had ever seen Marianne Catherine in her infancy would have supposed her born to be a heroine. Her situation in life, the character of her father and mother, her own person and disposition, were all equally against her.

Her form, though not so correct as her elder sister's, in having the advantage of height and other endowments, was more striking; and her face was so lovely, that when in the common cant of praise, she was called a beautiful girl, truth was less violently outraged than usually happens. Her skin was very brown, but, from its transparency, her complexion was uncommonly brilliant; her features were all good; her smile was sweet and attractive; and in her eyes, which were very dark, there was a life, a spirit, an eagerness, which could hardily be seen without delight.

Such were her propensities – her abilities were quite as extraordinary. She never could learn or understand anything before she was taught; and sometimes not even then, for she was often inattentive and dreamy. Not that Marianne Catherine was always stupid – by no means, even when attempting to fashion a gown from live squirrels; she was a great reader, and could most often be found sighing over a romantic novel, in which the heroine sadly wasted herself away for want of love. Marianne also was particularly fond of gothic novels, especially those by Mrs Radcliffe. She loved a good shiver, though she could often be found huddled under the bed with the cat soon after. But from fifteen to eighteen she was in training for a heroine; she read all such works as heroines must read to supply their memories with those quotations which are so serviceable and so soothing in the vicissitudes of their eventful lives.

So far her improvement was sufficient – and in many other points she came on exceedingly well; for though she could not write sonnets, she brought herself to read them; and though there seemed no chance of her throwing a whole party into raptures by a prelude on the pianoforte, of her own composition, she could listen to other people's performance, even Scary's, with very little fatigue. Her greatest deficiency was in the pencil – she had no notion of drawing – not enough even to attempt a sketch of her lover's profile, that she might be detected in the design. There she fell miserably short of the true heroic height. At present she did not know her own poverty, for she had no lover to portray. She had reached the age of eighteen, without having seen one amiable youth who could call forth her sensibility, without having inspired one real passion, and without having excited even any admiration but what was very moderate and very transient. This was strange indeed! But strange things may be generally accounted for if their cause be fairly searched out. Before the arrival at the party the night before, there had not been one lord in the neighbourhood; no – not even a baronet. There was not one family among their acquaintance who had reared and supported a boy accidentally found at their door – not one young man whose origin was unknown. Her father had no ward, and the squire of the parish no children. Such was her greatest disappointment.

On Wednesdays, she would go outside to sing with bluebirds and coax the squirrels to share their nuts (an act, admittedly, close to cannibalism on her part). She befriended all the woodland creatures and used to bring them home as pets until a deer bite became infected and the squirrels organized and turned against her.

But when a young lady is to be a heroine, the perverseness of forty surrounding families cannot prevent her. Something must and will happen to throw a hero in her way. She was determined in all ways to win herself the Luxury of living in every Distress that Poverty can inflict, with the object of her tenderest Affection.

When she heard that Netherbum Park was let, Marianne Catherine began to envision the hero awaiting her. He would be dreamy and handsome, with chiselled jaw, violet eyes, and long hair tossing in the breeze. They would meet on a hill of flowers perhaps, or she might stumble upon him asleep in a shady glen (that she knew of no such glen bothered her not a little) and their eyes would meet. She would soon be his, heart, body and soul.

However, her plans hit a faint snag.

"He's eighty-three!" she burst out, upon learning further details regarding what sort of man had accompanied Captain Wentworth. If a man might ever be said to be in safety from the determined perseverance of disagreeable lovers and the cruel persecutions of obstinate mothers, surely it must be at such a time of life. The man had ten thousand a year, to be sure, the perfect sum she had always envisioned as belonging to her soulmate, but some details must be considered a deterrent.

"He's such a handsome gentleman, though rather proud," her mother responded, unworried. "And he's hardly the eldest in the village. I daresay Mrs Bates is nearly ninety."

"Admiral Haughtyton is certainly younger than Mrs Bates, but he is old enough to be *my* grandfather; and if he were ever animated enough to be in love, must have long outlived every sensation of the kind."

"Come now. Surely God's granting him all that money he never earned and setting him over everyone shows his blessings falling on a worthy soul, kind and virtuous in every way."

"It is too ridiculous! When is a man to be safe from such wit, if age and infirmity will not protect him?"

"Infirmity!" said Dilemma, "do you call Admiral Haughtyton infirm? I can easily suppose that his age may appear much greater to you than to my mother; but a rich gentleman is eligible forever, unlike the ladies, who have only the job of producing countless babies, then dying so a younger woman can take over the task. Besides, you can hardly deceive yourself as to his having the use of his limbs! It is Captain Wentworth who seems to have lost most of his. And, no, you cannot have him; that would be far too cruel to our cousin Fanny Anne, who was to wed him you know."

"Did not you hear him complain of the rheumatism? and is not that the commonest infirmity of declining life?"

"My dearest child," said her mother, face forming into a pout, "at this rate you must be in continual terror of *my* decay; and it must seem to you a miracle that my life has been extended to the advanced age of forty. Although if my nerves keep on as they have been, I daresay I shall not see next summer."

Marianne ignored her mother's typical complaints with a wave of her hand, eager as she was to deal with the current crisis. "Mamma, you are not doing me justice. I know very well that Admiral Haughtyton may live many years longer. But eighty-three has nothing to do with matrimony."

"Perhaps," said Dilemma, "eighty-three and nineteen-and-a-half had better not have any thing to do with matrimony together. But if there should by any chance happen to be a woman who is single at three and twenty, I should not think Colonel Brandon's being eighty-three any objection to his marrying *her*." As all girls knew, twenty-one might be the age of majority, but at twenty-three and a half, all unmarried ladies were condemned as spinsters, their chances at matrimony terribly unlikely. And Fanny Anne lacked only a few months to that date.

"A woman of three and twenty," said Marianne, after pausing a moment, "can never hope to feel or inspire affection again, and if her home be uncomfortable, or her fortune small, I can suppose that she might bring herself to submit to the offices of a nurse, for the sake of the provision and security of a wife. In his marrying such a woman therefore there would be nothing unsuitable. It would be a compact of convenience, and the world would be satisfied. In my eyes it would be no marriage at all, but that would be nothing. To me it would seem only a commercial exchange, in which each wished to be benefited at the expense of the other."

Fanny Anne, who all this time had been dusting Mr Fussbudget's knickknacks, mainly unnoticed as she always was, stifled a hopeless sob. A spinster, in Marrytown, had no hopes but to grow old and die alone, a burden on her family and a shame that would be murmured about by supercilious and catty matrons forever. And she was nearly twenty-four!

"It would be impossible, I know," replied Dilemma to the earlier point, "to convince you that a woman of three and twenty could feel for a man of eighty-three anything near enough to love, to make him a desirable companion to her. But I must object to your dooming the admiral and his wife to the constant confinement of a sick chamber, merely because he chanced to complain yesterday (a very cold damp day) of a slight rheumatic feel in one of his shoulders."

"But he talked of flannel waistcoats," said Marianne; "and with me a flannel waistcoat is invariably connected with aches, cramps, rheumatisms, and every species of ailment that can afflict the old and the feeble. It may be the least romantic garment in all the world, matched only by the accordion for its ability to destroy even a touch of romance." She gazed at her sister in dismay. Dilemma was so oblivious to the magic of the world that she was clearly touched in the head.

"Had he been only in a violent fever, you would not have despised him half so much. Confess, Marianne, is not there something interesting to you in the flushed cheek, hollow eye, and quick pulse of a fever?"

At this image, Marianne was hard pressed not to swoon in deep delight. "Indeed, if he were dying of a consumption, he might be a devastatingly attractive figure."

"Or perhaps left on a doorstep, his ancestors a mystery," Fanny Anne added from across the room, unable to stop herself.

"Oh, do you think he was?"

"Or if he had a wicked past," said Dilemma. "You might like him if he had been a figure of scandal and romance, repenting from a youth of license and debauchery."

"Ohhhh!" Marianne now swooned in truth, and it was lucky there was a hard nineteenth century chair to catch her, or she would have tumbled to the floor. Little more need be said of Marianne.

Chapter 5: Dilemma

Dilemma Fussbudget, handsome, clever, and rich, with a comfortable home and happy disposition, seemed to unite some of the best blessings of existence; and had lived nearly twenty-one years in the world with very little to distress or vex her. An amateur matchmaker by profession, she had fixed upon their new neighbour as the perfect consort for her unfortunate cousin.

Oh not Captain Wentworth. For as Dilemma knew, to her eternal discomfiture, they had a tragic past, and now Captain Wentworth was unlikely to return her aging spinster cousin's affections. Worse yet, Dilemma had been the one to introduce them, considering it a perfect match before Mr Collins and his parents had contrived to spoil it all. Mr Collins, indeed, had all the wit and grace of an outhouse in summer, but as he was to inherit, Dilemma had plans for him.

That morning, Fanny Anne had come to her in a great state of resolution. "Now," said she, "that this first meeting is over, I feel perfectly easy. I know my own strength, and I shall never be embarrassed again by his coming. We meet only as common and indifferent acquaintance."

"Yes, very indifferent indeed," said Dilemma sympathetically. "Oh, Fanny Anne, take care." Dilemma eyed Miss Collins thoughtfully. "What a pity we have no brothers. If we did, you could marry your cousin and stay with us forever."

"What, as a companion and helper to Mr and Mrs Fussbudget for all my life?" Fanny Anne smiled politely even as her soul writhed at the idea. "I'm afraid I must seek my own path in life, though I thank you for the wish. I saw you watch me all to-day, Dilemma, and I know I appeared distressed. But don't imagine it was from any silly cause. I was only confused for the moment, because I felt that I *should* be looked at. I do assure you that his return does not affect me either with pleasure or pain."

In spite of what her cousin declared, and really believed to be her feelings at his arrival, Dilemma could easily perceive that her spirits were affected by it. They were more disturbed, more unequal, than she had often seen them. "May I ask, dearest, how far things went between you? I know I shall seem an interfering busybody, but indeed, my curiosity and prurience will wait no longer."

Fanny coloured several becoming shades. "I confess, he had a kiss from me when he asked that we should marry, and, on another occasion, at dinner, the back of his ungloved hand brushed my upper arm when he was reaching for a plate of muffins. I know it was terribly immodest of me to allow such a liberty, but I vow, it was an accident!"

"No more than that?"

Under Dilemma's scrutiny, Fanny Anne turned red, and then finally went up to her room and procured a small but dainty chest fashioned from cardboard, twine, and old newspaper. "I am now going to destroy – what I ought to have destroyed long ago – what I ought never to have kept – I know that very well (blushing as she spoke). – However, now I will destroy it all – and it is my particular wish to do it in your presence, that you may see how rational I am grown. Cannot you guess what this parcel holds?" said she, with a conscious look.

"Not the least in the world. – Did he ever give you any thing?"

"No – I cannot call them gifts; but they are things that I have valued very much." She held the parcel towards her, and Dilemma read the words *Most precious treasures* on the top. Her curiosity was greatly excited. Fanny Anne unfolded the parcel, and she looked on with impatience. Within it was well lined with the softest cotton; but, excepting the cotton, Dilemma saw only a small piece of court plaister.

"Now," said Fanny Anne, "you *must* recollect."

"No, indeed I do not."

"Dear me! I should not have thought it possible you could forget what passed! – Do not you remember his cutting his ear off at swordplay – so terribly sad as he was showing off for us young ladies at the time, and your recommending court plaister? – But, as you had none about you, and knew I had, you desired me to supply him; and so I took mine out and cut him a piece; but it was a great deal too large, and he cut it smaller, and kept playing some time with what was left, before he gave it back to me. And so then, in my nonsense, I could not help making a treasure of it – so I put it by never to be used, and looked at it now and then as a great treat."

"My dearest Fanny Anne!" cried Dilemma, putting her hand before her face, and jumping up, "I have no words for how much you need a good paint set or embroidery silks, which I am sure would provide far better entertainment."

"That is because you have never been in love," Fanny Anne said a bit hotly. "Though I know you intervened for my benefit, it all came to naught, and I blame only myself."

"You make me more ashamed of myself than I can bear. Remember it? Aye, I remember it all now; all, except your saving this relick – I knew nothing of that till this moment – but the cutting the finger, and my recommending court plaister, and saying I had none about me! – Oh! my sins, my sins! – And I had plenty all the while in my pocket! – One of my senseless tricks! – I deserve to be under a continual blush all the rest of my life. – Well – (sitting down again) – go on – what else?"

"And had you really some at hand yourself? – I am sure I never suspected it, you did it so naturally."

"And so you actually put this piece of court plaister by for his sake!" said Dilemma, recovering from her state of shame and feeling divided between wonder and amusement. And secretly she added to herself, "Lord bless me! when should I ever have thought of putting by in cotton a piece of court plaister that any young man had been pulling about! I never was equal to this."

"Here," resumed Fanny Anne, turning to her box again, "here is something still more valuable, I mean that *has been* more valuable, because this is what did really once belong to him, which the court plaister never did."

Dilemma was quite eager to see this superior treasure. It was the end of an old pencil, – the part without any lead.

"This was really his," said Fanny Anne. – "Do not you remember one morning? – no, I dare say you do not. But one morning – I forget exactly the day – but perhaps it was the Tuesday or Wednesday before *that evening*, he wanted to make a memorandum in his pocket-book; it was about spruce beer; but when he took out his pencil, there was so little lead that he soon cut it all away, and the tip of his finger along with it, and it would not do, so you lent him another, and this was left upon the table as good for nothing. But I kept my eye on it; and, as soon as I dared, caught it up, and never parted with it again from that moment."

"I do remember it," cried Dilemma; "I perfectly remember it. Well, go on."

Here Fanny Anne coloured a bit. "It is hardly the thing to have done, but on the pretext of an errand I visited his elderly nurse, now retired, and asked about his childhood. She showed me a fair pile of treasures, and I contrived, through artifice to steal – "

"Indeed, to steal what?"

Blushing, Fanny Anne moved aside the court plaister in her little box to reveal a tiny baby tooth.

"Dear lord!" was all Dilemma could say.

"And indeed, she also showed me in imprint of his hand in clay, and while I could not take such a treasure from her, I secretly scraped away a dusting of it." Fanny Anne solemnly pointed to a few speaks of dirt in one corner of the box that Dilemma had mistaken for, well, a few specks of dirt.

"And once, he had something between his teeth, and used a toothpick to clear it. Afterwards, I must confess that I – "

"No more!" Dilemma managed. "For God's sake, no more!"

"Oh! that's all. I have nothing more to show you, or to say – except that I am now going to throw them all behind the fire, and I wish you to see me do it."

"My poor dear Fanny Anne! and have you actually found happiness in treasuring up these things?"

"Yes, simpleton as I was! – but I am quite ashamed of it now, and wish I could forget as easily as I can burn them. It was very wrong of me, you know, to keep any remembrances, after he left me. I knew it was – but had not resolution enough to part with them."

"But, Fanny Anne, is it necessary to burn the court plaister? – I have not a word to say for the bit of old pencil, but the court plaister might be useful. And the tooth – " here Dilemma cringed, but could not say more than "Please do not."

"I shall be happier to burn them all," replied Fanny Anne. "They have a disagreeable look to me. I must get rid of every thing. – There it goes, and there is an end, thank Heaven! of Captain Wentworth. Now I believe I shall see if Jane Harriet is about and would care to venture into town." She departed the room with what fragments remained of her dignity.

Yes, Dilemma resolved, her cousin most certainly required a suitable match, before she went 'round the bend completely. But how to begin?

"Mr Tightly-Wound's come, Miss."

Mr Tightly-Wound! The very advisor she needed. Dilemma hastily set down her endless embroidery and hurried into the parlour.

Mr Tightly-Wound, a sensible man about seven or eight-and-thirty, was not only a very old and intimate friend of the family, but particularly connected with it as the younger brother of Mrs Fussbudget's third cousin twice removed's man of business. He lived about a mile from Longbore, was a frequent visitor and always welcome. Mr Tightly-Wound had a cheerful manner which always did him good; and his many inquiries after Mr Fussbudget's health and his collections were answered most satisfactorily by their object. Mrs Fussbudget called for tea, and the tables were soon loaded. She then did all the honours of the meal with many a flutter, and helped and recommended the minced chicken and scalloped oysters, with an urgency which she knew would be acceptable to the early hours and civil scruples of their guest.

Upon such occasions poor Mr Fussbudget's feelings were in sad warfare. He loved to have the cloth laid, because it had been the fashion of his youth, but his conviction of suppers being very unwholesome made him rather sorry to see any thing put on it; and while his hospitality would have welcomed his visitors to every thing, his care for their health made him grieve that they would eat. His own stomach could bear nothing rich, and he could never believe other people to be different from himself. What was unwholesome to him, he regarded as unfit for any body; and he had, therefore, earnestly tried to dissuade them from having any cake at all and being terribly careful about the oysters.

Such another small basin of thin gruel as his own was all that he could, with thorough self-approbation, recommend; though he might constrain himself, while his daughters were comfortably clearing the nicer things, to say:

"Mr Tightly-Wound, let me propose your venturing on one of these eggs. An egg boiled very soft is not unwholesome. Hill understands boiling an egg better than any body. I would not recommend an egg boiled by any body else; but you need not be afraid, they are very small, you see – one of our small eggs will not hurt you. Or, sir, let Dilemma help you to a *little* bit of tart – a *very* little bit. Ours are all apple-tarts. You need not be afraid of unwholesome preserves here. I do not advise the custard. However, the boiled pork and pease pudding with bacon fat is very well boiled indeed, so much so that nothing unwholesome can remain in it, I am sure."

Dilemma allowed her father to talk – but supplied everyone besides himself in a much more satisfactory style. When all had supped, and most of his daughter had departed, Mr Fussbudget gratefully observed, "We have quite a family party, with Fanny Anne Collins and her brother to visit. If they had not both gone for a walk into Marrytown, I declare, I would never have had a quiet hour for our conference."

"And where is your cousin, Miss Fussbudget? Your mother said she was indisposed this morning."

"I blame myself," Dilemma said forthrightly. "For it was I who persuaded her to fix on Captain Wentworth. I made the match, you know, seven years ago; and to have it not take place, and be proved in the wrong, when so many people said they were unsuited, may shame me forever. My cousin, I believe, is filled with sorrow that she should come here to escape her troubles and then that they should inadvertently follow her here!"

"How long do the Collinses plan to stay?" Mr Tightly-Wound inquired.

"If I have my will, until my sister Scary has wed the brother and I have found a better match for the sister," Dilemma replied promptly. "Admiral Haughtyton is the best available, and she is so skilled at nursemaiding that I am sure both would find the match ideal."

Mr Tightly-Wound shook his head at her. Her father fondly replied, "Ah! my dear, I wish you would not make matches and foretell things, for whatever you say always comes to pass. Pray do not make any more matches."

"I promise you to make none for myself, papa; but I must, indeed, for other people. I would have everybody marry if they can do it properly: I do not like to have people throw themselves away; but everybody should marry as soon as they can do it to advantage."

"No match for yourself," Tightly-Wound asked curiously, with a tremor of some strong emotion in his voice. "You do not seek to wed?"

"No, indeed, unless he be a great figure of mystery and romance, one new to town with an air of fascination about him," she said dreamily. "A true knight indeed. I hear so many delightful rumours of Mr Wickham – if I were to seek a romance, there are worse choices. But making matches for others, it is the greatest amusement in the world! And after such a disappointment, I must try again, you know! – Every body said that Captain Wentworth and our Fanny Anne were perfectly suited, so alike in steady temperament, and so quickly fond of one another. I made up my mind on the subject. I planned the match from that hour; And yet that came to naught. So I am determined to find my cousin a fine match, before I even think of my own happiness. When such disappointment has found me in this instance, dear papa, you cannot think that I shall leave off match-making."

Mr Tightly-Wound shook his head and gave Dilemma a gravely disappointed look. "Disappointment supposes endeavour. Your time has been properly and delicately spent, if you have been endeavouring to bring about this marriage. A worthy employment for a young lady's mind! But if, which I rather imagine, your making the match, as you call it, means only your planning it, your saying to yourself one idle day, 'I think it would be a very good thing for Miss Collins if Captain Wentworth were to marry her,' and saying it again to yourself every now and then afterwards, – why, you made a guess; and that is all that can be said."

"And have you never known the pleasure and triumph of a lucky guess? – I pity you. – I thought you cleverer – for, depend upon it a lucky guess is never merely luck. There is always some talent in it. And as to my poor word 'success,' which you quarrel with, I do not know that I am so entirely without any claim to it. You have drawn two pretty pictures – but I think there may be a third – a something between the do-nothing and the do-all. If I had not promoted Captain Wentworth's visits, and given many little encouragements, and smoothed many little matters, it might not have come to any thing after all. No one ever gives credit to the one who has done all the work."

"What, the servants?"

"No, indeed! What a foolish thing to say!"

He sighed. "A straight-forward, open-hearted man, like Captain Wentworth, and a practical, self-effacing woman, like Miss Collins, may be safely left to manage their own concerns. You have done harm to yourself and them, by interference."

"Dilemma never thinks of herself, if she can do good to others;" rejoined Mr Fussbudget, understanding but in part. "But, my dear, pray do not make any more matches, they are silly things, and break up one's family circle grievously. If you wed, my dear Dilemma, who will arrange my antique teakettles, and polish them each morning?"

"Only one more, papa; only for Admiral Haughtyton and Fanny. Poor Admiral Haughtyton! He is so well-off and advantaged in every way that it would be a shame to have him single any longer. Luckily, Captain Wentworth has promised to hold a ball, and it will be an excellent time to match the pair of them."

Mr Tightly-Wound lifted a dripping spoonful of gruel and lowered it, shaking his head. "Leave him to chuse his own wife, Dilemma. Depend upon it, a man of three or four-and-eighty can take care of himself."

Though Dilemma nodded politely, it seemed to her that everyone in her life lacked any sense at all, excepting, of course, herself.

NONSENSIBILITY

Chapter 6: Preparation

The prospect of the Netherbum ball was extremely agreeable to every female of the family. Mrs Fussbudget chose to consider it as given in compliment to her fetching daughters, and was particularly flattered by receiving the invitation from Captain Wentworth himself, instead of a ceremonious card; Marianne pictured to herself a happy evening in raptures over Captain Wentworth's tragic wounds or the Admiral's frigid glare; and Dilemma thought with pleasure of throwing her cousin together with Admiral Haughtyton and seeing them well-matched at last. Fanny Anne…well, who could say. But she indeed took a great deal of care with her new gown. The happiness anticipated by Lydia depended less on any single event, or any particular person, for though she meant to dance half the evening with Mr Wickham and Mr Denny by turns, they were by no means the only partners who could satisfy her, and a ball was at any rate, a ball. Jane Harriet enjoyed a ball, as her sisters needed someone with whom to gossip, or stroll away in a huff with when required. And even Scary could assure her family that she had no disinclination for it.

"While I can have my mornings to myself," said she, "it is enough. – I think it no sacrifice to join occasionally in evening engagements. Society has claims on us all; and I profess myself one of those who consider intervals of recreation and amusement as desirable for every body."

Poor Scary had long been passed over in the changing

passions of village life, so much so that she had set herself on another path before spinsterhood should overtake her at the daunting age of twenty-four. At eighteen or nineteen she was, as far as such an early age can be qualified for the care of children, fully competent to the office of instruction herself; but she was too much beloved to be parted with. If she were to leave, no one would read out instruction to them or play booming tuba music as they sewed, and Lydia's loud laughter would quite overwhelm them. The evil day was put off. It was easy to decide that she was still too young; and Scary remained with them, sharing, as another daughter, in all the rational pleasures of an elegant society, and a judicious mixture of home and amusement, with only the drawback of the future, the sobering suggestions of her own good understanding to remind her that all this might soon be over. She had long resolved that one-and-twenty should be the period. With the fortitude of a devoted novitiate, she had resolved at one-and-twenty to complete the sacrifice, and retire from all the pleasures of life, of rational intercourse, equal society, peace and hope, to penance and mortification for ever as an instructor of young ladies in French, Italian, and long, dreary ballads.

Dilemma's spirits were so high on the occasion that, though she did not often speak unnecessarily to Mr Collins, she could not help asking him whether he intended to accept Captain Wentworth's invitation, and, if he did, whether he would think it proper to join in the evening's amusement; and she was rather surprised to find that he entertained no scruple whatever on that head, and was very far from dreading a rebuke either from the Archbishop, or society, by venturing to dance.

"I am by no means of opinion, I assure you," said he, "that a ball of this kind, given by a young man of character to respectable people, can have any evil tendency; and I am so far from objecting to dancing myself, that I shall hope to be honoured with the hands of all my fair cousins in the course of the evening, and I take this opportunity of soliciting yours,

Miss Fussbudget, for the two first dances especially."

Dilemma felt herself completely taken in. There was no help for it however. Her happiness was perforce delayed a little longer, and Mr Collins's proposal accepted with as good a grace as she could. She was not the better pleased with his gallantry from the idea it suggested of something more – that *she* was selected from among her sisters as worthy of being the mistress of his own Dumbsford Parsonage. The idea soon reached to conviction, as she observed his increasing civilities toward herself, and heard his frequent attempt at a compliment on her wit and vivacity; and though more astonished than gratified herself by this effect of her charms, it was not long before her mother gave her to understand that the probability of their marriage was exceedingly agreeable to *her*. Dilemma, however, did not chuse to take the hint, being well aware that a serious dispute must be the consequence of any reply. Mr Collins might never make the offer, and till he did, it was useless to quarrel about him.

Mr Collins was not a sensible man, and the deficiency of nature had been but little assisted by education or society or the nurse that had tried to teach him to tuck his shirttails in after using the privy; the greatest part of his life having been spent under the guidance of an illiterate and miserly father. The subjection in which his father had brought him up had given him originally great humility of manner, but it was now a good deal counteracted by the self-conceit of a weak head, living in retirement, and the consequential feelings of early and unexpected prosperity. A very good opinion of himself, of his authority as a clergyman, and his rights as a rector, combined with a fervent need to be close to those in power made him altogether a mixture of pride and obsequiousness, self-importance and humility, complete with a feeble comb-over and periodic flatulence.

Having now a good house and very sufficient income, he intended to marry; and in seeking a reconciliation with the Longbore family he had a wife in view, as he meant to chuse one of the daughters. This was his plan of amends – of atonement – for inheriting their father's estate; and he thought it an excellent one, full of eligibility and suitableness, and excessively generous and disinterested on his own part. His plan had not varied on seeing them. – Miss Dilemma Fussbudget's lovely face and other physical endowments confirmed his views, and established all his strictest notions of what was due to seniority; and consequently she was his settled choice.

If there had not been a Netherbum ball to prepare for and talk of, the younger Miss Fussbudgets would have been in a pitiable state at this time, for from the day of the invitation to the day of the ball, there was such a succession of rain with bursts of hail and even a brief rain of sardines as prevented their walking to Marrytown once. There was nothing to do but decorate more cushions and an entire hatrack's worth of bonnets, as the watercolours had been depleted. No aunt, no officers, no news could be sought after; – the very shoe-roses for Netherbum were got by proxy. Nothing less than a dance on Tuesday, could have made such a Friday, Saturday, Sunday, and Monday endurable to Marianne and Lydia. And as the young ladies sat about quietly embroidering slippers for the cat, a storm was brewing within the house as well.

"Marianne, may I borrow your blue sash?" Lydia asked, prancing into her sister's room without knocking.

"Indeed, no! You spilled gravy on the last one I lent you."

"It's not fair!" Lydia cried, pouting in a manner she mistakenly thought appealing. "All I have are hand-me-downs! You're nearly eldest, so everything comes to you."

There were several responses Marianne might have made, namely that a sash need not be passed down from largest to smallest, and that she had, in fact, sewn this one herself and embroidered it with daisies of which she was quite fond. Or that Lydia had plenty of new gowns and trimmings, as her father had observed loudly on finding her dressmakers' bills. Marianne chose instead silence.

"Fanny Anne, you must curl my hair. Sarah is busy with

Dilemma's, and I shan't get a turn before it's time to leave," Jane Harriet said hopefully.

"Where is the housekeeper?"

"She said a ball was important, but not as much as her husband dying downstairs. Mean old thing!"

With a resigned shrug, Fanny Anne abandoned her own hair to tend her young cousin's.

"Oh, Fanny, you're so competent!" Jane smiled as Fanny began.

"You should watch that, dear cousin," Dilemma replied, emerging from her own room into the hall. She carried herself as if quite aware how her white gown accentuated her figure. A trail of orchids in her hair looked careless but had taken an hour to arrange, and a bit of netting somehow suggested a bride's veil in a terribly subtle manoeuvre. "Resolutely displaying total helplessness, even to the degree of brushing one's own hair, is the sign of a true lady."

"I see no need for excessive adornment," said Scary, who nonetheless was wearing a startlingly yellow gown with large, ugly cabbage roses adorning the bodice. "For it is said, the character of a man is known from his conversations." Her reticule bulged with so much sheet music that she could not quite keep it shut. "When he hears my music, Admiral Haughtyton shall be quite enthralled."

"You're only nineteen and should give way to your betters," Dilemma, retorted. While the admiral's eligibility was quite a heady aphrodisiac, Mr Wickham's excessive sideburns and toothy smile continued to float before her eyes. "He's not suited to you anyway. You need someone who is always reading and trying to impress others, like our cousin Mr Collins." Dilemma's generosity in this match might be considered less than selfless, as she had a distinct inkling of where his unwelcome attentions tended.

"I have no inclination for him," Scary said coldly. She had had no inclination for him since precisely three in the afternoon the previous day, when she had beheld him tweezing his nostril hairs. Of such small things are matches broken up.

"He is a respectable gentleman, and with little beauty, Scary, you should wed to save your family from ruin."

"Will next week suit you?" Scary asked ironically.

"Surely not. The eldest should marry before the youngest. And who is older than our cousin?"

Fanny Anne winced, though she knew it hadn't been meant unkindly. Dilemma's words often stung more than she knew. "Fanny Anne!" Jane Harriet squeaked, reacting to the inadvertent tug on her curls. "She said it, not me!"

"No, I didn't – that is, I beg pardon indeed," Fanny Anne began, but the other girls had entered the room.

"What'd she do, make you look a fright to increase her own chances?" Lydia asked. She tied the blue sash languidly about her waist. "For if Dilemma's the loveliest and I'm the most vivacious, Fanny Anne surely has nothing to recommend her."

Fanny Anne kept her hands steady as she wound another curl, though she was tempted to bind them around Lydia's saucy neck.

"Give that back at once!" Marianne had spied Lydia's new possession. She ripped it from the other girl's waist, tearing the thin muslin skirt.

"You've destroyed it!" Lydia shrieked in rage. Fanny Anne took up a needle and thread, but before she could try to salvage the dress, Lydia had launched herself at Marianne, pummelling her and shoving her to the floor in a full brawl. "You're determined to have me a shambles for the ball so Admiral Haughtyton can be all yours!" She pounded Marianne's head into the carpet, oblivious to the fact that she was ruining both their appearances.

"Stop it at once! I'll get Mama, I will," Jane Harriet threatened.

"We aren't six, Jane," Dilemma responded. "Girls, such a lack of decorum reminds one of the meanest of tenant farmers. Leave off this display at once and tend to your appearances." Both girls ignored her.

Scary eyed them with distaste. "Without an acquaintance with the rules of propriety, it is impossible for the character to be established."

"Yes, *thank you Scary*, terribly helpful as always." Dilemma eyed the girls, who seemed to have slowed down, as Lydia was sitting on Marianne's back, pushing her face into the carpet with one hand and prying the sash from her hand with the other. "Perhaps a bucket of water…"

"Perhaps Admiral Haughtyton is seeking a smug, bossy girl with more forcefulness than sense!" Marianne murmured from the carpet.

"We're all grown up girls – "

"Some older than others!"

"Ooh!" Heedless of Lydia or her own new gown, Dilemma launched herself onto Marianne.

"Stop that!" Scary hit Dilemma with her reticule, and then shrieked in dismay when its delicate beading caught in Dilemma's perfect curls. Pages flew everywhere, and Scary dashed about gathering them, heedless of which sister she stepped upon. Fanny Anne eyed the chaos and resigned herself to their all being late to the ball. "Jane, I'll finish your hair in my room. And then, I think your sisters will need all our help to complete their toilet."

NONSENSIBILITY

Chapter 7: The Netherbum Ball

Till Dilemma entered the drawing-room at Netherbum and looked in vain for Mr Wickham among the cluster of red coats there assembled, a doubt of his being present had never occurred to her. The certainty of meeting him had not been checked by any of those recollections that might not unreasonably have alarmed her. She had dressed with more than usual care in her most frolicsome gown and largest shoe-roses, and prepared in the highest spirits for the conquest of all that remained unsubdued of his heart, trusting that it was not more than might be won in the course of the evening. Though she wasn't sure she would willingly surrender her single status for the burden of a husband, she had looked forward to breaking a man's heart at least once in her life. But in an instant arose the dreadful suspicion of his being purposely omitted for Admiral Haughtyton's pleasure in Captain Wentworth's invitation to the officers; and though this was not exactly the case, the absolute fact of his absence was pronounced by his friend Mr Denny, to whom Lydia eagerly applied, and who told them that Wickham had been obliged to go to town on business the day before, and was not yet returned; adding, with a significant smile,

"I do not imagine his business would have called him away just now, if he had not wished to avoid a certain gentleman here."

This part of his intelligence, though unheard by Lydia, was caught by Dilemma, and as it assured her that

Haughtyton was not less answerable for Wickham's absence than if her first surmise had been just, every feeling of displeasure against the former was so sharpened by immediate disappointment, that she determined to avoid him, no matter how rich and eligible he might be. Since he was doing the same to her, indeed to everyone at the party, this was a task easily accomplished. She was resolved against any sort of conversation with him, and turned away with a degree of ill humour, which she could not wholly surmount even in speaking to Captain Wentworth, whose blind partiality provoked her.

But Dilemma was not formed for ill-humour, only for ruling over her sisters and everyone else of her acquaintance. She peeked into the next room and beheld a delightful supper had been assembled, of swallows' beaks in cream, glazed and perfumed suckling pig, gold-plated truffles, ducked goose, creamed cream, and all that was rich and luxurious. The anticipation of all this truly doubled the feast's delight. The room was all light and colour and heat, with such dainty muslin dresses and sweet shoe-roses flicking round and round with the dancers, feathers and flowers atop ponderous curls, gentlemen in dark coats or bright regimentals.

The two first dances, however, brought a return of distress; they were dances of mortification. Mr Collins, awkward and solemn, apologizing instead of attending, and often moving wrong without being aware of it, gave her all the shame and misery which a disagreeable partner for a couple of dances can give. Though everyone else in Marrytown had mastered the dances until they knew each step perfectly, and could even maintain complex conversations while dancing, Mr Collins was an outsider and had not learned such grace. Worse yet, his shoe polish was adhering to the beeswax on the floors and made a nasty squelching sound when he pulled his feet free. The moment of her release from him was ecstasy.

Dilemma continued to entertain no doubt of her being in love with the handsome and charming Mr Wickham. Her ideas only varied as to the how much. At first, she thought it was a good deal; and afterwards, but little. But, on the other hand, she could not admit herself to be unhappy, nor, at such a sparkling ball, to be less disposed for employment than usual; she was still busy and cheerful; and, pleasing as he was, she could yet imagine him to have faults; and farther, though thinking of him so much, and, as she danced and smiled, forming a thousand amusing schemes for the progress and close of their attachment, fancying interesting dialogues, and inventing elegant letters; the conclusion of every imaginary declaration on his side was that she *refused him.* Their affection was always to subside into friendship. Every thing tender and charming was to mark their parting; but still they were to part. When she became sensible of this, it struck her that she could not be very much in love; for in spite of her previous and fixed determination never to quit her father, never to marry, a strong attachment certainly must produce more of a struggle than she could foresee in her own feelings.

"I do not find myself making any use of the word *sacrifice*," said she. – "In not one of all my clever replies, my delicate negatives, is there any allusion to making a sacrifice. I do suspect that he is not really necessary to my happiness. So much the better. I certainly will not persuade myself to feel more than I do. I am quite enough in love. I should be sorry to be more."

Upon the whole, she was equally contented with her view of his feelings, based on a brief introduction at the assembly and the large-toothed smile he had offered her along with his nod and the immortal words, "Miss Fussbudget."

"*He* is undoubtedly very much in love – every thing denotes it – very much in love indeed! – and when he comes again, if his affection continue, I must be on my guard not to encourage it. – It would be most inexcusable to do otherwise, as my own mind is quite made up. Not that I imagine he can think I have been encouraging him hitherto. No, if he had believed me at all to share his feelings, he would not have been so wretched. Could *he* have thought himself encouraged, his looks and language at parting would have been different. – Still, however, I must be on my guard. This is in the supposition of his attachment continuing what it now is; but I do not know that I expect it will; I do not look upon him to be quite the sort of man – I do not altogether build upon his steadiness or constancy. – His feelings are warm, but I can imagine them rather changeable. – Every consideration of the subject, in short, makes me thankful that my happiness is not more deeply involved. – I shall do very well again after a little while – and then, it will be a good thing over; for they say every body is in love once in their lives, and I shall have been let off easily."

The ball proceeded pleasantly. Every body seemed happy; and the praise of being a delightful ball, which is seldom bestowed till after a ball has ceased to be, was repeatedly given in the very beginning of the existence of this. Of very important, very recordable events, it was not more productive than such meetings usually are. There was one, however, which Dilemma thought something of. – The two last dances before supper were begun, and Scary had no partner; – the only young lady sitting down; – and so equal had been hitherto the number of dancers, that how there could be any one disengaged was the wonder! – But Dilemma's wonder lessened soon afterwards, on seeing Mr Collins sauntering about. Apparently her pressure that he wed Scary had offended him. He would not ask Scary to dance if it were possible to be avoided: she was sure he would not – and she was expecting him every moment to escape into the card-room.

Escape, however, was not his plan. He came to the part of the room where the sitters-by were collected, spoke to some, and walked about in front of them, as if to show his liberty, and his resolution of maintaining it. He did not omit being sometimes directly before Scary, or speaking to those who were close to her.

Unable to resist more meddling in the face of this defiance, Dilemma had left her seat to join him and say, "Do not you dance, Mr Collins?" to which his prompt reply was, "Most readily, Miss Fussbudget, if you will have the great charm of manner to dance with me again." He gaped at her, treating her to his prodigious onion-breath.

She supressed a shudder. "Me! – oh! no – I would get you a better partner than myself."

"If Mrs Moneygrubber wishes to dance," said he, "I shall have great pleasure, I am sure."

"Mrs Moneygrubber does not mean to dance, but there is a young lady disengaged whom I should be very glad to see dancing – my sister, Miss Scary." She smiled triumphantly at the unleashing of her clever trap.

"Miss Scary! – oh! – I had not observed. – You are extremely obliging – and if I were not suddenly stricken by a terrible leg cramp, I surely would." And he comically stumbled from the room, managing to bumble into several couples on his way out.

Dilemma said no more, and winced at what surprise and mortification her unattractive sister must be feeling. This was Mr Collins! the amiable, obliging, gentle Mr Collins. – She looked round for a moment; he had joined Captain Wentworth at a little distance, and was arranging himself for settled conversation, while a smile of high glee passed over his features.

She would not look again. Her heart was in a glow, and she feared her face might be as hot.

"Is this because I'm a nag?!" she heard Scary ask sadly.

Fanny heard one of the Miss Moneygrubbers assure her that her equine resemblance had nothing to do with the cruel slight.

In another moment a happier sight caught her; – Admiral Haughtyton leading Scary to the set! – Never had she been more surprised, seldom more delighted, than at that instant. She was all pleasure and gratitude, both for Scary and herself, and longed to be thanking him; and though too distant for speech, her countenance said much, as soon as she could catch his eye again.

His dancing proved to be extremely good as he adroitly managed both walking stick and girl; and Scary would have seemed almost too lucky, if it had not been for the cruel state of things before, and for the very complete enjoyment and very high sense of the distinction which her happy features announced. It was not thrown away on her, though she had rarely danced (or indeed been asked) at all, she bounded higher than ever, flew farther down the middle, and was in a continual course of smiles. Such a moment of attention was enough for her – indeed the most eligible gentleman in the room had chosen her, and raised her above all others in esteem. Yet as she watched him, something calculating and yet delightful came over her features as she perhaps considered a life of ease as mistress of the admiral's grand estate, and convinced herself that his generous gesture might conceal true affection.

For her own part, Dilemma observed a party of young men were standing engaged in very lively consultation; and soon afterwards she saw the smartest officer of the set walking off to the orchestra to order the dance, while Lydia, passing before her to her little expecting partner, hastily said: "Edward, I beg your pardon for not keeping my engagement, but I am going to dance these two dances with Colonel Mustard. I know you will excuse me, and I will certainly dance with you after I meet him in the library with the candlestick"; and without staying for an answer, in another minute was led by Colonel Mustard to begin the set. If the poor little boy's face had in its happiness been interesting to Dilemma, it was infinitely more so under this sudden reverse; he stood the picture of disappointment, with crimsoned cheeks, quivering lips, and eyes bent on the floor. His mother, stifling her own mortification, tried to soothe his with the prospect of Lydia's second promise; but though he contrived to utter, with an effort of boyish bravery, "Oh, I do not mind it!" it was very evident, by the unceasing agitation of his features, that he minded it as much as ever.

Dilemma did not think or reflect; she felt and acted. "I

shall be very happy to dance with you, sir, if you like it," said she, holding out her hand with the most unaffected good-humour. The boy, in one moment restored to all his first delight, looked joyfully at his mother; and stepping forwards with an honest and simple "Thank you, ma'am," was instantly ready to attend his new acquaintance. Upon applying to his mother for an introduction (for Dilemma recalled the lady was known to her mother), she discovered they were distant relations from Snoreland Park, and indeed, as she vaguely recollected, Edward Edmunds was in fact next in the entail after Mr Collins.

The thankfulness of Mrs Edmunds was more diffuse; with a look most expressive of unexpected pleasure and lively gratitude, she turned to her neighbour with repeated and fervent acknowledgments of so great and condescending a kindness to her boy. Dilemma, with perfect truth, could assure her that she could not be giving greater pleasure than she felt herself; and they joined the set which was now rapidly forming, with nearly equal complacency. It was a partnership which could not be noticed without surprise. It gained her a broad stare from the Miss Moneygrubbers as they passed her in the dance. "Upon my word, Edward, you are in luck," called one of his friends, who was dancing with one of said sisters, "you have got a better partner than me"; to which the happy Edward answered "Yes."

When the dance had concluded, Dilemma saw Admiral Haughtyton whisper a brief word to Scary, and her beaming assent. She led him directly to her sister, who had just returned to her seat.

After being in raptures over Captain Wentworth upon their first meeting, and then transferring them to Admiral Haughtyton, and then repenting and perhaps repenting again, Marianne was quite emotionally exhausted. Pausing for a moment to sit, she found herself suddenly addressed by Admiral Haughtyton, who took her so much by surprise in his application for her hand, that, without knowing what she did, she accepted him. He walked away again immediately, and she was left to fret over her own want of presence of mind; Jane Harriet, who timed her arrival perfectly to comfort her sister, tried to console her.

"I dare say you will find him very agreeable."

"Heaven forbid! – *That* would be the greatest misfortune of all! – To have a pleasant time and be satisfied in love, rather than longing and suffering and having obstacles in one's way! – Do not wish me such mundanity."

When the dancing recommenced, however, and Haughtyton approached to claim her hand, Jane Harriet could not help cautioning her, in a whisper, not to be a simpleton, and allow her fancy for disappointment to make her appear unpleasant in the eyes of a man of such eligibility. Marianne made no answer, and took her place on the floor, amazed at the dignity to which she was arrived in being allowed to stand opposite to Admiral Haughtyton, and reading in her neighbours' looks their equal amazement in beholding it. Marianne felt quite uncomfortable on the arm of Admiral Haughtyton who had snubbed her sisters at the previous assembly and now so transformed as to rescue Scary from disgrace, but there was nothing to be done. They stood for some time without speaking a word; and she began to imagine that their silence was to last through the two dances, and at first was resolved not to break it; till suddenly fancying that it would be the greater punishment to her partner to oblige him to talk, she made some slight observation on the dance. He replied, and was again silent. "Have you a first name?" she enquired, and was dissatisfied to hear he did not. She then remarked on how delightful the evening was, and he replied, "Oh yes, it is astonishing! The dancers are laughing with passion, abandon, excitement!... All the things I've managed to suppress in all the years of my buttoned-up existence." An ominous, almost angry silence followed. She smiled. Perhaps there would be misery and disappointment after all.

"Oh here you are, Marianne!" Lydia cried, rushing up to

them with her friend Mr Denny in hand. He had been much the especial focus of Lydia's flirtations, at least for that week. "Do you need more for your set?"

As four couples were needed for the cotillion, the answer was obvious. Mr Haughtyton craned his head, no doubt hoping to find his friends, but before he could locate them, Scary arrived, with a lately-come Wickham himself in tow. Admiral Haughtyton stiffened in horror, but Mr Collins was following them close behind, Dilemma tugging feebly to disengage her hand, and there was nothing to do but accept their finished set.

First the two head ladies were to walk to the centre and curtsy. Scary, opposite Marianne, took an extra large step forward to tread squarely on her sister's toes. Marianne blinked. That had certainly been on purpose, and terribly ungraceful as well. Clearly, her sister resented being rescued from disgrace and elevated beyond all others only in order to procure an introduction to her prettier sister. Then the head gentlemen walked to the centre and bowed, Admiral Haughtyton glowering as he eyed Wickham.

The head ladies chained across, each taking the other's hand (Scary actually tried to trip Marianne!) and then having the opposite gentleman spin her around. As Marianne spun, she witnessed Scary actually rubbing against Admiral Haughtyton, like a cat desiring petting. A muscle in his face jumped and Marianne decided at that moment he would never again ask any of the Fussbudget sisters to dance. Then Mr Wickham, whose outside hand rested on her waist, lowered it to grope her posterior. Marianne jumped, eyes widening in horror. Then before her, she saw Scary's outstretched hand and grasped it gratefully to return to her cold but hardly licentious partner.

The gentlemen formed a star, with opposites taking hands. As Admiral Haughtyton took Mr Wickham's hand, he could be seen to barely touch the edge of it, as if handling a slimy dead thing. Mr Denny, releasing Mr Collins' hand, could be seen to wipe it carefully on his trousers.

Now it was the side ladies' turn. Dilemma and Lydia curtsied, though Lydia was staring at Admiral Haughtyton, not her sister. When they chained, Dilemma (who clearly believed Lydia too young or otherwise undeserving of Admiral Haughtyton) elbowed her hard in the ribs. Mr Collins spun Lydia around, and as the girls chained back, Lydia wiped a large handful of Collins-sweat on her sister in retaliation. Dilemma shuddered, but maintained a frozen smile as she returned to Mr Collins. The girls walked in a star, and Lydia, who was in front of Marianne, tossed her hair and arched her neck, catching the attention of all four men in the circle. Marianne doubled her pace, deliberately tripping on Lydia, and sending the vain girl stumbling in the middle of her presentation. Behind her, there was a lurch in the star, and she concluded that Dilemma had deliberately stumbled, probably to trip Scary. Thankfully, the star concluded.

Each girl was to dance the next figure with her corner. Marianne advanced to Denny. While he spun her quite energetically, until she felt quite dizzy, he did nothing improper. Marianne heard a gleeful giggle from Lydia, and guessed Wickham had groped her, to a more eager reception. "Marianne looks well tonight, even with her country complexion," Marianne heard Dilemma whispering behind her, and guessed Dilemma had relented in throwing Fanny Anne at Admiral Haughtyton long enough to try snatching him up for herself. After they all set and turned (with nothing more disastrous than more giggling and whispering), each girl moved on to the next gentleman. Wickham spun Marianne, this time stretching his fingers inappropriately up from her waist. Marianne considered shouting or flinging herself away, but a quick glance at Admiral Haughtyton's miserable features (Scary was murmuring something to him) made it clear there was enough of a scene. Marianne stomped hard on Mr Wickham's toes and was rewarded by having him drop his hands as if she'd burned him. She smiled and finished the figure. Next she was passed on to Mr Collins, who indeed dripped buckets of sweat from his thinning hair and down his

Wound replied coolly. "Miss Collins is a sweet and gentle lady. I found her more conversable than I expected."

Dilemma's thoughts, which had heretofore been engaged in her own affairs, all at once directed themselves toward an eligible man complimenting a young lady of her acquaintance. Mr Tightly-Wound was indeed most eligible, and poor Fanny Anne had few prospects, save that of tending to her brother for all her days, so the match seemed most suitable on both sides. Nonetheless, something deep down revolted her about such an alliance.

They were interrupted by the bustle of Captain Wentworth proposing a waltz. This dance was quite *fast* for a country ball, with the man clutching the lady so close in his arms that he was touching far far more than her gloved hand, and yet so many of the ladies were eager to try it. Dilemma spied Wickham leading Lydia to the floor, and Admiral Haughtyton speaking animatedly to a gentleman of his acquaintance in order to pretend he did not see Scary hovering behind him. Fanny Anne was sinking into her chair, handkerchief once more over her face as if by this she planned to disappear entirely. And Captain Wentworth seemed to have lighted on Marianne as his prospective partner, and they set off, his wooden leg clattering in a manner that did not detract from his great wealth and attractiveness. Even his hook for a hand was not a great deterrent, as he had covered it with an elegant white glove and tied on a small nosegay.

"Whom are you going to dance with?" asked Mr Tightly-Wound.

Dilemma hesitated a moment, and then replied, "With you, if you will ask me."

"Will you?" said he, offering his hand.

"Indeed I will. You have shown that you can dance, and you know you are not such a close connexion as to make it at all improper."

"No, indeed."

And with that puzzling comment, Mr Tightly-Wound led

her to the floor.

The rest of the evening brought her little amusement. She was teazed by Mr Collins, who continued most perseveringly by her side, and though he could not prevail with her to dance with him again, put it out of her power to dance with others. In vain did she entreat him to stand up with somebody else, and offer to introduce him to any young lady in the room (and perhaps, by doing so, find him a far better match as she hoped). He assured her that as to dancing, he was perfectly indifferent to it; that his chief object was by delicate attentions to recommend himself to her, and that he should therefore make a point of remaining close to her the whole evening. There was no arguing upon such a project. He continued to stand with her, in a corner where the candelabra were dripping on them both, importuning her for attention.

The supper was delicious, but Mr Collins (who escorted her in of course) slurped the wine and (though the gentlemen eating at such a time was quite insupportable) devoured many boiled potatoes, over which he fell into raptures concerning their taste, colour, and consistency, until Dilemma was heartily wishing Columbus had never procured even a specimen.

Fanny Anne, in turn, spent most of the evening pretending to be unaware of Captain Wentworth's existence. When they sat down to supper, Fanny Anne considered it a most unlucky perverseness which placed them within one of each other; and deeply was she vexed to find that her aunt was talking to Lady Moneygrubber freely, openly, and of nothing else but of her expectation that Marianne would be soon married to Admiral Haughtyton as surely as Dilemma would wed Mr Collins, only on the proof of their single disastrous dance. "For I am sure they should suit each other well. He is so cold, and she so romantic, that their opposite personalities must attract, as all my novels promise," she added. It seemed she shared her daughter's predisposition for romances. For the occasion, Mrs Fussbudget wore an ostrich feather the size of an umbrella, which had the distinction of being the largest in town and also protecting her plump face from the dripping candelabra overhead.

Hers was an animating subject, and Mrs Fussbudget seemed incapable of fatigue while enumerating the advantages of the match. His being such a charming man, and so rich, and so close to his demise, were the first points of self-gratulation. It was, moreover, such a promising thing for her younger daughters, as Marianne's marrying so greatly must throw them in the way of other rich men, perhaps by catapult if she had any say; and lastly, it was so pleasant at her time of life to be able to consign her single daughters to the care of their sister, that she might not be obliged to go into company more than she liked. It was necessary to make this circumstance a matter of pleasure, because on such occasions it is the etiquette but no one was less likely than Mrs Fussbudget to find comfort in staying at home at any period of her life. She concluded with many good wishes that Lady Moneygrubber might soon be equally fortunate, though evidently and triumphantly believing there was no chance of it. In fact, at the thought of this, she began laughing loudly enough that she soon took on the tones of a cawing jay, to her niece's dismay.

In vain did Fanny Anne endeavour to check the rapidity of her aunt's words, or persuade her to describe her felicity in a less audible whisper; for to her inexpressible vexation, she could perceive that the chief of it was overheard by Captain Wentworth. Fanny Anne blushed and blushed again with shame and vexation. She could not help frequently glancing her eye at Captain Wentworth, though every glance convinced her of what she dreaded; for though he was not always looking at her aunt, she was convinced that his attention was invariably fixed by her and her heart began to beat quite faster.

At length however Mrs Fussbudget had no more to say; and Lady Moneygrubber, who had been long yawning at the repetition of delights which she saw no likelihood of sharing, was left to the comforts of supreme sweetbread aux truffles and sugared squab. Fanny Anne now began to revive. But not long was the interval of tranquillity; for Mr Collins came up to them and told her with great exultation that he had just been so fortunate as to make a most important discovery.

"I have found out," said he, "by a singular accident, that the vicarage at Admiral Haughtyton's estate is currently vacant, and indeed, he is seeking a discerning gentleman to fill the post. Imagine such a distinguished and refined admiral as my patron! How wonderfully these sort of things occur! Who would have thought of my meeting with – perhaps – a new patron in this assembly! – I am most thankful that the discovery is made in time for me to pay my respects to him, which I am now going to do, and trust he will excuse my not having done it before. My total ignorance of the available situation must plead my apology."

"Oh fiddlesticks and jam! You are not going to introduce yourself to Admiral Haughtyton?"

"Indeed I am. I shall intreat his pardon for not having done it earlier. I believe him to be in need of someone with just my very talents. It will be in my power to offer him a vicar of whom he has never *dreamed*."

His sister tried hard to dissuade him from such a scheme; assuring him that Admiral Haughtyton would consider his addressing him without introduction as an impertinent freedom, rather than an offer of assistance; that it was not in the least necessary for Mr Collins to press his suit at a ball, and that it must belong to Admiral Haughtyton, the superior in consequence, to begin the acquaintance. As she pleaded, it was not clear to her aunt, or indeed to herself, whether she more dreaded the ill opinion of Admiral Haughtyton or of his friend Captain Wentworth, only that she prayed her brother would not make himself ridiculous before them both.

Mr Collins listened to her with the determined air of following his own inclination and when she ceased speaking, replied, "My dear sister, I have the highest opinion in the world of your excellent judgment in all matters within the scope of your understanding, but permit me to say that there must be a wide difference between the established forms of ceremony amongst the laity, and those which regulate the clergy; for give me leave to observe that I consider the clerical office as equal in point of dignity with the highest rank in the kingdom – provided that a proper humility of behaviour is at the same time maintained. You must therefore allow me to follow the dictates of my conscience on this occasion, which leads me to perform what I look on as a point of duty. Pardon me for neglecting to profit by your advice, which on every other subject shall be my constant guide, though in the case before us I consider myself more fitted by education and habitual study to decide on what is right than a young lady like yourself." And with a low bow he left her to attack Admiral Haughtyton, whose reception of his advances she eagerly watched, and whose astonishment at being so addressed was very evident. Her cousin prefaced his speech with a solemn bow, and though she could not hear a word of it, she felt as if hearing it all, and saw in the motion of his lips the words "apology," "excellent situation." – It vexed her to see him expose himself to such a man. Admiral Haughtyton was eyeing him with unrestrained wonder, and when at last Mr Collins allowed him time to speak, replied with an air of distant civility. Nonetheless, his expression suggested that Haughtyton seemed to be seriously considering choking Mr Collins with his own comb-over. Mr Collins, however, was not discouraged from speaking again, and Admiral Haughtyton's contempt seemed abundantly increasing with the length of his second speech, and at the end of it he only made him a slight bow, and moved another way. Mr Collins then returned to Fanny Anne.

"I have no reason, I assure you," said he, "to be dissatisfied with my reception. Admiral Haughtyton seemed much pleased with the attention. He answered me with the utmost civility, and even paid me the compliment of saying that he was so well convinced of my skill, he should very much like to employ me in entering the village square each

Thursday to bring a greater feeling of religious fervour among the village sheep and to quiet the caterwauling of cats by setting myself in competition with them. Clearly, he perceives that my oration could extend to even the humblest creatures among us. It was really a very handsome thought. Upon the whole, I am much pleased with him. He is fine and stately and gentlemanly and rich...why, I should really attempt to wed him myself."

When supper was over, singing was talked of, and she had the mortification of seeing Scary, after very little entreaty, preparing to oblige the company. By many significant looks and silent entreaties, did she endeavour to prevent such a proof of complaisance, – but in vain; Scary would not understand them; such an opportunity of exhibiting was delightful to her, and she began her song. Fanny Anne's eyes were fixed on her with most painful sensations; and she watched her progress through the several stanzas with an impatience which was very ill rewarded at their close; for Scary, on receiving amongst the thanks of the table, the hint of a hope that she might be prevailed on to favour them again, after the pause of half a minute began another. Scary's powers were by no means fitted for such a display; her voice was weak, and her manner affected. Further, her bagpipes had sprung an unfortunate leak – Fanny Anne was in agonies. She looked at Dilemma, to see how she bore it; but Dilemma was very composedly talking to Mr Tightly-Wound.

Outside, the dogs howled in despair. Cats screeched and tumbled off their fences. One of the carriage horses tore loose from its harness and galloped into the night.

Inside, Scary continued to sing.

By the time her second song had ended, no one was in much mood for the excellent anchovies or snails in aspic.

Fanny Anne looked at her uncle to entreat his interference, lest Scary should be singing all night. He took the hint, and when Scary had finished her second song, said aloud, "That will do extremely well, child. You have delighted us long enough. Let the other young ladies have time to exhibit."

Scary, though pretending not to hear, was somewhat disconcerted; and Fanny Anne, sorry for her, and sorry for her uncle's speech, was afraid her anxiety had done no good. – Others of the party were now applied to.

"If I," said Mr Collins, "were so fortunate as to be able to sing, I should have great pleasure, I am sure, in obliging the company with an air; for I consider music as a very innocent diversion, and perfectly compatible with the profession of a clergyman. – I do not mean however to assert that we can be justified in devoting too much of our time to music, for there are certainly other things to be attended to. The rector of a parish has much to do. – In the first place, he must make such an agreement for tithes as may be beneficial to himself and not offensive to his patron. He must write his own sermons; and the time that remains will not be too much for his parish duties, and the care and improvement of his dwelling, which he cannot be excused from making as comfortable as possible. And I do not think it of light importance that he should have attentive and conciliatory manners towards every body, especially towards those to whom he owes his preferment." And with a bow to Admiral Haughtyton, he concluded his speech, which had been spoken so loud as to be heard by half the room. – Many stared. – Many smiled; while Mrs Fussbudget seriously commended Mr Collins for having spoken so sensibly, and observed in a half-whisper to Lady Moneygrubber, that he was a remarkably clever, good kind of young man.

Meanwhile, Scary's father was dragging her forcibly from the pianoforte. "But I love this song!"

"Then you should learn the tune," he said with finality.

To Fanny Anne it appeared, that had her family made an agreement to expose themselves as much as they could during the evening, it would have been impossible for them to play their parts with more spirit, or finer success; and happy did she think it for Captain Wentworth that some of the exhibition had escaped his notice, thanks to his glass eye, and that his generous feelings were not of a sort to be much distressed by the folly which he must have witnessed.

The Longbore party were the last of all the company to depart; and by a manoeuvre of Mrs Fussbudget in which she spooked the horses by appearing outside without her concealing face powder, had to wait for their carriages a quarter of an hour after every body else was gone, which gave them time to see how heartily they were wished away by some of the family. Indeed, the captain and admiral both seemed prepared to whack her with the silver servingware if that would banish her from their vestibule. When at length they arose to take leave, Mrs Fussbudget was most pressingly civil and addressed herself particularly to Admiral Haughtyton, to assure him how happy he would make them by eating a family dinner with them at any time, without the ceremony of a formal invitation. The Admiral looked at her as if hoping by remaining motionless he could go unseen, but finally deigned to say some polite triviality that promised nothing at all. His friend, Captain Wentworth, was more civil, bidding an individual good night to each lady and finishing with "Goodnight, Miss Collins."

Oh, how Fanny Anne's cheeks warmed at such address! So kind, so solicitous, so clearly overwhelmed with things he might not say. She saw nothing, thought nothing of the brilliancy of the room. Her happiness was from within. Her eyes were bright, and her cheeks glowed; but she knew nothing about it. She was thinking only of the last half-hour, and as they passed to their carriage, her mind took a hasty range over it. His direct address, his expressions, and still more his manner and look, had been such as she could see in only one light. His half-averted eyes, and more than half-expressive glance, all, all declared that he had a heart returning to her at least; that anger, resentment, avoidance were no more; and that they were succeeded, not merely by friendship and regard, but by the tenderness of the past. Yes, some share of the tenderness of the past! She could not contemplate the change as implying less. He must love her.

Mrs Fussbudget, meanwhile, was perfectly satisfied; and quitted the house under the delightful persuasion that, allowing for the necessary preparations of settlements, new carriages, and wedding clothes, she should undoubtedly see her flighty daughter Marianne settled at in the course of three or four months. Of having another daughter married to Mr Collins, she thought with equal certainty, and with considerable, though not equal, pleasure. Dilemma (or perhaps Scary, she conceded mentally, aware already of her oldest daughter's intentions for the middle sister) – whichever might end up with the gentleman – were the least dear to her of all her children; and though the man and the match were quite good enough for either of *them*, the worth of each was eclipsed by Admiral Haughtyton and his income.

NONSENSIBILITY

Chapter 8: An Infelicitous Tête-à-tête

After the ball, Fanny Anne joined her cousins in their carriage, as if to keep an eye on them after the disaster of the ball. Dilemma, who was last to climb up and therefore crowded out, found, on being escorted and followed into the second carriage by Mr Collins, that the door was to be lawfully shut on them, and that they were to have a tête-à-tête drive. It would not have been the awkwardness of a moment, it would have been rather a pleasure, previous to the insult of this very day; she could have talked to him of Scary, and the three-quarters of a mile would have seemed but one. But now, she would rather it had not happened. After he had snubbed her sister so publicly, and shown such a preferred attachment to her, Dilemma felt she would do anything, including shatter the widows with her coiffured head, to break out of his presence.

To restrain him as much as might be, by her own manners, she was immediately preparing to speak with exquisite calmness and gravity of the weather and the night; but scarcely had she begun, scarcely had they passed the sweep-gate and joined the other carriage, than she found her subject cut up – her hand seized – her attention demanded, and Mr Collins actually making violent love to her: availing himself of the precious opportunity, declaring sentiments which must be already well known, hoping – fearing – adoring, overly perspiring; but flattering himself that his ardent attachment and unequalled love and unexampled passion could not fail of having some effect, and in short, very much resolved on being seriously accepted as soon as possible.

The idea of Mr Collins, with all his solemn composure, being run away with by his feelings, made Dilemma so appalled that she could not use the short pause he allowed in any attempt to stop him, and he continued:

"My reasons for marrying are, first, that I think it a right thing for every clergyman in easy circumstances (like myself) to set the example of matrimony in his parish. Secondly, that I am convinced it will add very greatly to my happiness; and thirdly – which perhaps I ought to have mentioned earlier, that it is the particular mirroring of the man who may soon be my patron. If he is indeed fixing on your sister Marianne (as your esteemed mother is so certain), then it behooves me to join, nay, anticipate him and wed myself, before I unite him and his lady into that holy state. Thus much for my general intention in favour of matrimony; it remains to be told why my views were directed to Longbore instead of my own neighbourhood, where I assure you there are many amiable young women with ample fortunes and other …charms. But the fact is, that being, as I am, to inherit your estate after the death of your honoured father (who, however, may live many years longer despite the mortality rate in this age), I could not satisfy myself without resolving to chuse a wife from among his daughters, that the loss to them might be as little as possible, when the melancholy event takes place – which, however, as I have already said, may not be for several years as he continues to stubbornly postpone it. I must add here that primogeniture is a marvellous custom, though, indeed, your mother and sisters may find it less so.

"This has been my motive, my fair cousin, and I flatter myself it will not sink me in your esteem. And now nothing remains for me but to assure you in the most animated language of the violence of my affection. To fortune I am perfectly indifferent, and shall make no demand of that nature on your father, since I am well aware that it could not be complied with; and that half a pittance, which will not be yours till after your mother's decease, is all that you may ever be entitled to. On that head, therefore, I shall be uniformly silent; and you may assure yourself that no ungenerous reproach shall ever pass my lips when we are married, but only demands for endless cups of tea and sandwiches."

He leaned in for a slobbery kiss, licking his plump lips as if to augment their objectionable dampness and Dilemma shrank back in horror, shielding herself with one of the nearby cushions of her carriage seat. It was absolutely necessary to interrupt him now.

"You are too hasty, Sir," she cried. "You forget that I have made no answer. Let me do it without farther loss of time. Accept my thanks for the compliment you are paying me, I am very sensible of the honour of your proposals, but it is impossible for me to do otherwise than *decline* them. I have *no thoughts* of matrimony at present."

"I am not now to learn," replied Mr Collins, with a formal wave of the hand, "that it is usual with young ladies to reject the addresses of the man whom they secretly mean to accept, when he first applies for their favour; and that sometimes the refusal is repeated a second or even a third time. I am therefore by no means discouraged by what you have just said, and shall hope to lead you to the altar ere long." And as he leaned forward, he dared to pet her knee in an altogether forward and thoroughly condescending manner.

"Upon my word, Sir," cried Dilemma, slapping his hand hard enough that he withdrew it. "Your hope is rather an extraordinary one after my declaration. I do assure you that I am not one of those young ladies (if such young ladies there are) who are so daring as to risk their happiness on the chance of being asked a second time."

Here he opened his mouth to interrupt her, but a happy thought seized her. Dilemma reached down to pull a pincushion bristling with pins from her reticule, happy beyond words that she had brought it to mend the little emergencies of dress that ladies may encounter during a ball. Turning it to catch the light on its silvery pins, she uttered, "I am perfectly serious in my refusal. – You could not make *me* happy, and I am convinced that I am the last woman in the world who would make *you* so. In making me the offer, you must have satisfied the delicacy of your feelings with regard to my family, and may take possession of Longbore estate whenever it falls, without any self-reproach." With this, she turned the pincushion in her hand as if prepared to throw it with its sharp contents into Mr Collins' readily available lap. "This matter may be considered, therefore, as finally settled."

He leaned forward once more, but at her steely glare, merely shifted on his seat. "When I do myself the honour of speaking to you next on this subject I shall hope to receive a more favourable answer than you have now given me; though I am far from accusing you of cruelty at present, because I know it to be the established custom of your sex to reject a man on the first application, and perhaps you have even now said as much to encourage my suit as would be consistent with the true delicacy of the female character."

"Really, Mr Collins," cried Dilemma with some warmth, "you puzzle me exceedingly." She gripped the pincushion tightly enough to cause discomfort even through her glove as she struggled to master her fury and not release her missile. "If what I have hitherto said can appear to you in the form of encouragement, I know not how to express my refusal in such a way as may convince you of its being one." Though the pincushion gave her a particular idea in how to do so.

"You must give me leave to flatter myself my dear cousin that your refusal of my addresses is merely words of course. My reasons for believing it are briefly these: – It does not appear to me that my hand is unworthy of your acceptance, or that the establishment I can offer would be any other than highly desirable. My situation in life, my upcoming situation, and my relationship to your own, it into farther consideration that in spite of your manifold attractions (here he gazed at her low neckline), it is by no means certain that another offer of marriage may ever be made you. As I must therefore conclude that you are not serious in your rejection of me, I shall chuse to attribute it to your wish of increasing my love by suspense, according to the usual practice of elegant females."

Here Dilemma faced her last ounce of patience, and was prepared to throw the pincushion when she happened on a happy thought. A pair of scissors, too, were lodged in her reticule. While the pincushion seemed too small to alarm Mr Collins, and Dilemma hesitated to do serious harm to even so aggravating a man by throwing it, the pointed scissors had a longer reach and might intimidate the man into ceasing his addresses. She withdrew the scissors, and had the satisfaction of seeing his prominent Adam's apple move with great rapidity. She pointed the scissors directly at his heart, adding nearly a foot to her reach by doing so, and spoke thusly:

"I do assure you, Sir, that I have no pretension whatever to that kind of elegance which consists in tormenting a respectable man. I would rather be paid the compliment of being believed sincere. I *thank* you again and again for the honour you have done me in your proposals, but to accept them is *absolutely impossible*."

She gave him her steeliest, coldest stare, willing him to accept her words before she must plunge the scissors into his heart and leave him to jut his very life's blood onto her new gown and ultimately perish, all for want of any ability to listen. "Please," she thought. "Hear my words and accept them. Let us finish this interminable carriage ride in blessed uncomfortable silence."

For a moment he paused, gazing at the scissors. Apparently, on some level, Dilemma had penetrated through to his dense understanding. Suddenly seized by a happy thought, he snatched up one of the cushions beside him and clasped it before his chest, shielding himself from the assault. "You are uniformly charming!" cried he, with an air of awkward gallantry; "and I am persuaded that when sanctioned by the express authority of both your excellent parents, my proposals will not fail of being acceptable."

To such perseverance in wilful self-deception Dilemma would make no reply, except that of an infuriated scream, torn from her soul and directed entirely at the most infuriating creature to have ever drawn breath.

He was too stunned by this response to say another word; her manner too decidedly horrified to invite supplication; and in this state of swelling resentment, and mutually deep mortification, they had to continue together a few minutes longer. If there had not been so much anger, there would have been desperate awkwardness; but their straightforward emotions left no room for the little zigzags of embarrassment. Without knowing when the carriage turned into her lane, or when it stopped, they found themselves, all at once, at the door of her house; and she was out before another syllable passed. – Dilemma then felt it indispensable to wish him a good night. The compliment was just returned, coldly and proudly; and, just as Dilemma stepped from the coach, she casually tossed the pincushion into her tormentor's lap. His howl as she shut the door indicated that it had found its target.

Chapter 9: Terribly Romantic Tumbles

The whole country about the Fussbudget home abounded in beautiful walks. The high downs, which invited them from almost every window to seek the exquisite enjoyment of air on their summits and breathe air that didn't abound with crochet lint and smothered dreams, were a happy alternative when the dirt of the valleys beneath shut up their superior beauties; and towards one of these hills did Marianne and Jane Harriet one memorable morning direct their steps, attracted by the partial sunshine of a showery sky and a cessation from Scary's caterwauling, and unable longer to bear the confinement which the settled rain of the preceding days had occasioned. The weather was not tempting enough to draw the others from their latest chore of embroidering matching aprons and bonnets for the tea tables (the pets already fully supplied); and the two girls set off together.

They gaily ascended the downs, rejoicing at every glimpse of blue sky; and when they caught in their faces the animating gales of a high south-westerly wind, with smatterings of pine needles and dagger-sharp hail, they pitied the fears which had prevented their mother and sisters from sharing such delightful sensations.

"Is there a felicity in the world," said Marianne, "superior to this? Oh how I adore the rain, so cool and sweet on my eyelids. And the hail pounding on my new bonnet with the force of arrows, how wild and freeing. Jane Harriet, we will walk here at least two hours!"

The nearby gophers, who put up with this sort of nonsense not less than twice a week, began to snicker in their dry holes, and it must be admitted that several squirrels began hurling pinecones from above. Several times, Marianne had tried adopting their furry brethren as pets and the squirrels did not soon forget.

The heedless girls pursued their way against the wind, resisting it with laughing delight for about twenty minutes longer, despite the showers of pinecones, when suddenly the clouds united over their heads, and a driving rain blasted full in their faces. Still Marianne longed to frolic in the sheeting torrent, until bursts of lightning began striking, one toppling a slender tree she had been in the process of having wild raptures over. Nonetheless, upon being nearly brained (assuming she had such an organ of which to be so deprived), she reluctantly agreed to turn back. One consolation however remained for the over-emotional girl, to which the exigence of the moment gave more than usual propriety; it was that of running with all possible speed down the steep side of the hill which led immediately to their garden gate, heedless of the boulders, thornbushes, etcetera that adorned her path. Clearly she was a total fruitcake with extra nuts smothered in crazy sauce.

They set off. Marianne had at first the advantage, but a false step in a maliciously dug gopher hole brought her suddenly to the ground; and Jane Harriet, unable to stop herself to assist her, or cease from crying "Eeeee!" in a silly and delightful manner, was involuntarily hurried along, and reached the bottom in safety.

A gentleman carrying a gun, with two hunting poodles frolicking round him, was passing up the hill and within a few yards of Marianne, when her accident happened. He dropped his gun, nearly causing a permanent disfigurement, and ran to her assistance. She had raised herself from the ground, but her foot had been twisted in her fall, and she was scarcely able to stand. The gentleman offered his services; and, upon gazing up at him, Marianne realized that it was indeed Mr Wickham. Here was all she had wished! The stormy skies, his wind-tossed hair, the ardour in his expression as a bolt of lightning struck far too close. Marianne was prepared to swoon at the romance of it all. Upon perceiving that her modesty declined what her situation rendered necessary, he took her up in his arms without further delay, and carried her down the hill. She felt all a flutter at being touched by a man in several forbidden places, such as the back of her knees, and would have enjoyed the novel sensation thoroughly, except for her fears of getting with child. Then passing through the garden, the gate of which had been left open by Jane Harriet, he bore her directly toward the house. This sweeping rescue would have been everything Marianne's storybooks promised, if not for his prompt step onto an abandoned garden rake. It sprang up, whanging his upturned nose, and causing him to drop his fair lady straight into the mud.

Stammering apologies, he lifted her aloft once more, bearing her straight to the door, until, alas, he slipped on a muddy patch and fell straight into the wheelbarrow. Once he had scrambled muddily from atop his spilled heroine, he finally managed to convey her safely through the door, and quitted not his hold till he had seated her in a chair in the parlour. She squelched.

The young ladies, who had finished their bonnet experiment and now sat about sketching the newly festooned parlour, rose up in amazement at their entrance, and while the eyes of all the so-bored-and-sheltered young ladies were fixed on him with an evident wonder and a secret admiration which equally sprung from his appearance, he apologized for his intrusion by relating its cause, in a manner so frank and so graceful that his person, which was already so uncommonly handsome, received additional charms from his voice and expression. Had he been even old, ugly, and vulgar, the gratitude and kindness of the Fussbudget girls would have been secured by any act of attention to their sister; but the influence of youth, beauty, and elegance on the newest gentleman of their acquaintance, gave an interest to the action which came home to their most devout feelings.

Dilemma, alerted to the sudden possibility of another match already made, as well as fine features that made her own heart jolt to an uncommon quickness, thanked him again and again; and, with a sweetness of address which always attended her upon meeting rich, romantic young men, invited him to be seated. But this he declined, as he was dirty and wet. Within moments, he departed, to make himself still more interesting, in the midst of a heavy rain, his cloak billowing, eyes smouldering, and all that he might use to entice doing quite well its job.

"Oh! do not leave," Dilemma suddenly cried, the protest bursting from deep within. "My sister Jane Harriet and myself were accosted by the gypsies just two days previous. Or at least I believe them to be gypsies as they were lurking outdoors. They might have been traveling salesmen. Regardless, with no young man around to rescue us, I was forced to seize the horsewhip and give them a fright. But now my knees are so shaky that I might beg for a trusted friend to stay close and protect us while my father is away." Her eyes rolled up in her head in a terrible display of pained weakness.

"No, I need a gallant to soothe me after my latest nightmares," Lydia squealed. "For I am far more traumatized thanks to my overactive imagination, which is even greater than Marianne's." She picked up one of the poodles and began kissing it to ingratiate herself to its owner, despite the mud getting smeared fetchingly all over her cheeks.

"Mr Wickham, do you care for music?" Scary asked sweetly, her own sensibilities succumbing to the rising emotions in the parlour. "I might offer more witty entertainment than my sisters, who indeed all have brains the size of walnuts."

At this over-display of female repression suddenly given voice from all quarters, Mr Wickham only paused to bow before running for the lane.

His manly beauty and more than common gracefulness were instantly the theme of general admiration, and the laugh which his gallantry raised against Marianne received particular spirit from his exterior attractions. Their imaginations were busy, their reflections were pleasant, and the pain of Marianne's sprained ankle was disregarded. When the recollection passed about her sisters that Mr Willoughby Wickham had indeed had a *wet shirt,* one made by the storm far wetter than any shirt of the famed Mr Darcy's, a round of happy shrieking swept through the Fussbudget home. As the ladies rhapsodized over his well-defined musculature, it seemed all thought of Admiral Haughtyton's eligibility had quite dropped beneath their remembrances.

Marianne's preserver called at the house early the next morning to make his personal enquiries. He was received by the young ladies with more than politeness; all five at once seemed to have set their caps for him. Dilemma thought him a charming puzzle, Lydia, a flirtatious dancer, Jane Harriet, a powerful walker if he could carry her sister so smoothly. Even Scary seemed to have caught in the excitement that transferred all of their affections from brooding Haughtyton to fair-faced Wickham, though she rendered an observation that his wits had not been proven to exceed the size of his gratifyingly large muscles. Only Fanny Anne, sighing over a few yellowed letters, seemed to be proof from his charm.

Marianne, who had feared all night that she might catch pneumonia and die before realizing her fondest hopes, found herself still alive in the morning, much to her wonderment. But when the gentleman arrived in the flesh and she beheld him, still so tall and fair (though to her dismay, his shirt was fresh and his locks not inclined to toss in the still air of the house), she was captivated anew. When she saw that to the perfect good-breeding of the gentleman, he united frankness and vivacity, and above all, when she heard him declare, that of music and dancing he was passionately fond, she gave him such a look of approbation as secured the largest share of his discourse to herself for the rest of his stay. He began by speaking on general topics, Marrytown, especially, in a voice that both enthralled and soothed.

"It was the prospect of constant society, and good society," he added, "which was my chief inducement to enter the – shire. I knew it to be a most respectable, agreeable corps, and my friend Denny tempted me farther by his account of their present quarters, and the very great attentions and excellent acquaintance Marrytown had procured them. Why, I believe there are fully three families here of repressed young ladies desperate for a gentleman's attention. Society, I own, is necessary to me. I *must* have employment and society. A military life is not what I was intended for, but circumstances have now made it eligible. Harlequin college *ought* to have been my profession – I was brought up for it, and I should at this time have been in possession of a most valuable living with an itinerant circus, had it pleased Admiral Haughtyton."

"Indeed!"

"Yes – his father bequeathed me the next presentation of the best living in his gift. He was my godfather, and excessively attached to me. I cannot do justice to his kindness. He meant to provide for me amply, and thought he had done it; but when the living fell, it was given elsewhere."

"Good heavens!" cried Marianne, bosom heaving with the injustice of it all; "but how could *that* be? – How could his will be disregarded?"

"Why did not you seek legal redress?" Dilemma enquired. One of the poodles barked and she condescendingly dropped it a sardine left over from tea. The dog gulped it down, choked a bit, then was noisily sick on the imported throw rug. The girls paid it no notice as the floors were the servants' province.

"There was just such an informality in the terms of the bequest as to give me no hope from law. A man of honour could not have doubted the intention, but the admiral chose to doubt it – or to treat it as a merely conditional recommendation, and to assert that I had forfeited all claim to becoming a jokester by extravagance, imprudence, in short any thing or nothing. I cannot accuse myself of having really done any thing to deserve to lose it. I have a warm, unguarded temper, and I may perhaps have sometimes spoken my opinion *of* him, and *to* him, too freely. There was also the time I was practicing my pie-throwing in expectation of my new position, and managed to coat him liberally with custard and gooseberries. I can recall nothing more. But the fact is, that we are very different sort of men, and that he hates me."

"This is quite shocking! – He deserves to be publicly disgraced," Marianne protested, rising up against her many embroidered cushions. In this instant, the admiral was forever vilified to her, despite his all-too-attractive disdain.

"Some time or other he *will* be – but it shall not be by *me*. Till I can forget his father, I can never defy or expose *him*."

Marianne honoured him for such feelings, and thought him handsomer than ever as he expressed them.

"But what," said she, after a pause, "can have been his motive? – what can have induced him to behave so cruelly? Did he suffer a great disappointment that left him in a fit of melancholy?"

"It *is* wonderful," – replied Wickham, – "for almost all his actions may be traced to pride; and with that a great deal of prejudice."

"It is like something in a novel," Marianne mused. And with that, the subject moved on. It was only necessary to mention any favourite amusement to engage her to talk. She could not be silent when such points were introduced, and she had neither shyness nor reserve in their discussion. She proceeded to question him on the subject of books; her favourite authors were brought forward and dwelt upon with so rapturous a delight, that any young man of five and twenty must have been insensible indeed, not to become an immediate convert to the excellence of such works, however disregarded before. Their taste was strikingly alike. The same books, the same passages were idolized by each – or if any difference appeared, any objection arose, it lasted no longer than till the force of her arguments and the brightness of her eyes could be displayed. Even the maid mopping up the dog-sick was no deterrent.

At last, Marianne Catherine ventured to bring up a question which had been long uppermost in her thoughts: "Have you ever read *Udolpho,* Mr Wickham?"

"*Udolpho!* Oh, Lord! Not I; I never read novels; I have something else to do. Novels are all so full of nonsense and stuff; there has not been a tolerably decent one come out since *Tom Jones,* except *The Monk;* I read that t'other day; but as for all the others, they are the stupidest things in creation."

Fanny, sitting nearby, recalled her brother's scathing critique of *The Monk* (though he had not of course read it) as being filled with the horrors of vice and salaciousness to which no God-fearing eyes must be subjected, and gave her own prayer of gratitude that her brother was not in the room.

"Oh! You must like *Udolpho,* if you were to read it; it is so very interesting!"

"Not I, faith! No, if I read any, it shall be Mrs Radcliffe's; her novels are amusing enough; they are worth reading; some fun and nature in them."

"But *Udolpho* was written by Mrs Radcliffe," she said with some hesitation, from the fear of mortifying his fragile male ego.

"No sure; was it? Aye, I remember, so it was; I was thinking of that other stupid book, written by that woman they make such a fuss about, she who married the French emigrant."

"I suppose you mean *Camilla?*"

"Yes, that's the book; such unnatural stuff! Women who operate without a need for the man as central hero! There's a strange turn of events indeed! But many of the romantics are quite fine! (Here his voice inflamed with such passion that strange capital letters erupted in his speech.) If Scott has a fault, it is the want of Passion. – Tender, Elegant, Descriptive

– but Tame. – The Man who cannot do justice to the attributes of Woman is my contempt. – Sometimes indeed a flash of feeling seems to irradiate him – as in the Lines "Oh! Woman in our hours of Ease." Imagine the sweetness, the kindness, of woman in total service to man:

> *O woman! In our hours of ease*
> *Uncertain, coy, and hard to please,*
> *And variable as the shade*
> *By the light, quivering aspen made;*
> *When pain and anguish wring the brow,*
> *A ministering angel thou!*

(Here he continued, without seeing Marianne's look of revulsion at the sentiment) – But Burns is always on fire. – His Soul was the Altar in which lovely Woman sat enshrined, his Spirit truly breathed the immortal Incence which is her Due – "

At this passion, Marianne felt a swoon coming on and a shiver trembled all through her body. Her own capital letters seemed imminent. "I have read several of Burns' poems with great delight," she said, as soon as she had breath to speak, "but I am not poetic enough to separate a Man's Poetry entirely from his Character; – and poor Burns's known Irregularities greatly interrupt my enjoyment of his Lines. – I have difficulty in depending on the *Truth* of his Feelings as a Lover. I have not faith in the *sincerity* of the affections of a Man of his Description. He felt & he wrote & he forgot."

"Oh! no no – " exclaimed Wickham, in an extasy. "He was all ardour & Truth! – His Genius & his Susceptibilities might lead him into some Aberrations – But who is perfect? – It were Hyper-criticism, it were Pseudo-philosophy to expect from the soul of high toned Genius, the grovellings of a common mind. – The Coruscations of Talent, elicited by impassioned feeling in the breast of Man, are perhaps incompatible with some of the prosaic Decencies of Life; – nor can you, loveliest Miss Marianne" – (speaking with an air of deep sentiment) – "nor can any Woman be a fair Judge of what a Man may be propelled to say, write, or do, by the sovereign impulses of illimitable Ardour. Oh how sorrowful I am that it is no longer legal for men to cry."

Yet except for this one disagreement, they were perfectly in accord. True, he had little interest in sewing strange costumes for his pets, and expressed his mild horror that his fine little black poodles might be subject to such a fate, but when the dog and cat were brought out in their fetching new bonnets, he was forced to describe them as not nearly as repulsive as he had envisioned. The dog had gotten into the laudanum, possibly to insulate itself against the next costume, but the cat's behaviour was all that might be wished. He acquiesced in all Marianne's decisions, caught all her enthusiasm; and long before his visit concluded, they conversed with the familiarity of a long-established acquaintance.

"Well, Marianne," said Dilemma, as soon as he had left them, "for *one* morning I think you have done pretty well. You have already ascertained Mr Willoughby's opinion in almost every matter of importance. You know what he thinks of Cowper, Radcliffe, and Scott; you are certain of his estimating their beauties as he ought, and you have received every assurance of his admiring Pope no more than is proper. He even shares your views on the Funny Pages. But how is your acquaintance to be long supported, under such extraordinary despatch of every subject for discourse? You will soon have exhausted each favourite topic. Another meeting will suffice to explain his sentiments on admiring dead leaves on the walk and tossing his hair artfully in the wind, and then you can have nothing farther to ask. If his mystery vanishes so quickly, how much longer can I – that is, you, esteem him?"

"Dilemma," cried Marianne, "is this fair? is this just? are my ideas so scanty? But I see what you mean. I have been too much at my ease, too happy, too frank. I have erred against every common-place notion of decorum; I have been open and sincere where I ought to have been reserved, spiritless, dull, and deceitful – had I talked only of the weather and the roads, and had I spoken only once in ten minutes, this reproach would have been spared."

"You ought to have more sense."

"And you, more sensibility!"

"Oh Lord!" said Lydia, who was watching the sisterly competition as she had watched the visiting gentleman, with sly and arch amusement. "You must not be offended with Dilemma – she was only in jest. How droll! But if she does urge caution, it is only because she has an interest in the gentleman. Did you not observe her immodest behaviour at the ball? I declare, she has certainly set her cap for him, and now *you* have unfairly drawn his attention with your fortuitous tumble and desperate need for rescue."

Dilemma's eyes flashed in anger. "I *set my cap?* How vulgar you are indeed. But you showed that well enough last night, giggling and draping yourself against the men until I was sure you would elope with one that very night."

"To my mind, all this time spent dwelling on the male form rather than the good of our souls is a waste of effort," Scary said, pinning up her hair and gazing anxiously in the mirror. "For it is for them to offer and us to sit and wait, until of course, one of us should be asked to exhibit our talents." It was perfectly clear that in this area she felt herself completely superior to the others.

The tension was growing thick enough that a spat like the one before the Netherbum Ball was presenting itself. Until at last, thunder burst across the hills. This outward break in tension seemed to release an internal one, and the girls' glares soon turned to shrugs of ennui.

"Well, it's raining out. What do you say we dress the pets as a bride and groom?" Marianne said, by way of a peace-offering.

"Perhaps they'll kiss," Lydia squealed. Fanny Anne, watching from the kitchen, shook her head mournfully. This much repression couldn't be good for anyone.

Though Mrs Fussbudget was all in a flutter over Marianne's ankle, her daughters could do nothing to help, and indeed, were rather eager to quit the house for an afternoon if not for all eternity. Marianne was satisfied to wait at home for days, staring longingly out the window and waiting for callers. The other girls, however, could hardly stand her raptures over her saviour's dark eyebrows and smouldering eyes. Luckily, Dilemma was bursting with ideas and suggested an excursion to the nearby Box Hill where they all might have a picnic the next day. Marianne's sisters and both Collins cousins were eager to agree, and they clambered up towards the hill, vast components of a traditional English tea weighing them down like lead stones.

On the way, who should they spy but Mr Wickham, making the acquaintance of a bored and put-upon looking Mr Tightly-Wound. As they approached, Dilemma discerned the words "clown college" and "the admiral." She was eager to discover more of Mr Wickham's character, and she invited both along with alacrity, to which they readily agreed.

They had a very fine day for Box Hill; and all the other outward circumstances of arrangement, accommodation, and punctuality, were in favour of a pleasant party. On a snowy cloth, they laid out rhubarb tarts, teacakes, and delicate crystal bowls of cherries, all atop lacy doilies. There was a cold pigeon pie, a cold turkey, a cold tongue, roast saddle of saddle, a mayonnaise of mayonnaise and half a dozen jellies. And at their father's insistence, a steaming kettle of gruel. The poodles began to whine and beg, but a single steely glare from Mr Tightly-Wound soon sent them cringing in apology.

At first it was downright dullness to Dilemma. She had never seen Mr Tightly-Wound so silent and stupid. He spoke of hunting and horses and cravats, all the gentlemanly pursuits until Dilemma feared they might never talk of doily-making or embroidery. While he was so dull, it was no wonder that Jane Harriet, Fanny Anne, and Mr Collins should be dull likewise; they were all far less clever than she. Scary was always talking nonsense, though on this occasion a book of terrible puns and scandalous rhymes was keeping her silent. Dilemma had seated Mr Collins beside her and hoped the pair would soon form an attachment and leave all settled. Lydia kept giggling to herself as she devoured strawberries and blackcurrants, getting covered in sticky juice, and Mr Tightly-Wound was looking bored indeed. Why were the men of Marrytown so unfitting as suitors, she asked herself.

When they all sat down it was better; to her taste a great deal better, for Mr Wickham grew talkative and gay, making her his first object. He sensed, perhaps, that he was being weighed as suitable (or not) for Dilemma's sister's attentions, and appeared eager to oblige her. Every distinguishing attention that could be paid, was paid to her. To amuse her, and be agreeable in her eyes, seemed all that he cared for – and Dilemma, glad to be enlivened, not sorry to be flattered, was gay and easy too, and gave him all the friendly encouragement, the admission to be gallant, which she had ever given anyone; but which now, in her own estimation, meant nothing, though in the judgment of most people looking on it must have had such an appearance as no English word but flirtation could very well describe. "Mr Wickham and Miss Fussbudget flirted together excessively." They were laying themselves open to that very phrase. Not that Dilemma was gay and thoughtless from any real felicity; it was rather because she felt less happy than she had expected. She laughed because she was disappointed; and though she liked him for his attentions, and thought them all, whether in friendship, admiration, or playfulness, extremely judicious, they were not winning her heart. She began to calculate whether he might be a better choice for Marianne rather than a future in which she must stare at his too-bright teeth over breakfast each morning.

"How much I am obliged to you," said he, "for telling me to come to day! – If it had not been for you, I should certainly have lost all the happiness of this party. I had quite determined to go away again, for I thought you had quite overlooked me, with captains and admirals in town."

Dilemma carefully ignored this last. "Yes, you were very ungenerous, ignoring all of us except Marianne when you visited; and I do not know why."

"Don't say I was ungenerous. I was fatigued. Carrying your delightful twenty-stone sister overcame me."

"You are not tired now?"

"No, indeed. I am perfectly comfortable to-day."

"You are comfortable because you are under command."

"Your command? – Yes."

"Perhaps I intended you to say so, but I meant self-command. You had, somehow or other, broken bounds yesterday, and allowed all your sensibilities of poetry and novels to hold sway to the point where you were gushing quite immodestly; but to-day you are got back again – and as I cannot be always with you, it is best to believe your temper under your own command rather than mine." She sighed. "I do so enjoy bossing around those who befriend me."

"It comes to the same thing. I can have no self-command without a motive. You order me, whether you speak or not. And you can be always with me." He gave her a cheeky grin. "There are so few people to talk to, without demeaning oneself to spend time with the lower class. Why, aside from your family and Mr Tightly-Wound there is nearly nobody in town."

His discernment that the Moneygrubber children, lately jumped up while her family had been thieving and pillaging in the Norman Conquest, were not of her class pleased and flattered her. "Yes indeed. But (lowering her voice) – nobody speaks except ourselves, and it is rather too much to be talking nonsense for the entertainment of six silent people."

"I say nothing of which I am ashamed," replied he, with lively impudence. "Our companions are excessively stupid. What shall we do to rouse them? Any nonsense will serve. They *shall* talk. Ladies and gentlemen, I am ordered by Miss Fussbudget (who, wherever she is, presides,) to say, that she desires to know what you are all thinking of?"

Some laughed, and Fanny and Jane mumbled good-humouredly. Mr Tightly-Wound's answer was the most distinct. "Is Miss Fussbudget sure that she would like to hear what we are all thinking of?" While he eyed her, there seemed a certain penetration of his blazing glare that seemed to make Dilemma feel cold then warm. Then a bit of seasonal allergies.

"Oh! no, no" – cried Dilemma, laughing as carelessly as she could – "Upon no account in the world. It is the very last thing I would stand the brunt of just now. Let me hear any thing rather than what you are all thinking of. I will not say quite all. There are one or two, perhaps, (glancing at Fanny then her brother) whose thoughts I might not be afraid of knowing, for if they be in love at all, I would know everything."

"It is a sort of thing," cried Mr Collins emphatically, "which *I* should not have thought myself privileged to inquire into." He shuddered in horror at the thought of such immodest behaviour.

As a retort, Mr Wickham rubbed Mr Collins' long forehead and leaned in close. "Look, I can see myself!" He glanced around but saw the others weren't taking any delight in his unrefined humour, and took on a more dignified tone. "Very well then," said Wickham. "Ladies and gentlemen – I am ordered by Miss Fussbudget to say, that she waives her right of knowing exactly what you may all be thinking of, and only requires something very entertaining from each of you, in a general way. Here are six of you, besides myself, (who, she is pleased to say, am very entertaining already,) and she only demands from each of you either one thing rather naughty, be it prose or verse, original or repeated – or two things moderately naughty – or three things not a bit naughty indeed, and she engages to laugh heartily at them all."

Lydia began giggling and could not stop, even to voice what she was thinking.

"Oh! I can think of many things," Fanny said. "But you all must judge how naughty they are."

Dilemma could not resist.

"Ah! Fanny dear, but there may be a difficulty. Pardon me – but you will be limited as to number – only three perfectly clean and proper things at once. I daresay there is no danger to see you flirt or even laugh with any one. Perhaps this is why Captain Wentworth has stayed away until now."

Fanny immediately caught her meaning; it could not anger, though a deep blush showed that it could pain her. "Ah! – well – to be sure. Yes, I see what she means, (turning to her brother) and I will try to hold my tongue. I must be in horrible disgrace, or she would not have said such a thing to me." She looked from person to person with the mournful eyes of a martyr. True, her speeches marked her as dull, obedient, and patient. But to be named as such was a trial beyond enduring. Her brother would not meet her eyes, possibly contemplating the burden she might pose him all her life, or more possibly, entranced by the excellent basket of cheeses on which he munched. Beside her brother, Mr Tightly-Wound was glaring quite quellingly at Dilemma, though Fanny failed to see it.

"I like your plan," cried Lydia, oblivious to the exchange. "Agreed, agreed. I will do my best. I am making a limerick. How will a limerick reckon?" She made calf's eyes at Wickham.

"Low, I am afraid, very low," answered Wickham; – "but we shall be indulgent – especially to any one who leads the way."

"Or I might recite something of Shakespeare's," Scary said quickly before the limerick might be heard. "Some have quite a clever play on words, and yet are properly worthy. Or I recall an elegy in which a dead sparrow is evoked quite piteously, over and over – "

At this offer, the picnic hastily broke up.

On their stroll, Mr Wickham, who had previously been so lively with Dilemma, now fell into step by Jane. "Do you often walk this way?"

"No, sir; we find it too dirty."

"You should wear half-boots." After another pause: "Nothing sets off a neat ankle more than a half-boot; nankeen galoshed with black looks very well. Or those dainty dancing slippers with the pink ribbons, or perhaps spike heels," his words were tumbling out faster and faster, and he suddenly had to open his collar a bit and fan himself. "Do not you like half-boots?" he asked, voice forcibly steady.

"Yes; but unless they are so stout as to injure their beauty, they are not fit for country walking."

"Ladies should ride in dirty weather. Do you ride?"

"No, sir."

"I wonder every lady does not; a woman never looks better than on horseback."

"But every woman may not have the inclination, or the means."

"If they knew how much it became them, they would all have the inclination; and I fancy, Miss Jane, when once they had the inclination, the means would soon follow."

"You think we always have our own way. *That* is a point on which ladies and gentlemen have long disagreed; but without pretending to decide it, I may say that there are some circumstances which even *women* cannot control. Female economy will do a great deal: but it cannot turn a small income into a large one. Or make a habitual liar truthful."

At this, Mr Wickham recalled an errand and changed his direction. While he had been equal to Marianne's love of literature and Dilemma's of herself, he found such quiet, concealed wit combined with cool disinterest more than a match for his.

While walking back, Dilemma found Mr Tightly-Wound by her side. He looked around, as if to see that no one were near, and then said, "Dilemma, I must once more speak to you as I have been used to do all my life as an overbearing friend of your father's: a privilege rather endured than allowed, perhaps, but I must still use it. I cannot see you acting wrong, without a remonstrance. How could you be so unfeeling to Miss Collins? How could you be so insolent in your wit to a woman of her character and situation? – Dilemma, I had not thought it possible."

Dilemma recollected, blushed, was sorry, but tried to laugh it off. "Nay, how could I help saying what I did? – Nobody could have helped it. It was not so very bad. I dare say she did not understand me."

"I assure you she did. She felt your full meaning. She has talked of it since. I wish you could have heard how she talked of it – with what candour and generosity. I wish you could have heard her honouring your forbearance, in being able to pay her such attentions, as she was for ever receiving from yourself and your family, when her society must be so irksome. She has indeed been going on for half of the walk home, so much that I know little how to console her."

"Oh!" cried Dilemma, "I know there is not a better creature in the world: but you must allow, that she has quite squandered her own chances at happiness."

"She is a little ninny of a person," said he, "I acknowledge; and, were she prosperous, I could allow much for the occasional prevalence of the unfortunate over the good. I would not quarrel with you for any liberties of manner, were she your equal in situation – but, Dilemma, consider how far this is from being the case. She is poor; she has sunk from the comforts her family was born to to live in yours as a hanger-on and country cousin. Her situation should secure your compassion. It was badly done, indeed! – To have you now, in thoughtless spirits, and the pride of the moment, laugh at her, humble her – and before her brother, too (though he seemed to be terribly oblivious) – and before others, many of whom (certainly *some*,) would be entirely guided by *your* treatment of her. – This is not pleasant to you, Dilemma – and it is very far from pleasant to me; but I must, I will, – I will tell you truths while I can; satisfied with proving myself your friend by very faithful counsel. Badly done, Dilemma."

From just behind them both came the startling sound of applause. Scary, who stood there, raised her eyebrows. "That's exactly what I was going to say. It's as if we're – "

"Completely on the same page," they said at the same time, gazing at one another as if this was their first meeting. And from there, they were inseparable.

On the walk home, Dilemma found herself severely vexed beyond what could have been expressed – almost beyond what she could conceal. Never had she felt so agitated, mortified, grieved, at any circumstance in her life. She was most forcibly struck. The truth of his representation there was no denying. She felt it at her heart. How could she have been so brutal, so cruel to her cousin! – How could she have exposed herself to such ill opinion in any one she valued! And how suffer him to leave her without saying one word of gratitude, of concurrence, of common kindness! Her head was starting to ache. Why was she, a well-born lady, being called on to think and make decisions?

It wasn't only that Mr Tightly-Wound had lost his good opinion of her and showed how childishly she was in the wrong. It was also that he seemed to have transferred his watchful brotherly care of her to her sister Scary in an instant, and that this care seemed far more devoted than a simple fraternal attachment. In short, as he leaned close and patted Scary's hand in a familiar way, he appeared to be in love with her. Though Dilemma had been tempted to writhe in dismay, she found a surprising relief welling within her. While having a friend who cared enough to correct her behaviour made her feel protected and cared for in a way her distant father rarely managed, that care could also turn positively obnoxious in its determined overbearing nature. And for Dilemma, accustomed to ordering the world to her liking, Tightly-Wound's criticism was rather burdensome. Very well then, she thought, tossing her head proudly. While she would be attentive to her cruel tongue, she would choose a better suitor for herself – one handsome and young but also quite tractable. And so she set out to make herself a match at last.

Fanny and Marianne, finding themselves awake early the next morning, agreed to stroll, as Marianne's ankle was healing nicely. And, as always, Jane Harriet must come along. They broke their fast hastily, with curds and whey and the crumpled husks of stifled dreams. "I wish," said Marianne as they walked up the path, "I wish Mr Wickham was with us. He is so lively, you know."

Fanny Anne rolled her eyes at Jane (while admitting privately that Jane indeed provided a fine companion with whom she could share her boredom with the topic). This was the season of happiness to Marianne. Her heart was devoted to Willoughby Wickham, and nothing could alter it. Every thing he did, was right. Every thing he said, was clever. Even the squirrels plotting overhead and the robin who deliberately dropped a deposit on her new bonnet could not quell her spirits.

Fanny Anne had only time, however, for a general answer, before all subjects suddenly ceased, on seeing Lydia and Captain Wentworth coming towards them down Bunion Street. They had apparently met on their own stroll (a comment Fanny Anne had to reflect upon with suspicion); and Lydia had the bulge of a telescope under her cloak, suggesting she'd been loitering near the regiment. Recollecting that she had something to procure at a shop, Lydia invited them all to go with her into the town. They were all at her disposal.

When they came to the steps leading upwards to the wall by the river, a gentleman at the same moment preparing to come down politely drew back, and stopped to give them way. They ascended and passed him; and as they passed, Fanny Anne's face caught his eye, and he looked at her with a degree of earnest admiration, which she could not be insensible of. She was looking remarkably well; her very regular, very pretty features, having the bloom and freshness of youth restored by the fine wind which had been blowing on her complexion, and by the animation of eye which it had also produced. It was evident that the gentleman, (completely a gentleman in manner) admired her exceedingly. Nonetheless, his dress suggested a somewhat lower rank, so he was not destined to wed any of the six eligible ladies but must fix himself on a less impossible target such as a Miss Moneygrubber.

Captain Wentworth looked round at her instantly in a way which shewed his noticing of it. He gave her a momentary glance, – a glance of brightness, which seemed to say, "That man is struck with you, – and even I, at this moment, see something like Fanny Anne again and want to marry you on the spot or at least touch your ungloved hand for half an instant with my own." There was quite a crowd loitering about, as the day was fine, and as there was nothing thereabouts to do but go walking or stay in, hoping for visitors. Breakfast had not been long over, when they were joined by Mr and Mrs Fussbudget, who often walked together, as they were beginning to sense that staying in the house all day might be making them a bit peculiar.

There was too much wind to make the high part of the wall pleasant for the ladies, and they agreed to get down the steps to the lower, and all were contented to pass quietly and carefully down the steep flight, excepting Lydia Louisa; she must be jumped down them by Captain Wentworth. In all their walks, he had had to jump her from the stiles; the sensation was delightful to her. The hardness of the pavement for her feet made him less willing upon the present occasion; he did it, however; she was safely down, and instantly, to show her enjoyment, ran up the steps to be jumped down again. He advised her against it, thought the jar too great; but no, he reasoned and talked in vain; she smiled and said, "I am determined I will:" he put out his hands; she was too precipitate by half a second and his wooden leg slipped on the hard stone. With a terrible thud, she fell on the pavement, and was taken up lifeless!

There was no wound, no blood, no visible bruise; but her eyes were closed, she breathed not, her face was like death, and her breath had a cheesy smell. – The horror of the moment to all who stood around!

Captain Wentworth, who had caught her up, knelt with her in his arms, looking on her with a face as pallid as her own, in an agony of silence. "She is dead! she is dead!" screamed Mrs Fussbudget, catching hold of her husband, and contributing with his own horror to make him immoveable; and in another moment, Marianne, sinking under the conviction, lost her senses too, and would have fallen on the steps, but for Jane and Fanny Anne, who caught and supported her between them.

"Is there no one to help me?" were the first words which burst from Captain Wentworth, in a tone of despair, and as if all his own strength were gone.

"Go to him, go to him," cried Fanny Anne to Jane, "for heaven's sake go to him. I can support Marianne myself. Leave me, and go to him. Rub her hands, rub her temples; here are salts, and a Chinese fan, and a flask of cold ale and a dustcloth without too much dust on it – take them, take them." Even as she remained calm and collected herself, she wondered at Captain Wentworth's passion for Lydia. Had their walk been as innocent as they had claimed? Or had she interrupted something more passionate and ill-advised? Was the gap on the back of her dress from a missed button? True, she might have missed it this morning in the normal course of things, but – !

Jane obeyed, and Mr Fussbudget at the same moment, disengaging himself from his wife, they were both with him; and Lydia was raised up and supported more firmly between them, and every thing was done that Fanny Anne had prompted, but in vain; while Captain Wentworth, staggering against the wall for his support, exclaimed in the bitterest agony, "Oh God! What's to be done!"

"A surgeon!" said Fanny Anne. Jane, who had been silently but rationally sizing up Lydia's coat for its size and condition was startled into jumping up.

He caught the word; it seemed to rouse him at once, and

he cried, "Are you certain? Surgeons are ungentlemanly louts who actually demean themselves to touch patients – worse, surgeon's wives cannot be presented at court."

"Yes, yes!"

Clearly inclined to take any action at all, he said only, "Well then, a surgeon this instant," was darting away, when Fanny Anne eagerly suggested,

"Jane, would not it be better for Jane? She walks so quickly and knows where a surgeon is to be found."

Every one capable of thinking (which wasn't many of them) felt the advantage of the idea, and in a moment (it was all done in rapid moments) Jane had resigned the poor corpse-like figure entirely to her father's care, and was off for the town with the utmost rapidity.

As to the wretched party left behind, it could scarcely be said which of the three, who were completely rational, was suffering most, Captain Wentworth, Fanny, or Mr Fussbudget, who, really an affectionate father when his collections weren't present, hung over Lydia with sobs of grief, and could only turn his eyes from one daughter, to see the other in a state as insensible, or to witness the hysterical agitations of his wife, calling on him for help which he could not give.

Marianne roused from her stupor, only to turn to her own hysterics. "Oh, my sweet sister, how piteously you lie there, dead, dead," Marianne sobbed. "You were the youngest and fairest of all of us, so light and giddy and de-delightful!" She flung herself on the girl's prone body, which could not possibly have done any good, and wept harder and harder until she was loudly forced to use the other girl's sleeve as a handkerchief. "At your funeral I shall play all your favourite airs, as Scary would only make a mess of it and so I shall bid my farewells and you shall know I loved you best for all time! Look how you lie on the road like a slaughtered deer, pale as a white lily, motionless as a single glistening raindrop, soon to melt away and depart this world for ever."

"Oh! My girl, my youngest girl," Mrs Fussbudget chimed

in piteously. "Why were you so heedless? Why did I just stand here and not forbid you from jumping off the wall? Or at least try to restore you with a taste of this sherry rather than drinking all myself? Oh, my dear!"

Marianne continued to sob, now adding the words "Oh lay me down and I shall die beside you," perhaps in an attempt to vie with her mother for the most drama.

Mrs Fussbudget replied with "My nerves, my nerves!" and seemed well on the way to hysteria herself, especially with an empty bottle to cope with.

Fanny Anne, attending with all the strength and zeal and thought that instinct supplied, to Marianne, still tried, at intervals, to suggest comfort to the others, tried to quiet Mrs Fussbudget, to animate Mr Fussbudget, to assuage the feelings of Captain Wentworth. What could be affecting them all so? Lydia, though grievously injured, was certainly not dead. And in their fussing, Lydia's mother and sister had provided two more patients to distract them from the suffering girl. Truly, sensibility could be a deadly quagmire.

"Fanny, Fanny," cried Mr Fussbudget, "what is to be done next? What, in heaven's name, is to be done next?" Fanny Anne upgraded her count to three useless patients, all of whom needed her guidance.

Captain Wentworth's eyes were also turned towards her. Four, then.

"Had not she better be carried to the house? Yes, I am sure, carry her gently."

"Yes, yes, to the house," repeated Captain Wentworth, comparatively collected, and eager to be doing something. "I will carry her myself, or at least drag her by use of my good hand. Mr Fussbudget, take care of the others."

By this time the report of the accident had spread among the workmen and labourers, and many were collected near them, to be useful if wanted, at any rate, to enjoy the sight of a dead young lady, nay, two dead young ladies, for it proved twice as fine as the first report. To some of the best-looking of these good people Marianne was consigned, for, though partially revived from her excessive grief, she was quite helpless; and in this manner, Fanny Anne walking by her side, and Mr Fussbudget attending to his wife, they set forward, treading back with feelings unutterable, the ground, which so lately, so very lately, and so light of heart, they had passed along.

They were not off the wall, before the Moneygrubbers met them. Jane had been seen flying by their house, with a teary countenance which showed something to be wrong; and they had set off immediately, informed and directed as they passed, towards the spot. Shocked as Sir Moneygrubber was, he brought senses and nerves that could be instantly useful; and a look between him and his wife decided what was to be done. She must be taken to their house – all must go to their house (which was far closer than their own) – and await the surgeon's arrival there. True, the local surgeon was a quack, too fond of his own concoctions to be of much aid in emergencies, but he was the nearest, and occasionally could offer a lucid bit of advice. They would not listen to scruples: Sir Moneygrubber was obeyed; they were all beneath his roof; and while Lydia, under Mrs Moneygrubber's direction, was conveyed up stairs, and given possession of her own bed, assistance, cordials, restoratives, impeccably embroidered handkerchiefs, and large quantities of brandy were supplied by her husband to all who needed them.

Lydia had once opened her eyes, but soon closed them again, without apparent consciousness. This had been a proof of life, however, in those times when life or death was a judgement hesitated at by professionals; and Marianne, though perfectly incapable of being in the same room with Lydia, was kept, by the agitation of hope and fear, from a return of her own insensibility. Mrs Fussbudget, too, was growing calmer. She opened them a second time, and Mrs Fussbudget vowed to spoil her and care for her beyond all treasures in the world, and, indeed, grant her anything she wished if she would only recover. Lydia's eyelids fluttered for a moment, and then she whispered, "Perhaps a trip to

Brighton..."

The surgeon was with them almost before it had seemed possible. With a quick inquiry on whether he was to treat a man, a woman, or the far more valuable horse, and hearing it was a woman, he immediately set to. She was covered with a sheet from head to toe for her modesty, and then he got to work. They were sick with horror while he examined (rather appreciatively, it must be related); but he was not hopeless. The head had received a severe contusion, but he had seen greater injuries recovered from: he was by no means hopeless; he spoke cheerfully.

That he did not regard it as a desperate case – that he did not say a few hours must end it – was at first felt, beyond the hope of most; and the ecstasy of such a reprieve, the rejoicing, deep and silent, after a few fervent ejaculations of gratitude to Heaven had been offered, may be conceived.

The tone, the look, with which "By gads and by jingo with monkeys all around!" was uttered by Captain Wentworth, Fanny Anne was sure could never be forgotten by her; nor the sight of him afterwards, as he sat near a table, leaning over it with folded arms and face concealed, as if overpowered by the various feelings of his soul, and trying by prayer and reflection and perhaps a score of repeated limericks to calm them.

Lydia's limbs had escaped. There was no injury but to the head and, if significant, the brain. Fortunately she was a lady of quality.

It now became necessary for the party to consider what was best to be done, as to their general situation. They were now able to speak to each other, and consult. That Lydia must remain where she was, however distressing to her friends to be involving the Moneygrubbers in such trouble, did not admit a doubt. Her removal was impossible. The Moneygrubbers silenced all scruples; and, as much as they could, all gratitude. They had looked forward and arranged everything before the others began to reflect. They were only concerned that the house could accommodate no more; and yet perhaps, by "putting the children away in the maids' room, or swinging a cot somewhere, or putting some of the less attractive young people in the hayloft," they could hardly bear to think of not finding room for two or three besides, supposing they might wish to stay; though, with regard to any attendance on Miss Lydia, there need not be the least uneasiness in leaving her to Mrs Moneygrubber's care entirely. Mrs Moneygrubber was a very experienced nurse; and her nursery-maid, who had lived with her long, and gone about with her everywhere to devotedly wipe her chin when she drooled, was just such another. Between these two, she could want no possible attendance by day or night. And all this was said with a truth and sincerity of feeling irresistible. And if Mrs Moneygrubber, with her own five daughters to dispose of (who remained well behind the Fussbudgets in both beauty and silliness) cherished some deep-buried plan of keeping Lydia confined to bed and safe from flirting with the officers until one or more of her brood had found matches, or perhaps even cutting all her hair off to speed her recovery and dying the remainder dull green, well, it was not done in ill humour.

Mr Fussbudget and Captain Wentworth were the two in consultation, and for a little while it was only an interchange of perplexity and terror; but, after a while, Captain Wentworth, exerting himself, said, "We must be decided, and without the loss of another minute. Every minute is valuable. Some one must resolve on being off for Uppercrust to fetch a qualified doctor instantly, one who is at least a Fellow at Oxford. If he has not read the first century texts in Latin, he is worth nothing! Mr Fussbudget, either you or I must go."

Mr Fussbudget agreed; but declared his resolution of not going away. He would be as little encumbrance as possible to Sir and Lady Moneygrubber; but he was truly helpless upon a horse if any speed was needed. He had none of his collections here, but if he must stay more than a day, some of them might be sent by carriage. The plan had reached this point, when Fanny Anne, coming quietly down from Lydia's room, could not but hear what followed, for the parlour door was open.

"Then it is settled, Mr Fussbudget," cried Captain Wentworth, "that you stay, and that I summon the doctor. But as to the rest; – as to the others; – If one stays to assist Mrs Moneygrubber, I think it need be only one. If Fanny Anne will stay, no one so proper, so capable as Fanny Anne."

She paused a moment to recover from the emotion of hearing herself so spoken of, and indeed brought to others' notice at all. The other two warmly agreed with what he said, and she then appeared.

"You will stay, I am sure; you will stay and nurse her;" cried he, turning to her and speaking with a glow, and yet a gentleness, which seemed almost restoring the past. – She coloured deeply; and he recollected himself and moved away. – She expressed herself most willing, ready, happy to remain. "It was what she had been thinking of, and wishing to be allowed to do. – A bed on the floor in Lydia's room would be sufficient for her, or one of dirty rags smeared with coal dust, if Mrs Moneygrubber would but think so." Was his concern for her that of a gentleman for a girl in distress or that of a lover? She could not tell. The one great love of her life might be on the verge on proposing marriage to her heedless cousin (or true, their meeting might have been innocent, but such a view seemed unlikely indeed). Nonetheless, she would stay of course. She patted the copy of Cinderella in her pocket as a talisman.

Captain Wentworth now hurried off to get everything ready on his part, and to be soon followed by the two remaining ladies. So far it was decided; and Marianne, being prevailed upon, was soon persuaded to agree. The uselessness of her staying! – She, who had not been able to remain in Lydia's room, or to look at her, without sufferings which made her worse than helpless! She was forced to acknowledge that she could do no good; yet was still unwilling to be away, till touched by the thought of her frantic sisters, she gave it up; she consented, she was anxious to be at home to have hysterics among all her dearest ones.

When the plan was made known to Mrs Fussbudget, however, there was an end of all peace in it. She was so wretched, and so vehement, complained so much of injustice in being expected to go away instead of Fanny Anne; – Fanny Anne, who was nothing to Lydia, while she was her mother, and had the best right to stay! No, it was too unkind! And, in short, she said more than her husband could long withstand; and as none of the others could oppose when he gave way, there was no help for it: the change of Mrs Fussbudget for Fanny Anne was inevitable.

Fanny had never submitted more reluctantly to the jealous and ill-judging claims of her aunt; but so it must be, and they set off for home, bouncing up and down in a borrowed carriage.

NONSENSIBILITY

Chapter 10: To Go to Brighton

Several days later, Lydia arrived safely at Longbore, and escorting her was none other than Mr Wickham! Upon inquiring, he had made bold to attend upon her, and finally escort her back to her waiting family. This, as one might expect, endeared him still further to the fluttering Mrs Fussbudget, though Marianne appeared less certain.

Lydia, upon seeing her family, immediately demanded, before a single kiss or greeting, that her mother send her to Brighton as she had promised. "The season there has just begun, and La! It will be such a laugh." Apparently her fall had not stifled a single frivolous impulse; if anything it appeared to have strengthened them all.

Mr Fussbudget pulled a long face. "As you must be reminded, I detest Brighton above all things. One cannot find a single gentleman who collects even antique bowling pins there! Silly, frivolous place."

Mr Wickham gave them a charming smile. "I, however, happen to be traveling to Brighton quite soon with my regiment, as our campaign against the murderous squirrels here has ended in inglorious defeat. And I should be perfectly delighted to escort Miss Lydia."

Mr Fussbudget's eyes narrowed. "The impropriety – "

"Will be no difficulty if *I too* accompany them," Marianne said suddenly and loudly. "For *I too* should adore such a trip."

Mr Wickham's smile broadened. "I should indeed be

delighted to accompany both ladies."

Mrs Fussbudget fluttered. Desperate as she was to have all her daughters married, something in Wickham's eyes seemed a bit off.

"No one is going to Brighton," Mr Fussbudget said with a tone of (slightly quavering) finality. "You must go upstairs, my dears, and I recommend a little gruel to you before you go," he added to Mr Wickham. "You and I will have a nice basin of gruel together. My dear Mrs Fussbudget, suppose we all have a little gruel."

At his moment, Captain Wentworth tapped on the door. When he saw Mr Wickham there, he froze for a moment, and then, steeling himself as if for the worst, he walked in and made that gentleman a brief and correct bow. He had come to enquire after Lydia, he explained, though his eyes darted briefly in Fanny Anne's direction. Seeing her, he smiled, and as she answered him with her eyes, the two shared a brief moment of hidden rapport.

Lydia, sensing an exchange that left no part for her, bounded up to the Captain. "I am to go to Brighton with Mr Wickham! And Marianne may come too, if she is so insistent. I am sure Wickham can handle us both."

Her parents' protests that nothing had been decided were overridden by Lydia's squeal of dismay. Her face grew red, and as she balled her hands into fists, she appeared quite on the verge of a tantrum.

Captain Wentworth cleared his throat. "I have an alternate possibility."

Happily, Captain Wentworth and Admiral Haughtyton were scheduled to make their own trip quite near to Bath, to see the Admiral's daughter at Mansfield Abbey. When Captain Wentworth announced this, he smiled slightly, and Fanny Anne immediately found herself seized by a torment of jealousy so great that she half-swooned upon the sofa. In this, as in most things, she went quite unnoticed. The captain concluded that he should be pleased to escort the entire party safely to Bath.

"Sea bathing is quite healthful –" Lydia began, upon seeing her chances for adventure significantly diminished. To her, Brighton was the spot of all earthly happiness, not least for the scores of officers conveniently camped there. Famously, there was no bathing in Bath.

"I am sure you will find the waters of the pump room just as invigorating," the captain said, in the voice of one who has many times had to turn aside importuning relatives on the grounds of propriety. "Bath water is so delightful to be drunk with its acidic muddy tang and sulphur aftertaste. Yes, it reminds me of when we were starving at sea and I had to make soup from my old boots. Miss Collins, will you be of the party?" he inquired pleasantly. Fanny Anne flushed and recovered quite in an instant. Surely he could have no understanding with Miss Haughtyton if he were inviting her along.

"I-I do not care for Bath with all of its… people…and diversions…and direct sunlight," she confessed. "As you know, I am most comfortable cooking or cleaning or scrubbing Marianne's many handkerchiefs. I do thank you though." Her memories of running in childhood fields seemed far removed, like a story she had read about another young woman in a far distant time. What was it about this place that so transformed women into marriage-hungry desperate misses who, with nothing to do but read of others' lives or sew, were prone to all manner of nervous complaints? She found herself momentarily longing for her old country life, but of course, the perpetual diversions of Marrytown were no comparison.

"What! Of course we are going!" Mr Collins said beside her. "First of all, I deem the healing effects of drinking the Bath water will do us both such a great deal of good. And second, it is most appropriate that a close relative escorts my fair cousins. Thirdly, such an elegant and well-established man as Admiral Haughtyton will surely be wanting conversation along the way. I gladly volunteer myself for such a project."

Though Mr Collins' motives were clear enough to everyone who had heard of Admiral Haughtyton's available situation (which was everyone in the room, indeed, many times over), the plan was so quickly established, with so many participants, that there was no turning it aside. Mrs Fussbudget was diffuse in her good wishes for the felicity of her daughters, and impressive in her injunctions that they would not miss the opportunity of enjoying themselves as much as possible; advice, which there was every reason to believe would be attended to; to Fanny, she only enjoined that she take particular care of her cousins' gowns and dancing slippers to ensure that they should be ready whenever called for. And thus it was settled: Admiral Haughtyton, Captain Wentworth, Mr Collins, Mr Wickham, Fanny Anne, Marianne, and Lydia were all off to Mansfield Abbey. Together.

Chapter 11: Mansfield Abbey

As might be suspected, despite Mr Wickham's initial plans to join them, this became a vaguely-stated desire "to wait upon them once they had all settled themselves" when he discovered the admiral must necessarily be of the party. Certainly, this made for less tension, or in fact, actual violence, on their journey together.

Though Mr Collins had anticipated joining the two gentlemen of their party in the admiral's fashionable chaise and four – postilions handsomely liveried, rising so regularly in their stirrups, and numerous outriders properly mounted, he was disappointed when he discovered both captain and admiral (whose various infirmities prohibited them from riding their excellent hunters on such a journey) were instead to travel in the captain's new curricle. As the two seats were thus filled in advance, Mr Collins was left with no alternative but the chaise and four, which the admiral had thoughtfully provided for the ladies. The worthy gentleman thus settled himself in the coach beside his sister, with his fair cousins opposite. Though a trifle let down by such a derailment of his plans, Mr Collins satisfied himself by plying Marianne and Lydia with entire volumes of advice, though he seemed unaware that there were hardly two ladies in all of England less desirous of receiving it. He paid no particular addresses to either of his cousins, who had heard of his proposal to Dilemma and then noted his even-mannered parting from her. Whether he had a new design for his affections –

sensible Jane, self-important Mary, or one of the rather desperate Moneygrubbers, neither girl could say, as he was keeping his own counsel. Both indeed, were simply relieved to be passed by.

Marianne Catherine's spirits revived as they set out on the last leg of the journey; for with the interest of a road entirely new to her, of an abbey before, and a curricle behind, she caught the last view of the turnoff for Bath without any regret, and met with every milestone before she expected it. It has been said by some that after six weeks, Bath becomes the most tiresome place in the world, and she was assured that this might indeed be so. The tediousness of a two hours' wait at Petty France, in which there was nothing to be done but to eat without being hungry, and loiter about without anything to see, and bounce pennies off the heads of the begging destitute, next followed – and her admiration of the style in which they travelled, though tremendously grand, sunk a little under this consequent inconvenience.

Had their party been perfectly agreeable, the delay would have been nothing; but Admiral Haughtyton, though so correctly behaved a man, was a check upon Marianne and Lydia's lively spirits, and scarcely anything was said but by himself; the observation of which, with his discontent at whatever the inn afforded, and his angry impatience at the waiters, and his hurling of tea trays at them, made Marianne Catherine grow every moment more in awe of his commanding superiority to the point where she felt a bit breathless, though it appeared to lengthen the two hours into four. At last, however, the order of release was given; and much was Marianne Catherine then surprised by the admiral's proposal of himself and her taking the two places in his friend's curricle for the rest of the journey: "the day was fine, and he was anxious for her seeing as much of the country as possible."

Or, the captain said, upon hearing this plan, he might show Miss Collins the joys of the country. Fanny, upon hearing such a proposal, shrank so far into herself she seemed prepared to disappear if such a thing were possible. Mr Collins sprang to her defence at once, forbidding his sister to enter into such an immodest tête-à-tête – though it should be proper, nay, entirely suitable for himself to join the admiral.

While the discussion continued, excessive politeness further delaying their trip and leading to not a little aggravation on all sides, Lydia climbed unassisted aboard, hiking her skirts up quite immodestly to aid herself. Thus in possession of the vehicle, she announced that she admired the nimbleness and swiftness of such a contrivance. If one of the gallants about would be kind enough to drive her, she should lack nothing in the world to make her happy. With a long glance at Mr Collins, as if to remind himself of the alternative, the admiral reluctantly took the reins, admitting that, by making better time, he might at least prepare the house for their coming. Before he could depart beside the chattering Lydia, however, Marianne suddenly recalled that Lydia's health was fragile after her fall and that the younger girl must not endanger herself with such a ride. The admiral immediately seconded this, refusing to drive a single inch if his passenger's health would be so imperilled. At this, Lydia's face screwed up for a tantrum, but Fanny quickly offered to embroider her best slippers on the way, if Lydia would but order her around and pick out the colours and designs. With reluctance, Lydia disembarked, and the admiral quickly helped Marianne aboard, with many compliments at how solicitous she was for her sister's health. Without delaying a single moment longer, he sped off, leaving the rest of the party to arrange themselves in the coach. The party proceeded thus to his home.

In the course of a few minutes, Marianne Catherine found herself as happy a being as ever existed. A very short trial convinced her that a curricle was the prettiest equipage in the world; the chaise and four wheeled off with some grandeur, to be sure, but it was a heavy and troublesome business, and she could not easily forget the two pedestrians and a goat they had run over on the way. Half the time would have been enough for the curricle, and so nimbly were the light horses disposed to move, that, they had left behind the admiral's own carriage with ease in half a minute. But the merit of the curricle did not all belong to the horses; the admiral drove so well – so quietly – without making any disturbance, without parading to her, or swearing at them or picking his nose: so different from the coachmen whom it was in her power to compare him with! And then his hat sat so well, and the innumerable capes of his greatcoat looked so becomingly important!

To be sure, he was elderly indeed, but at the shine of his sideburns in the moonlight, added to the allure of his ancestral home, Marianne felt herself intrigued. Her eager imagination, thus offered an outlet, began stacking dozens of future plans, from the ride together to a week of being caught in darkened corners and discovering the secrets of the admiral's past to reassuring him that, whether he was the son of a murderer or himself a terrible vampire, Marianne had been touched to the depth of her soul and would love him through all! In addition to every other delight, she had now that of listening to her own praise; of being thanked at least, on his daughter's account, for her kindness in thus becoming her visitor; of hearing it ranked as real friendship, and described as creating real gratitude. His daughter, he said, was uncomfortably circumstanced – she had no female companion – and, in the frequent absence of her father, was sometimes without any companion at all. Even on her brief releases from being locked away from the eyes of man, she had entertained few visitors. All her life, he believed she had sought a friend, at least since her sister – but here he stopped abruptly.

Marianne, however, was imagining herself such a bosom friend. "How sorry you must be for that!"

"I am always sorry to leave Wallflora."

"Yes; but besides your affection for her, you must be so fond of the abbey! After being used to such a home as the abbey, an ordinary parsonage–house must be very disagreeable."

He smiled, and said, "You have formed a very favourable idea of the abbey."

"To be sure, I have. Is not it a fine old place, just like what one reads about?"

The admiral, so gruff and distant back at the inn, took on a surprisingly teazing tone. "And are you prepared to encounter all the horrors that a building such as 'what one reads about' may produce? Have you a stout heart? Nerves fit for sliding panels and tapestry?"

"Oh! yes – I do not think I should be easily frightened, because there would be so many people in the house – and besides, it has never been uninhabited and left deserted for years, and then the family come back to it unawares, without giving any notice, as generally happens."

"No, certainly. We shall not have to explore our way into a hall dimly lighted by the expiring embers of a wood fire – nor be obliged to spread our beds on the floor of a room without windows, doors, or furniture. But you must be aware that when a young lady is (by whatever means) introduced into a dwelling of this kind, she is always lodged apart from the rest of the family. While they snugly repair to their own end of the house, she is formally conducted by Dorothy, the ancient housekeeper, up a different staircase, and along many gloomy passages, into an apartment never used since some cousin or kin died in it about twenty years before. Can you stand such a ceremony as this? Will not your mind misgive you when you find yourself in this gloomy chamber – too lofty and extensive for you, with only the feeble rays of a single lamp to take in its size – its walls hung with tapestry exhibiting figures as large as life, and the bed, of dark green stuff or purple velvet, presenting even a funereal appearance? Will not your heart sink within you?"

"Oh! But this will not happen to me, I am sure." For Marianne, though delighted by the romance of it all, was just a bit sceptical that the house was as strange as all that.

"How fearfully will you examine the furniture of your

apartment! And what will you discern? Not tables, toilettes, wardrobes, or drawers, but on one side perhaps the remains of a broken lute, on the other a ponderous chest which no efforts can open, and over the fireplace the portrait of some handsome warrior, whose features will so incomprehensibly strike you, that you will not be able to withdraw your eyes from it. Dorothy, meanwhile, no less struck by your appearance, gazes on you in great agitation, and drops a few unintelligible hints. To raise your spirits, moreover, she gives you reason to suppose that the part of the abbey you inhabit is undoubtedly haunted, and informs you that you will not have a single domestic within call. With this parting cordial she curtsies off – you listen to the sound of her receding footsteps as long as the last echo can reach you – and when, with fainting spirits, you attempt to fasten your door, you discover, with increased alarm, that it has no lock."

"Oh! Admiral, how frightful! This is just like a book! But it cannot really happen to me. I am sure your housekeeper is not really Dorothy. Well, what then?"

"Nothing further to alarm perhaps may occur the first night. After surmounting your unconquerable horror of the bed, you will retire to rest, and get a few hours' unquiet slumber. But on the second, or at farthest the third night after your arrival, you will probably have a violent storm. Peals of thunder so loud as to seem to shake the edifice to its foundation will roll round the neighbouring mountains – and during the frightful gusts of wind which accompany it, you will probably think you discern (for your lamp is not extinguished) one part of the hanging more violently agitated than the rest. Unable of course to repress your curiosity in so favourable a moment for indulging it, you will instantly arise, and throwing your dressing–gown around you, proceed to examine this mystery. After a very short search, you will discover a division in the tapestry so artfully constructed as to defy the minutest inspection, and on opening it, a door will immediately appear – which door, being only secured by massy bars and a padlock, you will, after a few efforts, succeed in opening – and, with your lamp in your hand, will pass through it into a small vaulted room."

"No, indeed; I should be too much frightened to do any such thing."

"What! Not when Dorothy has given you to understand that there is a secret subterraneous communication between your apartment and the chapel of St. Anthony, scarcely two miles off? Could you shrink from so simple an adventure? No, no, you will proceed into this small vaulted room, and through this into several others, without perceiving anything very remarkable in either. In one perhaps there may be a dagger, in another a few drops of blood, and in a third the remains of some instrument of torture; but there being nothing in all this out of the common way, and your lamp being nearly exhausted, you will return towards your own apartment. In repassing through the small vaulted room, however, your eyes will be attracted towards a large, old–fashioned cabinet of ebony and gold, which, though narrowly examining the furniture before, you had passed unnoticed. Impelled by an irresistible presentiment, you will eagerly advance to it, unlock its folding doors, and search into every drawer – but for some time without discovering anything of importance – perhaps nothing but a considerable hoard of diamonds. At last, however, by touching a secret spring, an inner compartment will open – a roll of paper appears – you seize it – it contains many sheets of manuscript – you hasten with the precious treasure into your own chamber, but scarcely have you been able to decipher 'Oh! Thou – whomsoever thou mayst be, into whose hands these memoirs of the wretched Matilda may fall' – when your lamp suddenly expires in the socket, and leaves you in total darkness."

"Oh! No, no – do not say so. Well, go on."

But the admiral was too much amused by the interest he had raised to be able to carry it farther; he could no longer command solemnity either of subject or voice, and was obliged to entreat her to use her own fancy in the perusal of Matilda's woes. Marianne Catherine, recollecting herself, grew ashamed of her eagerness, and began earnestly to assure him that her attention had been fixed without the smallest apprehension of really meeting with what he related. "Her friend, she was sure, would never put her into such a chamber as he had described! She was not at all afraid."

As they drew near the end of their journey, he regaled her with further tales of suspense. There were, he revealed, many tales of a highwayman thereabouts, all shrouded in black, who a decade since terrorized all who traveled these roads.

"A decade ago! Is he supposed to have made a vast fortune and finally retired?" she asked, wondering whether she was being teased.

"Some say so," he said with a strangely melancholy smile. "It would certainly be a cure for vast gaming debts, would it not? Unless he turned to forgery or something less strenuous on the body."

As they sped along through the cold wind, her impatience for a sight of the abbey returned in full force, and every bend in the road was expected with solemn awe to afford a glimpse of its massy walls of grey stone, rising amidst a grove of ancient oaks, with the last beams of the sun playing in beautiful splendour on its high gothic windows.

Soon enough, they arrived at Mansfield Abbey, an ominous-looking actual turreted stone castle overlooking a lake. Its manner was everything Marianne Catherine had hoped, from its narrow windows and gothic arches to the dainty little footbridge they need cross over to approach. "Oh!" she cried, struck with its beauty. The admiral glanced over, and a small smile might be seen to play upon his features. "It pleases you then?"

"Oh, yes indeed! It puts me in mind of the country that Emily and her father travelled through, in *The Mysteries of Udolpho*. But you never read novels, I dare say?"

"Why not?"

"Because they are not clever enough for you – gentlemen read better books."

"The person, be it gentleman or lady, who has not

pleasure in a good novel, must be intolerably stupid. I have read all Mrs Radcliffe's works, and most of them with great pleasure. *The Mysteries of Udolpho,* when I had once begun it, I could not lay down again; I remember finishing it in two days – my hair standing on end the whole time."

"I am very glad to hear it indeed, and now I shall never be ashamed of liking *Udolpho* myself. But I really thought before, men despised novels amazingly."

"It is amazingly; it may well suggest amazement if they do – for they read nearly as many as women. I myself have read hundreds and hundreds. Do not imagine that you can cope with me in a knowledge of Wallfloras and Louisas. If we proceed to particulars, and engage in the never-ceasing inquiry of 'Have you read this?' and 'Have you read that?' I shall soon leave you as far behind me as – what shall I say? – I want an appropriate simile. – as far as your friend Emily herself left poor Valancourt when she went with her aunt into Italy. Consider how many years I have had the start of you. I had entered on my studies at Oxford, while you were not even thought of!" Here Marianna Catherine lowered her eyes modestly, as their age gap was one of the admiral's least attractive features, and focused instead on the eerie delights that would soon await her in his home.

All it lacked, she thought, as they entered the gloomy hall, decorated in velvety crimson with shaded lamps, was a vampire or long-concealed corpse to lend it more intrigue. The stonework was imposing, the hall long and ancient with years; everything, in short, recollected the spookiest of her novels.

They set forward; and, with a grandeur of air, a dignified step, which caught the eye, but could not shake the doubts of the well-read Marianne Catherine, Admiral Haughtyton led the way across the hall of his daughter's lodgings through the common drawing-room and one useless antechamber, into a room magnificent both in size and furniture – the real drawing-room, used only with company of consequence. It was very noble – very grand – very charming! – was all that Marianne Catherine had to say, for her indiscriminating eye scarcely discerned the colour of the satin; and all minuteness of praise, all praise that had much meaning, was supplied by the general: the costliness or elegance of any room's fitting-up could be nothing to her; she cared for no furniture of a more modern date than the fifteenth century, unless someone had had the drama to perish upon it quite tragically.

When the general had satisfied his own curiosity, in a close examination of every well-known ornament, from the occasional table that also spent time as a throw rug during the summer months to the shelves of miniature shoehorns and train whistles, they proceeded into the library, an apartment, in its way, of equal magnificence, exhibiting a collection of books, on which an humble man might have looked with pride (except of course for a few that were hidden in back). Marianne Catherine heard, admired, and wondered with more genuine feeling than before – gathered all that she could from this storehouse of knowledge, by running over the titles of half a shelf, though certainly not by bothering to read any.

They returned to the hall, that the chief staircase might be ascended, and the beauty of its wood, and ornaments of rich carving might be pointed out: having gained the top, they turned in an opposite direction. She was here shown successively into three large bed-chambers, with their dressing-rooms, most completely and handsomely fitted up; everything that money and taste could do, to give comfort and elegance to apartments, had been bestowed on these; and, being furnished within the last five years, they were perfect in all that would be generally pleasing, and wanting in all that could give pleasure to Marianne Catherine. As they were surveying the last, the general, after slightly naming a few of the distinguished characters by whom they had at times been honoured, turned with a smiling countenance to Marianne Catherine, and ventured to hope that henceforward some of their earliest tenants might be "our friends from Marrytown." She felt the unexpected compliment, but such a pleasant line of civility from such an otherwise disagreeable man did little to transform her, whose thoughts were still filled with the charms of Willoughby Wickham and had been from the moment she had espied the unromantically modern furnishings in this wing.

She was soon conveyed to her own apartment, where she discovered a far different turn of affairs. The house had mainly been modernized, true, but her own bedroom was just as the admiral had described it on their trip: narrow, iron-bound windows, a dark bed rich with velvet, ensconced in thick drapes of the same. The fireplace was ancient stone and large enough to roast a hog. The carpet, though thick and mossy in colour, did little to mitigate the icy chill of the stone floor. The housekeeper (whose name was Mrs Agatha Brown rather than Dorothy, but this was indeed the only particular in which the admiral had erred) named this room the "North Tower," and so it appeared to be. Before the woman could lock her in, Marianne Catherine rather timidly inquired whether there might be another room near her sister and cousin, for indeed, they had gone a different way, down a comfortable hallway papered in the latest style. With a smile only half-hidden, the housekeeper replied that while her master kept a room such as this for the entertainment of his more fanciful guests, he had many more modern suites awaiting her pleasure. Upon Marianne Catherine's blushing request, the housekeeper escorted her to such a one, noting slyly that the admiral's sense of humour had certainly managed to get the better of his guest though "It seems the pair of you share an affection for the same novels." With that intriguing thought, Marianne found herself abandoned in a very pretty apartment. The walls were papered, the floor was carpeted; the windows were neither less perfect nor more dim than those of the drawing room below; the furniture was handsome and comfortable, and the air of the room altogether far from uncheerful. With that triumph of the admiral's sly joke on her, and this revelation that he kept a true gothic chamber for his imaginative guests, Marianne found herself musing on the delights of a pair of fine sideburns, ones not in the least belonging to Mr Wickham.

Chapter 12: A Touch of Amateur Theatre

At supper, the party made the acquaintance of Miss Wallflora Haughtyton at last. The room was lush and dark, the china thin. Beside it on either side, a full set of forks and spoons diminished in size until they reached near-invisibility. The crystal was spotless, the courses so dainty and elegant that each was only a trifle bigger than the aforementioned absent spots.

Fanny watched with envy as their hostess sliced each blackcurrant into individual wedges. So elegant! She would never aspire to such a role. Throughout the dinner, Miss Haughtyton nodded, smiled, and once shook her head upon being offered the asparagus, but mainly sat, pretty as a statue and rather as useful to the conversation. She had clearly never set her dainty slippers in the muddy roads or worn practical pattens to keep her feet dry. No! There was likely a footman just to carry her at such occasions as a three mile walk to town. Her behaviour seemed only the more refined as Mr Collins let out several belches at the table.

As Marianne was certain from her timorous attitude, Miss Haughtyton customarily spent her time in a bricked-up tower at the behest of her father, to prevent fortune hunters from charming her. Her father, the admiral, must while away many happy hours pacing before her door, loaded gun at the ready.

In deference to the friendliness of her new acquaintances however, she had been released for a short time.

A few days followed, occupied with pleasant diversions, though the lady never became much more animated nor forward. While the admiral was away on business, Mr Wickham became all at once a frequent visitor. However, he was not the only eligible gentleman about, as the Honourable E. Legible, Miss Haughtyton's cousin, came by to visit the party. He came on the wings of disappointment, and with his head full of acting and more than a little gin, for he had been taking part in a theatrical party; and the play, in which he had borne a part, was within two days of representation, when the sudden death of one of the nearest connexions of the family had destroyed the scheme and dispersed the performers. To be so near happiness, so near fame, so near the long paragraph in praise of the private theatricals at Ecclesford, the seat of the Right Hon. Lord Ravenshaw, in Cornwall, which would of course have immortalised the whole party for at least a twelvemonth! and being so near, to lose it all, was an injury to be keenly felt, and Mr Legible could talk of nothing else. Ecclesford and its theatre, with its arrangements and dresses, rehearsals and jokes, was his never-failing subject, and to boast of the past his only consolation.

Happily for him, a love of the theatre is so general, an itch for acting so strong among young people, that he could hardly out-talk the interest of his hearers. From the first casting of the parts, to the epilogue, it was all bewitching, and there were few who did not wish to have been a party concerned, or would have hesitated to try their skill. The play had been *A Midsummer Night's Dream,* and Mr Legible was to have been Bottom. "A trifling part," said he, "and not at all to my taste, and such a one as I certainly would not accept again; but I was determined to make no difficulties. My fellow actors said that a donkey costume was the only one that would fit me, as the Elizabethan suits and even Grecian bathsheets had been designed for someone half my size, so indeed, I gave in with good grace. Our fairy queen was inimitable, and Demetrius was thought very great by many. And upon the whole, it would certainly have gone off wonderfully."

"It was a hard case, upon my word;" and, "I do think you were very much to be pitied;" were the kind responses of listening sympathy. Even Miss Haughtyton offered a sympathetic smile.

"It is not worth complaining about, but to be sure the poor old dowager could not have died at a worse time; and it is impossible to help wishing, that the news could have been suppressed for just the three days we wanted. It was but three days; and being only a grand-mother, and all happening two hundred miles off, I think there would have been no great harm, and it *was* suggested, I know; but Lord Ravenshaw, who I suppose is one of the most correct men in England, would not hear of it."

"Why, to make *you* amends, Mr Legible, I think we must raise a little theatre at Mansfield Abbey, and ask you to be our manager," Lydia chirped.

This, though the thought of the moment, did not end with the moment; for the inclination to act was awakened, and in no one more strongly than in her who was now lady of the house and had never seemed to have had a friend, or been invited to do any thing; and who, having so much leisure as to make almost any novelty a certain good, had likewise such a degree of lively talents and comic taste, as were exactly adapted to the novelty of acting. The thought returned again and again. "Oh! for the Ecclesford theatre and scenery to try something with." Miss Haughtyton was all a-gush; and the visiting Mr Wickham, to whom, in all the riot of his gratifications, it was yet an untasted pleasure, was quite alive at the idea. "I really believe," said he, "I could be fool enough at this moment to undertake any character that ever was written, from Shylock or Richard III down to the singing hero of a farce in his scarlet coat and cocked hat. I feel as if I could be any thing or every thing, as if I could rant and storm, or sigh, or cut capers in any tragedy or comedy in the

English language. For you know, I was to have been a great clown and only the unkindness of one in particular prevented me." One of his beloved poodles barked in agreement, the other leaving a deposit under a highbacked chair. "Let us be doing something. Be it only half a play – an act – a scene; what should prevent us? Not these countenances I am sure," looking towards the Miss Fussbudgets, "and for a theatre, what signifies a theatre? We shall be only amusing ourselves. Any room in this house might suffice."

Captain Wentworth eyed him suspiciously, but uttered nothing. His feelings toward Wickham were wary, but with his hostess's welcome of him, to say nothing of the Miss Fussbudgets' partiality, the captain was clearly in the minority and gave in with good grace.

"What is the nature of the play?" Lydia asked. "For Lord! I'm not much for books."

"Oh! It is so romantic!" Mr Wickham proclaimed, leaning in close to Lydia. "At the marriage of Theseus the Duke of Athens to Hippolyta, proud queen of the Amazons, the fair maid Hermia elopes with her betrothed, Lysander. Her father's choice of suitor, Demetrius, follows her into the woods, and his scorned love, Helena, chases him in turn. In the forest, the fairies play tricks on them, until each falls in love with the wrong suitor."

"And the couples both have a second chance," Fanny Anne smiled. She caught Captain Wentworth's eye for only the briefest of moments, but it seemed to her that he attached some sympathy to her comment.

"Oh, how I adore this play," Marianne Catherine added eagerly. "And I recall there's a subplot, just as romantic, as the fairy king Oberon forces his lady to fall for the donkey-headed churl Bottom. All to show his great love for her." She smiled dreamily at Wickham. With the admiral being out of sight, he appeared to have fallen out of mind as well. Or perhaps it was the blinding effect of Wickham's shining teeth.

"To be sure," Wickham said, smiling directly at her. "I believe fairy queen is a role that would suit you quite well. All you would need is a man of stature to be your monarch."

Mr Collins, presumably seeing himself in this role, beamed. "I am flattered, sir. My dear cousin Marianne, you tell the story well. However, I think it would be very wrong to hold this sort of entertainment. In a *general* light, private theatricals are open to some objections, but as *we* are circumstanced, I must think it would be highly injudicious, and more than injudicious, to attempt any thing of the kind. It would show great want of feeling on our host, Admiral Haughtyton's account, absent as he is, and in some degree of constant danger; and it would be imprudent, I think, with regard to Miss Haughtyton, whose constitution is a very delicate one, considering every thing, extremely delicate."

"Why shouldn't we hold a play?" Lydia demanded. "I say, Mr Collins, you're always determined to ruin our fun."

Mr Collins cleared his throat. "I am certain, cousin, you know the reputations of women in the theatre are not to be spoken of. It is not a thing I would subject my sister or my fair cousins to. And some of the lines, I hear, though I have not read them, no, concern such inappropriate sentiments as I should never wish to hear respectable ladies utter, even in fun. Especially in fun, I should say, for this seems to me an altogether frivolous occupation. I might offer instead to read an appropriate treatise of sermons to our company after supper."

"Oh, Lord!" Lydia groaned. "Anything but those."

Mr Collins cleared his throat. "I have often observed how little young ladies are interested by books of a serious stamp, though written solely for their benefit. It amazes me, I confess; – for certainly, there can be nothing so advantageous to them as instruction. But I will no longer importune my young cousin."

Now that Mr Collins had finished saying his piece, the others turned and began to discuss the notion of a play as if he'd never voiced an objection, and, indeed, as if he were not in the room.

"We must have a curtain," said Wickham; "a few yards of

green baize for a curtain, and perhaps that may be enough."

"Oh! quite enough," cried Mr Legible, "with only just a side wing or two run up, doors in flat, and three or four scenes to be let down; nothing more would be necessary on such a plan as this. For mere amusement among ourselves, we should want nothing more."

"I believe we must be satisfied with *less*," said Marianne. "There would not be time, and other difficulties would arise. We must rather adopt Mr Wickham's views, and make the *performance*, not the *theatre*, our object. Many parts of our best plays are independent of scenery."

"If you are resolved on acting," replied the persevering Mr Collins, "I must hope it will be in a very small and quiet way; and I think a theatre ought not to be attempted. – It would be taking liberties with our host's house in his absence which could not be justified."

"For every thing of that nature, I will be answerable," – said Miss Haughtyton, in a decided tone and in the longest speech her guests had heard her utter.

"Indeed," Lydia chirped. "Don't act yourself, if you do not like it, but don't expect to govern everybody else." She stared piercingly at her cousin, suddenly mesmerized by her reflection in his broad forehead.

"No, as to acting myself," said Collins, "*that* I absolutely protest against."

Collins had little to hope, but he was still urging the subject, when Lydia entered the room, calling out, "No want of hands in our theatre, Mr Collins. No want of under strappers – My sister Marianne desires her love, and hopes to be admitted into the company, and will be happy to take the part of any old Duenna or tame Confidante, that you may not like to do yourselves."

Miss Haughtyton cleared her throat. "What say you all? – Here are two capital tragic parts for Wickham and Wentworth as the quarrelling suitors, and here is the great Amazon queen for me – if nobody else wants it," voice hesitant at taking on something one of the others might be inclined towards.

The suggestion was generally welcome. Mr Legible was particularly pleased; he had been sighing and longing to do Oberon the fairy king instead of the foolish Bottom at Ecclesford, had grudged every rant of Lord Ravenshaw's, and been forced to re-rant it all in his own room. To do him justice, however, he did not resolve to appropriate it – for remembering that there was some very good ranting ground in Lysander, he professed an equal willingness for that. Captain Wentworth was ready to take either. Whichever Mr Legible did not choose, would perfectly satisfy him, and a short parley of compliment ensued. Miss Lydia feeling all the interest of a Hermia in the question, took on her to decide it, by observing to Captain Wentworth, that this was a point in which height and figure ought to be considered, and that *his* being the tallest, seemed to fit him peculiarly for the romantic hero. She was acknowledged to be quite right, and the two parts being accepted accordingly, Marianne, too, was certain of the proper tragic figure of romance from the rather maimed gentleman. The part of the fairy queen fell as a thing long-decided to Marianne, and so all was well-settled.

"Are we certain this is the best course," asked Mr Legible. "Titania is a character more difficult to be well represented than even Hermia. I consider Titania is the most difficult character in the whole piece. It requires great powers, great nicety, to give her playfulness and simplicity without extravagance. I have seen good actresses fail in the part. Simplicity, indeed, is beyond the reach of almost every actress by profession. It requires a delicacy of feeling which they have not. It requires a truly sensitive woman – a Miss Haughtyton. You *will* undertake it, I hope?" turning to her with a look of anxious entreaty, which softened her a little; but while she hesitated what to say, Mr Wickham interposed with Marianne's better claim.

"No, no, Miss Marianne must not be Hermia. It is not at all the part for her. She would not like it. She would not do well. She is too tall and robust. Hermia should be a small, light, girlish, skipping figure. It is fit for Miss Lydia, and Miss Lydia only. She looks the part, and I am persuaded will do it admirably. I shall be Demetrius, and make violent love to her, determined to woo her and carry her off, even against her will."

The influence of his voice was felt. Marianne wavered: but was he only trying to soothe and pacify her, and make her overlook his affronting words? She distrusted him. The slight had been most determined. He was, perhaps, but at treacherous play with her. She looked suspiciously at her sister; Lydia's countenance was to decide it; if she were smug or gleeful – but Lydia looked all serenity, and Marianne well knew that on this ground Lydia could not be happy but at her expense. With hasty indignation, therefore, and a tremulous voice, she agreed.

Mr E. Legible eyed Miss Haughtyton, whom he had envisioned as the fairy queen slowly seduced back to love and obedience by her dashing husband. Perhaps, too, thoughts of the thirty thousand pounds she was to have on her marriage quarrelled in his mind with Miss Marianne's single thousand.

A short silence succeeded this; but Captain Wentworth soon returned to business and *A Midsummer Night's Dream*, and was eagerly looking over the play, with Mr Legible's help, to ascertain what scenery would be necessary – while Lydia and Mr Wickham conversed together in an under voice, and the declaration with which she began of, "I am sure I would give up the part to Marianne most willingly, but that though I shall probably do it very ill, I feel persuaded *she* would do it worse," was doubtless receiving all the compliments it called for.

Fanny Anne, who had stood there all this time without a word spoken to her, took up the volume which had been left on the table, and begin to acquaint herself with the play of which she had heard so much. Her curiosity was all awake, and she ran through it with an eagerness which was suspended only by intervals of astonishment, that it could be chosen in the present instance – that it could be proposed and accepted in a private theatre! Hermia and Titania appeared to her in their different ways so totally improper for home representation – the romantic foolishness of one, and the boldfaced acts of the other, so unfit to be expressed by any woman of modesty, that she could hardly suppose her cousins could be aware of what they were engaging in; and longed to have them roused as soon as possible by the remonstrance which Mr Collins would certainly continue to make. Yet, at the beginning, a single speech caught her eye.

How happy some o'er other some can be!
Through Athens I am thought as fair as she.
But what of that? Demetrius thinks not so;
He will not know what all but he do know:

Poor Helena, passed over by her once-devoted lover, did manage to elicit a pang of sympathy from Fanny Anne.

Marianne, struck by a sudden recollection, exclaimed, "My good friends, pray let me know my fate. Who is to be Bottom? What gentleman among you am I to have the pleasure of making love to?" She gazed hopefully at Mr Wickham.

For a moment no one spoke; and then many spoke together to tell the same melancholy truth – that they had not yet got any Bottom.

"I should be but too happy in taking the part, if it were possible," cried Wickham, "but unluckily Demetrius and Bottom are in together. I will not entirely give it up, however – I will try what can be done – I will look it over again. To woo the fairy queen, court Hermia, and wed Helena would indeed be a thespian triumph."

"Your *brother* should take the part," said Captain Wentworth to Fanny Anne, in a low voice. He gestured emphatically and his hook-hand got caught in the bannister, forcing him to yank it free. "Do not you think he would?"

"Please excuse me, I cannot ask him," Fanny Anne replied, jumping a bit at actually being applied to.

Miss Haughtyton smiled at Mr Collins, who had been sitting in the corner all this while. "Mr Collins, as you do not act yourself, you will be a disinterested adviser; and, therefore, I apply to *you*. What shall we do for a Bottom? Is it practicable for any of the others to double it? What is your advice?"

"My advice," said he, calmly, "is that you change the play."

"*I* should have no objection," she replied; "for though I should not particularly dislike the part of Hippolyta if well supported – that is, if every thing went well – I shall be sorry to be an inconvenience – but as they do not chuse to hear your advice at *that table* – (looking round) – it certainly will not be taken."

Mr Collins said no more.

"If *any* part could tempt *you* to act, I suppose it would be Theseus," observed the lady archly, after a short pause – "for he is a great statesman you know."

"*That* circumstance would by no means tempt me," he replied, "for I should be sorry to make the character ridiculous by bad acting. Indeed, I frown on this sort of frivolous entertainment, and cannot, in good conscience, support it."

Miss Haughtyton was silenced; and with some feelings of resentment and mortification, moved her chair considerably nearer the tea-table. Perhaps she, like Marianne, was most intrigued by gentlemen who were rude and standoffish.

"Fanny Anne," cried Lydia, from the other table, where the conference was eagerly carrying on, and the conversation incessant, "we want your services."

Fanny Anne was up in a moment, expecting some errand, for the habit of employing her in that way was not yet overcome.

"Oh! we do not want to disturb you from your seat. We do not want your *present* services. We shall only want you in our play. You must be Helena."

"Me!" cried Fanny Anne, sitting down again with a most

frightened look. "Indeed you must excuse me. I could not act any thing if you were to give me the world. No, indeed, I cannot act." Putting herself forward in such a way shook her to her soul and made her feel like the kitchen maid suddenly called upon to perform an aria. And of course, Lydia would have her play the discarded heroine, the one neither hero found desirable until the end.

"Indeed but you must, for we cannot excuse you. It need not frighten you; it is a nothing of a part, a mere nothing, not above half a dozen speeches altogether, and it will not much signify if nobody hears a word you say, so you may be as creepmouse as you like, but we must have you to look at."

"It is not that I am afraid of learning by heart," said Fanny Anne, shocked to find herself at that moment the only speaker in the room, and to feel that almost every eye was upon her; "but I really cannot act."

"Yes, yes, you can act well enough for *us*. Learn your part, and we will teach you all the rest. You have only a few scenes, and you will do it very well I'll answer for it."

"No, indeed, Lydia, you must excuse me. You cannot have an idea. It would be absolutely impossible for me. If I were to undertake it, I should only disappoint you."

"Phoo! Phoo! Do not be so shamefaced. You'll do it very well. Every allowance will be made for you. We do not expect perfection. We can make you a large wig, perhaps from a mop."

"You must excuse me, indeed you must excuse me," cried Fanny Anne, growing more and more red from excessive agitation, and looking distressful. The cousins soon relented, for Mr Collins had glanced over the play and in a rapid turn-around, agreed that such a fine young man as Theseus would be no great suffering to play, at his wedding to such a stately lady. At this, he glanced up at Miss Haughtyton, eyes suddenly alive with hope.

It was, indeed, a triumphant day to Marianne and Lydia. Such a victory over Mr Collins's discretion had been beyond their hopes, and was most delightful. There was no longer any thing to disturb them in their darling project, and they congratulated each other in private on the jealous weakness to which they attributed the change, with all the glee of feelings gratified in every way. Mr Collins might still look grave, and say he did not like the scheme in general, and must disapprove the play in particular; their point was gained; he was to act, and he was driven to it by the force of selfish inclinations only. Mr Collins had descended from that moral elevation which he had maintained before, and they were both as much the better as the happier for the descent.

They behaved very well, however, *to him* on the occasion, betraying no exultation beyond the lines about the corners of the mouth. It was all good humour and encouragement. Marianne offered to contrive his dress, Mr Legible assured him that Theseus's last scene admitted a good deal of stage power and presence, and Lydia undertook to groom his hair into, as she called it, "Something quite nearly passable." Upon hearing that Marianne still required a lover, Wickham insisted that he would take on the part of Bottom as well as Demetrius, and contrive to make love to all the young ladies.

"Perhaps," said Lydia, "*Fanny* may be more disposed to oblige us now. Perhaps you may persuade *her.*"

"No, she is quite determined. She certainly will not act," Mr Collins said.

"Oh! very well." And not another word was said; but Fanny Anne felt herself again in danger, and her indifference to the danger was beginning to fail her already. The morning wore away in satisfactions very sweet, if not very sound. Miss Haughtyton had prevailed upon her rather illiterate nursemaid, who had been shut up in the attic until needed as servants often were, and the woman had, with her usual good-humour, agreed to undertake the part for which Fanny had been wanted

Now Fanny of course remained left out of their preparations. Every body around her was gay and busy, prosperous and important; each had their object of interest, their part, their dress, their favourite scene, their friends and confederates, all were finding employment in consultations and comparisons, or diversion in the playful conceits they suggested. She alone was sad and insignificant; she had no share in any thing; she might go or stay; she might be in the midst of their noise, or retreat from it to the solitude of the North Tower, without being seen or missed. She could almost think any thing would have been preferable to this.

Every thing was now in a regular train; theatre, actors, actresses, and dresses, were all getting forward: but though no other great impediments arose, Fanny Anne found, before many days were past, that it was not all uninterrupted enjoyment to the party themselves, and that she had not to witness the continuance of such unanimity and delight, as had been almost too much for her at first. Fanny Anne watched as Marianne exulted in her part of the tragically misled fairy queen, falling desperately in love with Mr Wickham as Bottom as she wound her arms around him.

Come, wait upon him; lead him to my bower.
The moon methinks looks with a watery eye;
And when she weeps, weeps every little flower,
Lamenting some enforced chastity.
Tie up my love's tongue bring him silently.

She threw herself so zealously into the part that real tears dripped down her cheeks. As she charmed and begged kisses from Mr Wickham, Fanny Anne felt her own eyes sting. If it had been permissible for a lady, Marianne might have been an exemplary actress, at least in the sentimental and dramatic roles.

Fanny Anne's services were under constant request, as a seamstress, confidante, carpenter, and theatre assistant. "Would you help me memorize my lines," Captain Wentworth asked one day. Fanny Anne meekly came forward to assist.

LYSANDER: How now, my love! why is your cheek so pale?

151

How chance the roses there do fade so fast?
    HERMIA: Belike for want of rain, which I could well Beteem
them from the tempest of my eyes.
    LYSANDER: Ay me! for aught that I could ever read,
Could ever hear by tale or history,
The course of true love never did run smooth; But, either it was
different in blood, —
    HERMIA: O cross! too high to be enthrall'd to low.

"No, no," Marianne interrupted, coming from her own scene with Bottom. "You read as if you read the grocery list. Cling to him, sob, beg Providence for a way to be together once more. Listen." And Marianne spoke the same lines, nearly swooning with the passion the words gave her. "Now you."

"Indeed, I have no talent for the stage as you have. I am only reciting the words to aid Captain Wentworth's memorization."

"And so he shall remember better with your emotions to guide him."

Fanny Anne read the lines, a little better, perhaps, than she had before.

"No, you are still too cold! Cling to him, place your arms around him!" Before Fanny Anne could protest, Marianne had taken her arms and physically wrapped them around Captain Wentworth. She could not look at him; this was too embarrassing. She could feel the warmth of his arms even through his substantial coat, and she felt an unaccustomed flush rise in her own cheeks. She said her lines warmly, still unable to look at the captain. He said his lines in return, Marianne coaching them both. And yet, Captain Wentworth's voice seemed to tremble when he said:

    hear me, Hermia.
I have a widow aunt, a dowager
Of great revenue, and she hath no child:
From Athens is her house remote seven leagues;

And she respects me as her only son.
There, gentle Hermia, may I marry thee;
And to that place the sharp Athenian law
Cannot pursue us. If thou lovest me then,
Steal forth thy father's house to-morrow night;
And in the wood, a league without the town,
Where I did meet thee once with Helena,
To do observance to a morn of May,
There will I stay for thee.

"Capital, capital," Marianne said. "You achieve so much more emotion when I direct you, I see." If Marianne had been her eldest sister, Fanny would have suspected a deliberate attempt to build a greater attachment through one of Dilemma's many little schemes. Marianne, however, had no talent for concealing her true feelings but only seemed to demand that everyone in the whole of England read the drama with a height of feeling. Besides, her personal ambition seemed to lie more seriously with Wickham. Lydia of course tended to flirt with the entire male population of their surroundings.

Fanny Anne swallowed and willed her voice to steadiness.

My good Lysander!
I swear to thee, by Cupid's strongest bow,
By his best arrow with the golden head,
By the simplicity of Venus' doves,
By that which knitteth souls and prospers loves,
And by that fire which burn'd the Carthage queen,
When the false Troyan under sail was seen,
By all the vows that ever men have broke,
In number more than ever women spoke,
In that same place thou hast appointed me,
To-morrow truly will I meet with thee.

"On 'I swear to thee' you must look at him," Marianne said. "Oh, Captain Wentworth is quite tall, is he not? Step back a place and take his hands."

Those too were quite warm, and Fanny Anne prayed her own did not tremble too hard as Wentworth took them and gazed fully upon her. "Keep promise, love." He paused a moment, gazing at her face, then suddenly seemed to recall their audience. "Look, here comes Helena."

"Excellent, excellent. So sweet and sincere. Now you must run this scene with me, that way I can direct you as we practice. Fanny, you've been so kind to help." With Marianne's oblivious dismissal, Fanny Anne was free to leave. But as she walked away, she could still feel Captain Wentworth's warmth all about her, as if she stood in the sun.

Fanny Anne would have been most uncomfortable running lines with her brother, who had so disapproved the play and was now one of its romantic heroes. He however, had cast another as his scene partner, whether she would or no.

"Oh, Miss Haughtyton, would you run lines with me once more? I'm not certain of my part," was his daily refrain, though his was nearly the shortest in the text.

One day Miss Haughtyton sought her out particularly, and Fanny Anne squirmed. If this conversation, for good or ill, concerned her brother, she should surely rather not be a part of it. As it turned out, Miss Haughtyton wanted only her hem shortened on her costume, which Fanny Anne was happy enough to do. And when Miss Haughtyton's conversation *did* turn to Mr Collins, her words were polite and genteel rather than afire with love. As the lady concluded, "Your brother is a good man, indeed, but his voice sometimes sounds a bit too much like my father's for me to take much comfort in it." Indeed, Fanny had noticed that his "Sweet friends, to bed" was more in the tone of a father insisting on bedtime than a bridegroom on his wedding night. And that was the end of that.

Fanny Anne, being always a very courteous listener, and often the only listener at hand, came in for the complaints and the distresses of most of them. *She* knew that Mr Legible was in general thought to rant dreadfully, that Mr Legible was disappointed in Captain Wentworth, that Mr Wickham spoke so quick he would be unintelligible, that Lydia spoilt every thing by laughing, that Mr Collins was behind-hand with his part. – So far from being all satisfied and all enjoying, she found every body requiring something they had not, and giving occasion of discontent to the others. – Every body had a part either too long or too short; – nobody would attend as they ought, nobody would remember on which side they were to come in – nobody but the complainer would observe any directions.

Fanny Anne believed herself to derive as much innocent enjoyment from the play as any of them; – Mr Wickham acted especially well, and it was a pleasure to *her* to creep into the theatre, and attend the rehearsal of the third act – in spite of the feelings it excited in some speeches for Lydia. – Lydia, she also thought, acted well – too well; – and after the first rehearsal or two, Fanny Anne began to be their only audience, and – sometimes as prompter, sometimes as spectator – was often very useful.

Fanny Anne felt herself quite swept away by the cavalier liveliness Mr Wickham brought to the young seducer determined to sweep away young Hermia. "O, why rebuke you him that loves you so? Lay breath so bitter on your bitter foe," he smirked.

As far as she could judge, Mr Wickham was considerably the best actor of all; he had more confidence than Mr Collins, more judgment than Captain Wentworth, more talent and taste than Mr Legible. – She did not like him as a man, but she must admit him to be the best actor, and on this point there were not many who differed from her.

Captain Wentworth seemed to have no particular animosity toward Mr Wickham, and yet seemed to watch him quite closely. On one occasion he walked up to Fanny Anne and said without preamble, "The selfish Demetrius is rehearsing lines alone with your cousin Lydia. Perhaps you might go watch them."

Fanny Anne blinked. "They are very good, certainly. But I'm obligated to hem this curtain."

Captain Wentworth looked even more uncomfortable, if such were possible. "Nonetheless, I think perhaps you should watch them."

Was the captain implying that the two young persons, unchaperoned, might be making mischief? It was possible, and Fanny Anne went to check on the pair.

As she entered the room, they were holding hands, murmuring in an undertone. To be sure, when they saw her, they said their lines fervently, as if to convince her that was all they had been doing, but Fanny Anne made sure to stay close by for the next hour. At Lydia's request, Wickham also read her the part of Lysander, her true love who stole away with her into the forest, defying her parents' laws for their shared passion. These lines too he read well, far better than the stodgy captain, Lydia insisted.

Fanny Anne thought of the morrow a great deal, – for Mr Wickham and Marianne would then be acting together for the first time; – the third act would bring a love scene between them which interested her most particularly, as he would be wearing an ass's head for the whole of it, and which she was longing with more than a little humour to see how they would perform.

The first regular rehearsal of the three first acts was certainly to take place in the evening; some of Mr Wickham's regimental companions were engaged to visit for that purpose as soon as they could after dinner; and every one concerned was looking forward with eagerness.

However, when Miss Haughtyton arrived, it was with the news that her governess had had the supremely bad taste and timing to fall ill. Here was disappointment! The woman's non-attendance was sad indeed. Her pleasant manners and cheerful stupidity made her always valuable amongst them, as a chaperone fully unaware of her charges' acts – but *now* she was absolutely necessary. They could not act, they could not

rehearse with any satisfaction without her. The comfort of
the whole evening was destroyed. What was to be done?
After a pause of perplexity, some eyes began to be turned
towards Fanny Anne, and a voice or two, to say, "If Miss
Collins would be so good as to *read* the part." She was
immediately surrounded by supplications; every body asked it,
even Captain Wentworth said, "Do, Miss Collins, if it is not
very disagreeable to you."

But Fanny Anne still hung back. She could not endure the
idea of it. Why had not she rather gone to her own room, as
she had felt to be safest, instead of attending the rehearsal at
all? She had known it would irritate and distress her to be
around strange gentlemen – she had known it her duty to
keep away. She was properly punished for appearing among
people.

"You have only to *read* the part," said her brother, with
renewed entreaty.

"And I do believe she can say every word of it," added
Marianne, "Fanny Anne, I am sure you know the part."

Fanny Anne could not say she did *not* – and as they all
persevered – as the captain repeated his wish, and with a look
of even fond dependence on her good nature, she must yield.
She would do her best. Every body was satisfied – and she
was left to the tremors of a most palpitating heart, while the
others prepared to begin.

They *did* begin – and being too much engaged in their
own noise, to be struck by an unusual noise in the other part
of the house, had proceeded some way, when the door of the
room was thrown open, and Miss Haughtyton appearing at it,
with a face all aghast, exclaimed, "My father is come! He is in
the hall at this moment."

How is the consternation of the party to be described? To
the greater number it was a moment of absolute horror.
Admiral Haughtyton in the house! All felt the instantaneous
conviction. Not a hope of imposition or mistake was
harboured any where. Miss Haughtyton's looks were an
evidence of the fact that made it indisputable; and after the

first starts and exclamations, not a word was spoken for half a minute; each with an altered countenance was looking at some other, and almost each was feeling it a stroke the most unwelcome, most ill-timed, most appalling! Mr Legible might consider it only as a vexatious interruption for the evening, or perhaps a blessing, but every other heart was sinking under some degree of self-condemnation or undefined alarm, every other heart was suggesting, "What will become of us? what is to be done now?" It was a terrible pause; and terrible to every ear were the corroborating sounds of opening doors and passing footsteps.

Miss Haughtyton was the first to move and speak again. She turned out of the room, saying, "*I* need not be afraid of appearing before him."

After she had left, Mr Legible volunteered that they might offer the admiral the best part – Theseus, say – and he might thus enjoy leading their little drama. However, Mr Collins let out a strangled whimper at the thought of his lost status.

The captain was more warm on the subject than Mr Legible, from better understanding his friend and judging more clearly of the mischief that must ensue. The ruin of the play was to him a certainty, he felt the total destruction of the scheme to be inevitably at hand; while Mr Legible considered it only as a temporary interruption, a disaster for the evening, and could even suggest the possibility of the rehearsal being renewed after tea, when the bustle of receiving Admiral Haughtyton were over and he might be at leisure to be amused by it. Mr Wickham laughed at the idea; and having soon agreed on the propriety of his walking quietly home and leaving the family to themselves, proposed Mr Legible's accompanying him for a drink or seven. But Mr Legible, having never been with those who thought much of parental claims, or family confidence, could not perceive that any thing of the kind was necessary, and therefore, thanking them, said, "he preferred remaining where he was that he might pay his respects to the old gentleman handsomely since he *was* come; and besides, he did not think it would be fair by the others to have every body run away." He glanced in the direction of the admiral, and indeed of his wealthy daughter. Wickham nodded and smiled at this, and yet scurried from the house within minutes.

Within moments, Admiral Haughtyton entered the room, followed by his daughter. He eyed the miscreants coolly. "I see a red curtain and a flat surface, suggesting a stage. And your strange and varied dress suggests much of a play. Is this so?"

"It is, Admiral," said his daughter, blushing and paling by turns.

One of the forgotten poodles of Wickham let out a bark from under a chair. The admiral turned and smoothly drop-kicked the unfortunate creature out the window and into the hedges, where it let out a pitiful yip and scurried back to his master.

Smoothly he returned to his daughter. "Indeed! and what have you been acting?"

"You will hear enough of it to-morrow, sir," cried she hastily, and with affected unconcern; "We have just been trying, just within the last week, to get up a few scenes, a mere trifle. We have had such incessant rains almost since October began, that we have been nearly confined to the house for days together. Whenever Miss Marianne goes out, the squirrels trip her and hurl pebbles, so much that I feared for her safety."

"And what is this play?" he asked again.

"A very fine work, with a great duke as the romantic figure," Mr Collins said proudly, waving his script toward the Admiral. Fanny Anne winced.

The Admiral flipped briefly through the play, and then eyed Lydia, Marianne, and his own daughter. Lydia and Marianne's costumes were quite romantic, down to the disarrayed necklines and half-sewn sleeves. Miss Haughtyton looked little better, with the flowers in her braids all askew and bare arms stretching from her one-strap Amazon gown. "And all three of you ladies have taken parts?"

"We have, sir," his daughter said.

"I think there are better uses for your leisure," was all the Admiral replied. But within hours, every trace of the play, from scripts to moved furniture, to costumes had quite vanished and the house and its occupants returned to their usual state.

Chapter 13: Trespass in the Abbey

By breakfast the next morning, Mr Wickham was nowhere to be found, and the cook was complaining of the absence of half-a-dozen silver spoons. Lydia did not come down to breakfast that morning, and whether she was sulking over Mr Wickham's departure or the play's cancelation was less than certain.

Marianne Catherine, herself a bit dispirited over the play, prevailed upon Miss Haughtyton for a tour of the house, which was readily granted. The admiral abruptly volunteered to lead this tour, and, a bit more dispirited by the admiral's stuffy presence, Marianne followed her two hosts through the garden, admiring the antique back garden privy and the adjoining cabbage yard before returning to the house.

The gallery was terminated by folding doors, which Miss Haughtyton, advancing, had thrown open, and passed through, and seemed on the point of doing the same by the first door to the left, in another long reach of gallery, when the admiral, coming forwards, called her hastily, and, as Marianne Catherine thought, rather angrily back, demanding whether she were going? – And what was there more to be seen? – Had not Miss Marianne already seen all that could be worth her notice? – And did she not suppose her friend might be glad of some refreshment after so much exercise? Miss Haughtyton drew back directly, and the heavy doors were closed upon the mortified Marianne Catherine, who, having seen, in a momentary glance beyond them, a narrower passage, more numerous openings, and symptoms of a

winding staircase, believed herself at last within the reach of
something worth her notice; and felt, as she unwillingly paced
back the gallery, that she would rather be allowed to examine
that end of the house than see all the finery of all the rest.
The admiral's evident desire of preventing such an
examination was an additional stimulant. Something was
certainly to be concealed; her fancy, though it had trespassed
lately once or twice, could not mislead her here; and what that
something was, a short sentence of Miss Haughtyton's, as
they followed the admiral at some distance downstairs,
seemed to point out: "I was going to take you into what was
my mother's room – the room in which she died – " were all
her words; but few as they were, they conveyed pages of
intelligence to Marianne Catherine. It was no wonder that the
admiral should shrink from the sight of such objects as that
room must contain; a room in all probability never entered by
him since the dreadful scene had passed, which released his
suffering wife, and left him to the stings of conscience.

She ventured, when next alone with Miss Haughtyton, to
express her wish of being permitted to see it, as well as all the
rest of that side of the house; and Miss Haughtyton promised
to attend her there, whenever they should have a convenient
hour. Marianne Catherine understood her: the admiral must
be watched from home, before that room could be entered.
"It remains as it was, I suppose?" said she, in a tone of
feeling.

"Yes, entirely."

"And how long ago may it be that your mother died?"

"She has been dead these nine years." And nine years,
Marianne Catherine knew, was a trifle of time, compared with
what admirably elapsed after the death of an injured wife,
before her room was put to rights. At home, she would have
been pleased to clean her room only once every nine years,
indeed.

"You were with her, I suppose, to the last?"

"No," said Miss Haughtyton, sighing; "I was unfortu-
nately from home. Her illness was sudden and short; and,

before I arrived it was all over. My sister was here, however."

"Sister?" She had thought Miss Haughtyton an only child.

The lady froze. "We no longer speak of her."

"And your mother?"

"My father, in time, has gotten over the loss, and now seeks a new wife."

Marianne Catherine's blood ran cold with the horrid suggestions which naturally sprang from these words. Could it be possible? Could the admiral – ? And yet how many were the examples to justify even the blackest suspicions! And, when she saw him in the evening, while she worked with her friend, slowly pacing the drawing-room for an hour together in silent thoughtfulness, with downcast eyes and contracted brow, she felt secure from all possibility of wronging him. It was the air and attitude of a monk! What could more plainly speak the gloomy workings of a mind not wholly dead to every sense of humanity, in its fearful review of past scenes of guilt? Unhappy man! And the anxiousness of her spirits directed her eyes towards his figure so repeatedly, as to catch Miss Haughtyton's notice. "My father," she whispered, "often walks about the room in this way; it is nothing unusual."

"So much the worse!" thought Marianne Catherine; such ill-timed exercise was of a piece with the strange unseasonableness of his morning walks, and boded nothing good. Clearly, she was in the midst of a dreadful mystery.

"I believe he experiences her loss with great feeling," Miss Haughtyton said timorously, and then her eyes welled with tears. Marianne stared in amazement. The lady was not haughty at all, but terribly reserved, most likely from the severity of her father. Beneath this, however, lurked a heart of pure sentiment.

After having been deprived during the course of several weeks of a real friend, one can only imagine her transports at beholding one most truly worthy of the name. Wallflora was charming, sweet, attentive, everything that touched Marianne's overwrought sensibilities even to her capitalization once again. Looking, Marianne saw that a soft languor spread over her lovely features, but increased their Beauty. – It was the Characteristic of her Mind. – She was all Sensibility and Feeling. Upon beholding their likemindness in that instant, they flew into each other's arms and after having exchanged vows of mutual (and particularly spelled) Freindship for the rest of their Lives, instantly unfolded to each other the most inward secrets of their Hearts. It was all too pathetic for the feelings of Wallflora and herself – The two sensitive ladies fainted alternately on a sofa.

By the next day when she had recovered, more mundane concerns eventually intruded upon the young heroine. When the evening produced no sign of Lydia, Marianne went to her room, and when pounding on the door produced no result, cautiously opened it. The bed was neatly made, the clothes gone, a note lay upon the dresser. This note, which Marianne promptly opened, was fortuitously addressed to her. Lydia begged her sister to understand that the events of the previous day had proved too much for her. The disappointment of losing both play and Wickham was all a terrible disappointment, and still she had not seen any of Brighton at all! She had therefore departed for Brighton by hired coach, determined to have at least a brief outing before having to return to their dull home. No servant or relative need trouble – she would manage all. She had an old school chum there (unnamed in the letter, which was quite strange and inconvenient, especially as Lydia had never been to school) who should be delighted to host her for as long as needed. Perhaps Marianne would be good enough to hem the slippers Lydia had left under the bed, for one had quite a shameful tear in it. Love to them all, etc.

Marianne discovered the slippers, and took them and the note with her. She was glad Lydia would take some pleasure on her outing after all and was only offended not to have been invited. But for Marianne, the locked room was such a great temptation that she felt all her imagination quite caught up in it.

After an evening, the little variety and seeming length of which made her peculiarly sensible of Mr Wickham's importance among them, she was heartily glad to be dismissed; though it was a look from the admiral not designed for her observation which sent his daughter to the bell. When the butler would have lit his master's candle, however, he was forbidden. The latter was not going to retire. "I have many pamphlets on the subject of being elderly and not liking today's music to finish," said he to Marianne Catherine teazingly, "before I can close my eyes, and perhaps may be poring over the affairs of the nation for hours after you are asleep. Can either of us be more meetly employed? My eyes will be blinding for the good of others, and your's preparing by rest for future mischief."

But neither the business alleged, nor the magnificent compliment, could win Marianne Catherine from thinking that some very different object must occasion so serious a delay of proper repose. To be kept up for hours, after the family were in bed, by stupid pamphlets about the clichéd elderly lifestyle was not very likely. There must be some deeper cause: something was to be done which could be done only while the household slept; and the probability that Mrs Haughtyton yet lived, shut up for causes unknown, and receiving from the pitiless hands of her husband a nightly supply of stewed rats with rat sauce, was the conclusion which necessarily followed. Shocking as was the idea, it was at least better than a death unfairly hastened, as, in the natural course of things, she must ere long be released. The suddenness of her reputed illness, the absence of her daughter, at the time – all favoured the supposition of her imprisonment. Its origin – jealousy perhaps, or wanton cruelty – was yet to be unravelled.

Marianne Catherine hurried away, quickly enough that she barely noticed the admiral opening a chest and lifting out stacks of identical banknotes, which if she had observed very closely indeed, might have revealed faint irregularities in the signatures, and, indeed, the shininess of fresh ink in the centres.

In revolving the fate of Mrs Haughtyton, while she undressed, it suddenly struck her as not unlikely that she might that morning have passed near the very spot of this unfortunate woman's confinement – might have been within a few paces of the cell in which she languished out her days; for what part of the abbey could be more fitted for the purpose? Marianne Catherine sometimes started at the boldness of her own surmises, and sometimes hoped or feared that she had gone too far; but they were supported by such appearances as made their dismissal impossible. Could this be the source of the admiral's animosity for Mr Wickham? The latter had described a childhood hatred, but what if in fact he had learned too much of the admiral's terrible imprisonment or murder of his wife! She nearly swooned at the momentousness of it all.

As she huddled there in her room, she resolved that when the clock had struck twelve, and all was quiet, she would, if not quite appalled by darkness, and not perceiving any frightening moans of ghosts or howls of wolves, steal out and look once more. At last, the clock struck twelve – and Marianne Catherine had been half an hour asleep. While it might be most traditional for her to lie awake all night in a frenzy of terror, it seemed the young heroine could not quite manage it.

The next day afforded no opportunity for the proposed examination of the mysterious apartments. It was Sunday, and the whole time between morning and afternoon service was required by the admiral in exercise abroad or eating cold quail, squab, and dodo bird at home; and great as was Marianne Catherine's curiosity, her courage was not equal to a wish of exploring them after dinner, either by the fading light of the sky between six and seven o'clock, or by the yet more partial though stronger illumination of a treacherous lamp. The day was unmarked therefore by anything to interest her imagination beyond the sight of a very elegant monument to the memory of Mrs Haughtyton, which immediately fronted the family pew. By that her eye was instantly caught and long retained; and the perusal of the highly strained epitaph, in which every virtue was ascribed to her by the inconsolable husband in painfully jingly and upbeat rhyme, affected her even to tears.

That the admiral, having erected such a monument, should be able to face it, was not perhaps very strange, and yet that he could sit so boldly collected within its view, maintain so elevated an air, look so fearlessly around, nay, that he should even enter the church, seemed wonderful to Marianne Catherine. It seemed he was no vampire, werewolf, or other creature of the night, despite his Gothic lair, and thus another blossoming theory was spoilt.

In the course of the next morning's reflections, she came to a resolution of making her next attempt on the forbidden door. Of the way to the apartment she was now perfectly mistress; the day was bright, her courage high; at four o'clock, the sun was now two hours above the horizon, and it would be only her retiring to dress half an hour earlier than usual. Her foray down a few corridors and through the unlocked door had been planned with the cunning of a master criminal and all was ready.

It was done; and Marianne Catherine found herself alone in the gallery before the clocks had ceased to strike. There was the wife's portrait, and beside it, a large blank space where a similar one might have stood, and beside that, one of Miss Haughtyton. That seemed natural enough; she hurried on, slipped with the least possible noise through the folding doors, and without stopping to look or breathe, rushed forward to the one in question. The lock yielded to her hand, and, luckily, with no sullen sound that could alarm a human being. On tiptoe she entered; the room was before her; but it was some minutes before she could advance another step. She beheld what fixed her to the spot and agitated every feature. She saw a large, well-proportioned apartment, an handsome dimity bed, arranged as unoccupied with an housemaid's care, a bright Bath stove, mahogany wardrobes, and neatly painted chairs, on which the warm beams of a western sun gaily poured through two sash windows! The watercolours of kittens and puppies were appallingly ugly, but aside from this, nothing seemed amiss.

She rifled through the desk. Willfully, she shoved aside numerous pawnshop tickets for diamond rings and brooches, and eagerly she dumped out a thick black hood and impressive revolver. What she sought here was the lady's diary or a packet of letters, but alas! There was no sign of these, nothing peculiar at all.

A search under the bed revealed a box stuffed with printing plates, and beneath them, a tidy stack of banknotes. The lady's closet revealed nothing of interest, save for a set of dark boy's clothes that might have fit Marianne herself, but surely not the admiral. Perhaps they were a memento of his childhood. Clearly, the woman who lived here had had a perfectly ordinary life, and most likely, death. Marianne Catherine had expected to have her feelings worked, and worked they were. Astonishment and doubt first seized them; and a shortly succeeding ray of common sense added some bitter emotions of shame, followed by a pulsing spotlight of self-loathing. She could not be mistaken as to the room; but how grossly mistaken in everything else!

She was sick of exploring, and desired but to be safe in her own room, hugging her collection of stuffed kittens, with her own heart only privy to its folly; and she was on the point of retreating as softly as she had entered, when the sound of footsteps, she could hardly tell where, made her pause and tremble. To be found there, even by a servant, would be unpleasant; but by the admiral (and he seemed always at hand when least wanted), much worse! She listened – the sound had ceased; and resolving not to lose a moment, she passed through and closed the door. At that instant a door underneath was hastily opened; someone seemed with swift steps to ascend the stairs, by the head of which she had yet to pass before she could gain the gallery. She had no power to move and felt the twist of her stomach that suggested a burst of flatulence would soon be upon her, though heroines of her time must never be found so afflicted. With a feeling of terror not very definable, she fixed her eyes on the staircase, and in a few moments it gave the admiral to her view. "Admiral Haughtyton!" she exclaimed in a voice of more than common astonishment. He looked astonished too. "Good God!" she continued, not attending to his address. "How came you here? How came you up that staircase?"

"How came I up that staircase!" he replied, greatly surprised. "It was only a matter of dragging myself up them one by one and clinging to the bannister."

Marianne Catherine recollected herself, blushed deeply, and could say no more, though her squirming stomach said it for her. A burst of unwelcome fragrance assaulted his nose, judging by the expression on his face as he hustled her towards the gallery. "And may I not, in my turn," said he, as he pushed back the folding doors, "ask how you came here? This passage is at least as extraordinary a road from the breakfast-parlour to your apartment, as that staircase can be from the stables to mine."

"I have been," said Marianne Catherine, looking down, "to see your wife's room."

"My wife's room! Is there anything extraordinary to be seen there?"

"No, nothing at all," she said quickly. "Is not it very late? I must go and dress."

"It is only a quarter past four" showing his watch – "and you are not in Bath or London. No theatre, no rooms to prepare for. Half an hour at Mansfield must be enough, though I might suggest some ivy leaves or sugar of lead for dyspepsia while you are there."

She could not contradict it, and therefore suffered herself to be detained, though her dread of further questions made her shiver. They walked slowly up the gallery. After a short silence, during which he had closely observed her, he asked, "Did you discover any thing of a surprising nature?" She shook her head meekly, and his brows raised nearly to the rafters. He added, "As there is nothing in the room in itself to raise curiosity, this must have proceeded from a sentiment of respect for my wife's character, as described by Wallflora, which does honour to her memory. The world, I believe, never saw a better woman. She was accomplished too, in every kind of frivolous indoor pursuit of which ladies are so fond, and several outdoor ones as well. Yes, she was adventurous and quite unconventional, the sort of woman unique in her class. She was also shrewd, with a talent for providing for her family. But it is not often that virtue can boast an interest such as this. The domestic, unpretending merits of a person never known do not often create that kind of fervent, venerating tenderness which would prompt a visit like yours. Wallflora, I suppose, has talked of her a great deal?"

"Yes, a great deal. That is – no, not much, but what she did say was very interesting. Her dying so suddenly" (slowly, and with hesitation it was spoken), "and you – none of you being at home – I thought – perhaps you had not been very fond of her. And then there is your treatment of Mr Wickham, a fine, charming man, yet you cannot stand to clap eyes on him." At the mention of the man's name, the admiral clenched his hand on the banister, trembling with such fury that the bannister seemed quite in danger of snapping. "Does he know your terrible secret?" she persisted boldly.

"And from these circumstances," he replied (his quick eye fixed on hers), "you infer perhaps the probability of some negligence – some" – (involuntarily she shook her head) – "or it may be – of something still less pardonable. Of that odious man, I cannot and will not speak." She raised her eyes towards him more fully than she had ever done before. "My wife's illness," he continued, "the shot – I mean, seizure, which ended in her death, was sudden. Still, she received every possible attention which could spring from the affection of those about her, or which her situation in life could command. Poor Wallflora was absent, and at such a distance as to return only to see her mother in her coffin."

"If I understand you rightly, you had formed a surmise of such horror as I have hardly words to – Dear Miss Fussbudget, consider the dreadful nature of the suspicions you have entertained. What have you been judging from? Remember the country and the age in which we live. Remember that we are stuffy English peerage, that we are Christians, that we never unbutton a single button unless compelled. Consult your own understanding, your own sense of the probable, your own observation of what is passing around you. Does our education prepare us for such atrocities? Could they be perpetrated without being known, in a country like this, though bleak and empty of most inhabitants, save travellers whom rogues might easily prey upon? Dearest Miss Fussbudget, what ideas have you been admitting?"

They had reached the end of the gallery, and with tears of shame she ran off to her own room. There she was confronted with her tall stack of novels, silently condemning her from the nightstand.

The visions of romance were over. Marianne Catherine was completely awakened. Admiral Haughtyton's address, short as it had been, had more thoroughly opened her eyes to the extravagance of her late fancies than all their several disappointments had done. Most grievously was she humbled. Most bitterly did she cry. Most horribly did she upchuck into her handy chamberpot. It was not only with herself that she was sunk – but with Admiral Haughtyton. Her folly, which now seemed even criminal, was all exposed to him, and he must despise her forever. The liberty which her imagination had dared to take with his character – could he ever forgive it? The absurdity of her curiosity and her fears – could they ever be forgotten? And the indelicate sight of Admiral Haughtyton is his very shirtsleeves, bony arms fully discernible – might those ever be unseen? She hated herself more than she could express, especially as the bony arms appeared once more before her eyes. He had – she thought he had, once or twice before this fatal morning, shown something like affection for her. But now – in short, she made herself as miserable as possible for about half an hour, went down when the clock struck five, with a broken heart, and could scarcely give an intelligible answer to Wallflora's inquiry if she was well. The formidable Admiral Haughtyton soon followed her into the room, and the only difference in his behaviour to her was that he paid her rather more attention than usual. Marianne Catherine had never wanted comfort more, and he looked as if he was aware of it.

"What have I done?" she asked herself. A moment later, her flighty mind recalled, "Oh yes, I acted like a total fluffhead in front of the most eligible man I ever met and now he will no longer want me."

The evening wore away with no abatement of this soothing politeness; and her spirits were gradually raised to a modest tranquillity. She did not learn either to forget or defend the past; but she learned to hope that it would never transpire farther, and that it might not cost her Admiral Haughtyton's entire regard. Her thoughts being still chiefly fixed on what she had with such causeless terror felt and done, nothing could shortly be clearer than that it had been all a voluntary, self-created delusion, each trifling circumstance receiving importance from an imagination resolved on alarm, and everything forced to bend to one purpose by a mind which, before she entered the abbey, had been craving to be frightened.

Her mind made up on these several points, and her resolution formed, of always judging and acting in future with the greatest good sense, she had nothing to do but to forgive herself and be happier than ever and pour the contents of the chamberpot into a handy chest, where they might only be discovered after her departure; and the lenient hand of time did much for her by insensible gradations in the course of another day. Admiral Haughtyton's astonishing generosity and nobleness of conduct, in never alluding in the slightest way to what had passed, was of the greatest assistance to her;

and sooner than she could have supposed it possible in the beginning of her distress, her spirits became absolutely comfortable, and capable, as heretofore, of continual improvement by anything he said. There were still some subjects, indeed, under which she believed they must always tremble – the mention of a guilty chest, for instance – but even she could allow that an occasional memento of past folly, however painful, might not be without use.

The next morning, she found a note slipped under her door, and upon opening it, found it to be from the admiral himself. It began with brief compliments and explained, nay, insisted, that the admiral's character required it to be written and read.

Pardon me for alluding to a discussion I am sure we would both rather forget. Along with your fears about my wife, you described Mr Wickham's ill treatment at my hands. I fear you may not know the full extent of Mr Wickham's perfidy. In the hopes of being of use to you, I wish you to understand the kind of match you have escaped, and I hope, you may take comfort for the future in finding one far better.

Mr Wickham is the son of a very respectable man, who had for many years the management of all his estates; and whose good conduct in the discharge of his trust, naturally inclined my father to be of service to him, and on Willoughby Wickham, who was his god-son, his kindness was therefore liberally bestowed. My father supported him at school, and afterwards at Cambridge; – most important assistance, as his own father, always poor from the extravagance of his wife's monogrammed tea-towel collection, would have been unable to give him a gentleman's education. My father was not only fond of this young man's society, whose manners were always engaging; he had also the highest opinion of him, and hoping clowning would be his profession, intended to provide for him in it. As for myself, it is many, many years since I first began to think of him in a very different manner. The vicious propensities – the want of principle and fashion which he was careful to guard from the knowledge of his best benefactor, could not escape the observation of a young man of nearly the same age with himself, and who had opportunities of seeing him in unguarded moments, which my father could

173

not have. He began spending time in low company and even appearing in public with neither hat nor cravat! I fear I shock you, but some such shocks are necessary.

Here again I shall give you pain – to what degree you only can tell. But whatever may be the sentiments which Mr Wickham has created, a suspicion of their nature shall not prevent me from unfolding his real character. It adds even another motive. My excellent father died about five years ago; and his attachment to Mr Wickham was to the last so steady, that in his will he particularly recommended it to me, to promote his advancement in the best manner that his profession might allow, and if he ventured to harlequin college desired that a valuable circus living as a ringleader might be his as soon as soon as it became vacant. There was also a legacy of a chest of gold, as a working man in the professions might not subsist on the pittances of which women are so fond. His own father did not long survive mine, and within half a year from these events, Mr Wickham wrote to inform me that, having finally resolved against taking the facepaint and rubber nose, he hoped I should not think it unreasonable for him to expect some more immediate pecuniary advantage, in lieu of the preferment, by which he could not be benefited. He had some intention, he added, of studying pigeon fancying, and I must be aware that the interest of one chest of gold would be a very insufficient support therein. I rather wished, than believed him to be sincere; but at any rate, was perfectly ready to accede to his proposal. I knew that Mr Wickham ought not to be an entertainer of young people.

The business was therefore soon settled. He resigned all claim to assistance in clowning, were it possible that he could ever be in a situation to receive it, and accepted in return ten chests of gold (for I had limited knowledge of financial matters. Even now I allow my man of business to handle all my arrangements and mail a healthy annual salary to his homes in Jamaica and the South of France). All connexion between us seemed now dissolved. In town I believe he chiefly lived, but his studying pigeon fancying, or indeed, anything connected with ornithology, was a mere pretence, and being now free from all restraint, his life was a life of idleness and dissipation. From untied cravats, he sank to a bowler hat, and from then, I know nothing, though a rumour suggested he shaved off his very muttonchops.

For about three years I heard little of him; but on the decease of the incumbent of the living which had been designed for him, he applied to me again by letter for the presentation. His circumstances, he assured me, and I had no difficulty in believing it, were exceedingly bad. He had found pigeons a most unprofitable study, and was now absolutely resolved on clowning, if I would present him to the living in question with a dozen or so more chests of gold – of which he trusted there could be little doubt, as he was well assured that I had no other person to provide for, and I could not have forgotten my revered father's intentions. You will hardly blame me for refusing to comply with this entreaty, or for resisting every repetition of it. His resentment was in proportion to the distress of his circumstances – and he was doubtless as violent in his abuse of me to others, as in his reproaches to myself. He ended his diatribe by hurling a pie, leaving me dripping with gooseberries and custard. After this period, every appearance of acquaintance was dropt. How he lived I know not.

But last summer he was again most painfully obtruded on my notice. I must now mention a circumstance which I would wish to forget myself, and which no obligation less than the present desire to justify myself to a near stranger should induce me to unfold to any human being. Having said thus much, I feel no doubt of your secrecy. About a year ago, my older daughter Inchastity was taken from school, and an establishment formed for her in London; and last summer she went with the lady who presided over it, Mrs Tongue, to Ramsgate, a wicked party town where women bathe publicly in costumes that reveal their very ankles and collarbones and elbows! I believe many sheep reside there as well, for some reason. Thither also went Mr Wickham, undoubtedly by design.

He so far recommended himself to my Inchastity, whose affectionate heart retained a strong impression of his kindness to her as a child when he would give her candy and take her on long walks far from her chaperones, that she was persuaded to believe herself in love, or at least heady, passionate feelings that we in this age deny any females possess, and to consent to an elopement. She was then but fifteen and three-quarters, which must be her excuse; and after stating her imprudence, I am happy to add, that I owed the knowledge of it to herself. I joined them unexpectedly a day or two before the intended elopement, and then Inchastity, unable to support the idea of grieving and offending a father, acknowledged the whole to me. You may imagine what I felt and how I acted. Regard for my daughter's credit and feelings prevented any public exposure, but I threw the poker at the scoundrel and then the entire fireplace. He hastened away, with more speed, perhaps, thanks to the dining room table that hurtled behind. Mrs Tongue was of course fired with several frowny faces and a "Not Satisfactory" box checked on the character I wrote her. Further, I locked my errant daughter away in an establishment for wayward young ladies set on the lonely moors to the north and have never spoken of her since. Mr Wickham's chief object was unquestionably my daughter's fortune, which is thirty thousand pounds; but I cannot help supposing that the hope of revenging himself on me, was a strong inducement. His revenge would have been complete indeed.

After this, he charmed my housekeeper with their old connexion and attempted to kidnap her at gunpoint, hoping I might pay a generous ransom for her safe release. I sent in several strong gardener's lads to save her, and once more I hushed up the scandal, before the shades of Mansfield Abbey could be exposed to gossip.

Following this, he began a scheme of blackmail, based on some of my…past irregularities in connexion with my fortune, particularly the chests of gold. Once more, I thwarted him, and once more I buried the scandal. From hence, I believe, he made his way into the army and from thence to Marrytown. Now, only yesterday, my younger Wallflora has told me she too has spent time with Mr Wickham, under our very roof here, though she adds that she would never disgrace me by eloping or indeed speaking to a visitor without my express permission, or allowing him to see her without her elbow-gloves. It would seem that my many nights walling her up in the North Tower and patrolling with a shotgun have had their effect.

I know I may rely on your discretion to allow him to keep charming all those around him, without summoning the constables or alerting the neighbourhood. Surely, such discretion is best.

I will only add, God bless you and for heaven's sake, take something for that stomach complaint.

Haughtyton

When Marianne read this account of Mr Wickham, a relation of events, which, if true, must overthrow every cherished opinion of his worth, and which bore so alarming an affinity to his own history of himself, her feelings were yet more acutely painful and more difficult of definition. For hours she pored over Samuel Johnson's dictionary, trying in vain to find the words to describe her distress. Astonishment, apprehension, and even horror, oppressed her. "Oh, why has no thesaurus yet been invented!" she cried. She wished to discredit the letter entirely, repeatedly exclaiming, "This must be false! This cannot be! This must be the grossest falsehood!"

"Who are you speaking to?" called Fanny who was situated next door, despite her request for a dimly-lit garret. "Did you want me?"

"No!" – and when she had gone through the whole letter, though scarcely knowing any thing of the last page or two, put it hastily away, protesting that she would not regard it, that she would never look in it again.

In this perturbed state of mind, with thoughts that could rest on nothing, she paced; but it would not do; in half a minute she escalated to galloping, then tried a handstand to relieve her perturbation. All was for naught! The letter was unfolded again, and collecting herself as well as she could, she again began the mortifying perusal of all that related to Wickham, and commanded herself so far as to examine the meaning of every sentence.

When she read, and re-read with the closest attention, the particulars immediately following of Wickham's resigning all pretensions to the living, of his receiving in lieu, so considerable a sum as ten chests of gold, again was she forced to hesitate. She put down the letter, weighed every circumstance with what she meant to be impartiality – deliberated on the probability of each statement – but with little success. On both sides it was only assertion. Again she read on. But for Admiral Haughtyton to accuse a gentleman of wearing a bowler hat! Such words could destroy a man's social standing for ever! Such a thing must then be true – it was too grievous a sin to be otherwise. Every line proved more clearly that the affair, which she had believed it impossible that any contrivance could so represent, as to render the admiral's conduct in it less than infamous, was capable of a turn which must make him entirely blameless and perhaps overgenerous throughout the whole.

She tried to recollect some instance of goodness, some distinguished trait of integrity or benevolence, that might rescue Wickham from the attacks of the admiral; or at least, by the predominance of virtue, atone for those casual errors, under which she would endeavour to class, what the admiral had described as the idleness and vice of many years continuance. But no such recollection befriended her. She could see him instantly before her, in every charm of air and address; but she could remember no more substantial good than the general approbation of the neighbourhood, and the regard which his social powers had gained him in the mess.

Once more in the space of a day she found herself grieved at her terrible naiveté and her eagerness to accept the worst in the admiral. Once more, she turned her harsh words over and over in her head and resolved to go forth as a changed woman, no longer bound by overimagination or dripping sentimentality. Further, she would be cheerful, trusting, charming. She would look on the kindly, forbearing admiral as he was, and perhaps, despite his age, might even fall into true love with him as much as with his fortune.

Just then, a knock sounded at the door.

Marianne Catherine had been a good deal disappointed in not finding a letter from Dilemma on their first arrival at the Abbey; and this disappointment had been renewed on each of the mornings that had now been spent there; but on this morning, her repining was over, and her sister justified, by the receipt of two letters from her at once, on one of which was marked that it had been missent elsewhere. Marianne Catherine was not surprised at it, as Dilemma had written the direction remarkably ill in order to enhance suspense. The one missent must be first attended to; it had been written five days ago. The beginning contained an account of all their little parties and engagements and proposed scheme to hurl Scary down the well with her sheet music after her, with such news as the country afforded; but the latter half, which was dated a day later, and written in evident agitation, gave more important intelligence. It was to this effect:

Since writing the above, dearest Marianne, something has occurred of a most unexpected and serious nature; An express came at twelve last night, just as we were all gone to bed, from Lydia's friends Colonel and Mrs Mustard, to inform us that poor Lydia was gone off to Scotland with one of his officers; to own the truth, with Wickham! – Imagine our surprise. So imprudent a match on both sides! Such dishonour in this ill-considered scandal. To be sure, this is the last match I would have recommended for her, if I thought Lydia ready for the responsibility of matrimony at all. Are you not completely surprised by the frivolous girl's behaviour? Our poor mother is sadly grieved. My father bears it better, though I caught him deliberately bending a collectable buckle sadly out of shape.. They were off Saturday night about twelve, as is conjectured, but were not missed till yesterday morning at ten, since her hosts like to sleep in. The express was sent off directly. Colonel Mustard gives us reason to expect him here soon. Lydia left a few lines for his wife, informing her of their intention. I must conclude, for I cannot be long from telling my frantic mother that this might occur.

Without allowing herself time for consideration, and scarcely knowing what she felt, Marianne, on finishing this letter, instantly seized the other, and opening it with the utmost impatience, read as follows – it had been written a day later than the conclusion of the first:

By this time, my dearest sister, you have received my hurried letter; I wish this may be more intelligible, but though not confined for time, my head is so bewildered that I cannot answer for being coherent. Dearest Marianne, I hardly know what I would write, but I have bad news for you, and it cannot be delayed. Imprudent as a marriage between Mr Wickham and our poor Lydia would be, we are now anxious to be assured it has taken place, for there is but too much reason to fear they are not gone to Scotland but to some more adventurous and heathen place, such as the Caribbean, and brought their bathing costumes with them! Colonel Mustard came yesterday, having left Brighton the day before, not many hours after the express. Though Lydia's short letter to Mrs M. gave them to understand that they were going to Gretna Green, something was dropped by Denny expressing his belief that W. never intended to go there, or to marry Lydia at all, which was repeated to Colonel M., who, instantly taking the alarm, set off from B. intending to trace their route. Do these initials not make my letter sound both urgent and folkishly picturesque? He did trace them easily to Clapcatch, but no farther; for on entering that place they removed into a hackney-coach and dismissed the chaise that brought them. All that is known after this is that they were seen to continue the London road. I know not what to think. After making every possible enquiry on that side London, Colonel M. came on into Marrytown, anxiously renewing them at all the turnpikes, but without any success; no such people had been seen to pass through. Our distress, my dear Marianne, is very great. This match, so imprudent and with such a low character, must disgrace us all. Our mother is really ill and keeps her room. All my lectures have failed to soothe her. Could she exert herself it would be better, but this is not to be expected; and as to my father, I never in my life saw him so affected. His buckle collection is quite neglected. I am truly glad, dearest Marianne, that you have been spared something of these distressing scenes, as I know they would cut to your very heart; but now, as the first shock is over, shall I own that I long for your return? Our father is going to London with Colonel Mustard instantly, to try to discover her. What he means to do, I am sure I know not; but his excessive distress will not allow him to pursue any measure in the best and safest way, and Colonel Mustard is obliged to be at Brighton again to-morrow evening. In such an exigence you must return. Fanny is so capable, she would be best to fetch and carry for Mama at all hours of the night. As for Mr Collins, he knows nothing of the world outside of sermons, but he may yet be of unexpected use. Perhaps I can turn his attention toward Scary and save us at least a little. Prevail upon him to bring you all home at once.

"Oh! where, where is my cousin?" cried Marianne Catherine, darting from her seat as she finished the letter, in eagerness to follow him without losing a moment of the time so precious; but as she reached the door, she found Mr Haughtyton just outside it. Her pale face and impetuous manner made him start, and before he could recover himself enough to speak, she, in whose mind every idea was superseded by Lydia's situation, hastily exclaimed, "I beg your pardon, but I must leave you. I must find Mr Collins this moment, on business that cannot be delayed; I have not a moment to lose."

"Good God! what is the matter?" cried he, with more feeling than politeness; then recollecting himself, "I will not detain you a minute, but let me, or let the servant, go after Mr and Miss Collins. You are not well enough; – you cannot go yourself."

Marianne Catherine hesitated, but her knees trembled under her, and she felt how little would be gained by her attempting to pursue them. Calling back the servant, therefore, she commissioned him, though in so breathless an accent as made her almost unintelligible, to fetch her cousins home instantly.

On his quitting the hall, she slumped on a nearby bench, unable to support herself, and looking so miserably ill that it was impossible for Haughtyton to leave her, or to refrain from saying, in a tone of gentleness and commiseration, "Let me call your maid. Is there nothing you could take, to give you present relief? – A glass of wine; – shall I get you one? – You are very ill."

"No, I thank you;" she replied, endeavouring to recover herself. "There is nothing the matter with me. I am quite well. I am only distressed by some dreadful news which I have just received from Longbore."

She burst into tears as she alluded to it, and for a few minutes could not speak another word. Haughtyton, in wretched suspense, could only say something indistinctly of his concern, and observe her in compassionate silence. At length, she spoke again. "I have just had a letter from Dilemma, with such dreadful news. It cannot be concealed from any one. My youngest sister has left all her friends – has eloped; – has thrown herself into the power of – of Mr Wickham. They are gone off together from Brighton. *You* know him too well to doubt the rest. She has no money, no connexions, nothing that can tempt him to – she is lost for ever."

"I am grieved, indeed," cried Haughtyton; "grieved – shocked. But is it certain, absolutely certain?"

"Oh yes! – They left Brighton together on Sunday night, and were traced almost to London, but not beyond; they are certainly not gone to Scotland."

"And what has been done, what has been attempted, to recover her?"

"My father is gone to London, where he can put up 'Missing Daughter' posters beside all those that advertise lost kittens and umbrellas. Dilemma has written to beg my immediate assistance, and we shall be off, I hope, in half an hour. But nothing can be done; I know very well that nothing can be done. How is such a man to be worked on? How are they even to be discovered? I have not the smallest hope. It is every way horrible!"

Haughtyton made no answer. He seemed scarcely to hear her, and was walking up and down the room in earnest meditation; his brow contracted, his air gloomy. Marianne Catherine soon observed and instantly understood it. Her power was sinking; every thing *must* sink under such a proof of family weakness, such an assurance of the deepest disgrace. She should neither wonder nor condemn, but the belief of his self-conquest brought nothing consolatory to her bosom, afforded no palliation of her distress. It was, on the contrary, exactly calculated to make her understand her own wishes; and never had she so honestly felt that she could have loved him, as now, when all love must be vain. She might have simply accepted her loss, but that would require strength of character and thoughts other than selfish longing, which would be unbecoming of a romantic heroine. Perhaps, she thought, she might walk about outdoors and catch a putrid fever and languish to death – that would indeed make everyone sorry.

But self, though it would intrude, could not engross her. Lydia – the humiliation, the misery, she was bringing on them all – soon swallowed up every private care; and covering her face with her handkerchief, Marianne Catherine was soon lost to every thing else; and, after a pause of several minutes, was only recalled to a sense of her situation by the voice of her companion, who, in a manner, which though it spoke compassion, spoke likewise restraint, said, "I am afraid you have been long desiring my absence, nor have I any thing to plead in excuse of my stay, but real, though unavailing, concern. Would to heaven that any thing could be either said or done on my part, that might offer consolation to such distress! – But I will not torment you with vain wishes, which may seem purposely to ask for your thanks. If your family desires the address of the ladies' establishment in Yorkshire, you need only ask." He readily assured her of his secrecy – again expressed his sorrow for her distress, wished it a happier conclusion than there was at present reason to hope, and, leaving his compliments for her relations, with only one serious, parting, look, went away.

As he quitted the hall, Marianne Catherine felt how improbable it was that they should ever see each other again on such terms of cordiality; and as she threw a retrospective glance over the whole of their acquaintance, so full of contradictions and varieties, sighed at the perverseness of those feelings which would now have promoted its continuance, and would formerly have rejoiced in its termination. She might have languished there and slowly perished of misery, but there was far too much to do.

She had never perceived, while the regiment was in Hertfordshire, that Lydia had any partiality for him, but she was convinced that Lydia had wanted only encouragement to attach herself to any body. Sometimes one officer, sometimes another had been her favourite, as their attentions raised them in her opinion. Her affections had been continually fluctuating, but never without an object. The mischief of neglect and mistaken indulgence towards such a girl. – Oh! how acutely did she now feel it.

She was wild to be at home – to hear, to see, to be upon the spot, to share with Dilemma in the cares that must now fall wholly upon her, in a family so deranged; a father absent, a mother incapable of exertion and requiring constant. Mr and Miss Collins had hurried back in alarm, supposing, by the servant's account, that their cousin was taken suddenly ill; – but satisfying them instantly on that head by, in her distress, vomiting on their shoes, she then eagerly communicated the cause of their summons, reading the two letters aloud, and dwelling on the postscript of the last with trembling energy. – Though Lydia had never been a favourite with them, Mr and Miss Collins could not but be deeply affected. Not Lydia only, but all were concerned in it; and after the first exclamations of surprise and horror, Miss Collins readily promised every assistance in their power. – Marianne, though expecting no less, thanked her with tears of gratitude. Mr Collins was seen to cough and mumble a bit, but at Marianne's wails of heartfelt gratitude, he looked up and ordered the carriage brought around. All three being actuated by one spirit, every thing relating to their journey was speedily settled. They were to be off as soon as possible. "But what is to be done about our visit?" cried Mr Collins suddenly. "Do you not fear that Admiral Haughtyton will be offended by our departure?"

"I told him it must be ended early. *That* is all settled." After hasty folding, packing, organizing, and ironing, as well as a hurried trip into town for traveling bonnets and visiting gloves, nothing remained to be done but to go; and Marianne Catherine, after all the misery of the morning, found herself, in a shorter space of time than she could have supposed, seated in the carriage, and on the road to Longbore.

Chapter 14: Lydia Exposes Herself to Talk

They travelled as expeditiously as possible; and, sleeping one night on the road (literally, as Fanny did not feel herself worthy of an inn), reached Longbore by dinner-time the next day. It was a comfort to Marianne to consider that Dilemma could not have been wearied by long expectations. As they drove through the night, she thought endlessly of Lydia, perhaps lost forever, of her suffering parents and sisters, but most of all, how bouncing up and down in the carriage was leaving the seat's rivulets imprinted in her tender bottom.

Upon arrival at Longbore, as she affectionately embraced her sisters, whilst tears filled her eyes and a flood of desperate emotions flooded her heart, she lost not a moment in asking whether any thing had been heard of the fugitives.

"Not yet," replied Dilemma. "But now that you all have come, and Marianne, you are here, embracing me so tightly I feel my stays shattering, I hope every thing will be well. Dear Fanny, might you oblige us by mopping the floor? All the maids are upstairs with Mama." Indeed the shrieks of hysteria alerted them all to this fact.

"Is my father in town?" Marianne asked as Fanny hurried for the mop.

"Yes, he went on Tuesday, as I wrote you word."

"And have you heard from him often?"

"We have heard only once. He wrote me a few lines on Wednesday, to say that he had arrived in safety, and to give me his directions and a pretty plumed bonnet, which I had particularly begged him to do. He merely added that he should not write again till he had something of importance to mention, such as the latest in cuckoo clocks."

"And my mother – How is she? How are you all?"

"My mother is tolerably well, I trust; though her spirits are greatly shaken and alcohol imbibement quite high. She is up stairs, and will have great satisfaction in seeing you all. She does not yet leave her dressing-room."

Mrs Fussbudget, to whose apartment they all repaired, after a few minutes conversation together, received them exactly as might be expected; with tears and lamentations of regret, invectives against the villainous conduct of Wickham, appeals to the heavens for the price of sugar to go down, and complaints of her own sufferings and ill usage; blaming every body but the person to whose ill-judging indulgence the errors of her daughter must be principally owing.

"If I had been able," said she, "to carry my point of going to Brighton, with all my family, *this* would not have happened; but poor dear Lydia had nobody to take care of her while surrounded by every one. I am sure there was some great neglect or other on their side, for she is not the kind of girl to do such a thing, even with those dirty magazines she always is reading. Poor dear inappropriate child! And now here's Mr Fussbudget gone away, and I know he will fight Wickham wherever he meets him, and with only his almanac of cravats against the other man's sword, then he will be killed, and what is to become of us all? The Collinses will turn us out, before he is cold in his grave; and if you are not kind to us, Fanny, I do not know what we shall do."

They all exclaimed against such terrific ideas; and Fanny vowed that her family would always have a place in her brother's house, though indeed, she had no authority to make such a promise. A prouder young woman might have lorded over her aunt, but Fanny truly only hoped to be helpful until the floor needed mopping once again.

"How are you aunt?" she asked meekly.

"How do you think, silly girl? It's all gone to poop!" She clutched at the arms of her chair for support, but as chairs of the time were stiff, armless affairs, she tumbled to the floor.

They soon left the lady of the house to her distress, unable to do anything to console her, as each assurance brought a new round of the lady's cries of woe. In the dining-room they were soon joined by Scary and Jane Harriet, who had been too busily engaged in their separate apartments to make their appearance before. One came from her books, and the other from her walk. The faces of both, however, were tolerably calm; and no change was visible in either, except that the loss of her favourite sister had given something more of fretfulness than usual to the placid face of Jane Harriet. As for Scary, she was mistress enough of herself to whisper to Marianne, with a countenance of grave reflection, soon after they were seated at table,

"This is a most unfortunate affair; and will probably be much talked of. But we must stem the tide of malice, and pour into the wounded bosoms of each other the balm of sisterly consolation."

Then, perceiving in Marianne no inclination of replying, she added, "Unhappy as the event must be for Lydia, we may draw from it this useful lesson: that loss of virtue in a female is irretrievable – that one false step involves her in endless ruin – that her reputation is no less brittle than it is beautiful, – and that she cannot be too much guarded in her behaviour towards the undeserving of the other sex." She bent with eagerness to their hasty meal of swan's tails and fox tongues in pie.

Across the table, Fanny Anne lifted up her eyes in amazement while her brother nodded in ponderous judgment. Scary, however, continued to console herself with such kind of moral extractions from the evil before them.

"As Thomas Fuller said, 'Trust thyself only, and another shall not betray thee,'" Scary quoted pontifically.

Mr Collins nodded eagerly beside her. "I sincerely sympathize with ladies, and all your respectable family, in your present distress, which must be of the bitterest kind, because proceeding from a cause which no time can remove. No arguments shall be wanting on my part that can alleviate so severe a misfortune."

Fanny Anne took her knitting needle and rammed it into her callous brother's heart. As he fell, she withdrew the needle in a swift tug, and then stabbed it directly into the overactive brain of her cousin Scary. The platitudes stopped forever.

Fanny Anne blinked. Her daydreams were becoming far too vivid and indeed vicious. It seemed a life of idleness and worry here at Marrytown was hardly conducive to a healthy aspect on life.

Mrs Fussbudget came in, swaddled in an afghan festooned with ugly embroidered kittens, and Mr Collins rushed to console her with words that did nothing of the kind. "This circumstance that must be of all others most afflicting to a parent's mind. The death of your daughter would have been a blessing in comparison. And it is the more to be lamented, because there is reason to suppose that this licentiousness of behaviour in your daughter has proceeded from a faulty degree of indulgence, though at the same time, for the consolation of yourself and Mrs Fussbudget, I am inclined to think that her own disposition must be naturally bad, or she could not be guilty of such an enormity at so early an age. Indeed, last month I partook of one of her magazines and swooned for not less than two hours! Howsoever that may be, you are grievously to be pitied. Let me advise you then, my dear lady, to console yourself as much as possible, to throw off your unworthy child from your affection for ever, and leave her to reap the fruits of her own heinous offence." As one might expect, this did nothing to comfort Mrs Fussbudget, and threw her instead into more paroxysms of grief and lamentation.

"She is truly lost to us," Dilemma noted sadly. "We can

never visit the cast-off mistress of a loutish seducer, though she was one our best-beloved sister. It grieves me so to lose her acquaintance."

"You would refuse to see her?" Fanny Anne asked. "True, she has disgraced herself forever, but she is still – "

"She has lost her station and honour. Without that she can be nothing to us," Dilemma said with the sadness and resolution of youth. "She is condemned to a life of sorrow, though we might banish her to a country cottage in disgrace, with only a hundred a year for bonnet allowance, and several maids, or perhaps Fanny, to do the cooking and scrubbing "

Jane Harriet shivered but did not contradict her sister. She stood, mumbled something about her sewing, and retreated upstairs.

"She has thrown herself out of all good society. We must give her up," Dilemma concluded. "No man will be tempted by any of us now, and we must all sit in this parlour, endlessly sewing and criticizing the cut of one another's bonnets, until we have the sense to die of shame."

"Dear me! – How should we bear it! It will kill me never to see Lydia any more!" Marianne cried. She hurled herself onto the sofa hard enough to make the piece shudder, and began to screech hysterically.

Mrs Fussbudget embraced her, and her own sobs doubled in volume.

Fanny helplessly ran from one to the other with a supply of handkerchiefs, but she began to fear the laundry would not be done fast enough.

Marianne shuddered and protested between hysterical gulps, "Dear affectionate creature! *She* is the one who will suffer! I wonder how such a handsome young man, so new in town, could tempt her to such a fate."

"It does seem, and it is most shocking indeed," replied Dilemma, "that a sister's sense of decency and virtue in such a point should admit of doubt." She sat up and began to lecture. "But she is very young; she has never been taught to think on serious subjects; and lately she has been given up to nothing but amusement and vanity. She has been allowed to dispose of her time in the most idle and frivolous manner. Since the – shire were first quartered in Marrytown, nothing but love, flirtation, and officers have been in her head. She has been doing every thing in her power, by thinking and talking on the subject, to give greater – what shall I call it? – susceptibility to her feelings, which are naturally lively enough. And we all know that Wickham has every charm of person and address that can captivate a woman." At this last, she sighed heavily.

Fanny Anne found herself considering Dilemma's and Marianne's own shameless behaviour toward Wickham, which must seem doubly regrettable to them now. Truly, all their fortunes might have reached a grievous end. Many disturbing reports had been reaching them – of tradesman's bills unpaid, maidservants interfered with, sheep insulted, and cattle tipped. It seemed Mr Wickham had been guilty of all sorts of misbehaviour, of which they had all been blissfully unaware.

Seeking another handkerchief, Marianne groped over the table, where she discovered a scrap of paper Jane Harriet had discarded. A quick glance showed her it was one of the girl's charades, light little rhymes she had been writing and collecting on her journeys. A second glance, however, had her gasping with dismay. "Mama! All of you! Look!"

When my first is a task to a young girl of spirit,
And my second confines her to finish the piece,
How hard is her fate! but how great is her merit
If by taking my whole she effects her release!

"What is that?" Mrs Fussbudget asked, distracted from her vapours.

"The riddle! Oh, and the solution, oh my dear Jane! Tell me not that we have lost two sisters all at once, one perhaps in shame at the other! Oh my, oh dear! Oh! I think I shall succumb to more hysterics!"

"Why, what does it mean?" Fanny asked.

Dilemma gasped at the riddle's contents. "The task! She said she was going up to sew. Or, one might say 'hem.' And if, like all of us, she feels locked in her task, why then – "

"Hemlock!" screeched their mother in horror, and she burst into nosier sobs.

"Let me go see," cried Fanny, rushing upstairs, as she was certain checking on Jane's welfare would me more helpful than hysterics.

Upstairs, she found no cousin expired on her bed, or under the window, or any sort of thing. In fact, Jane was perched at her desk, writing. When the door creaked, she jumped, and endeavoured to hide her paper. "What is it?"

"Are you well? What is it that you write?"

Jane hesitated. "A description of my family. I admit, I have literary ambitions, after observing so much of the country and so much of human behaviour. I had thought I might put it into print and aspire for publication. Lydia's misfortune, at least, aids my own work a bit, for all I wish she had not been so heedless."

"Have you additional literary ambitions?"

"Oh, a few. My novel about killer spiders from Mars may be a trifle outlandish, however."

"And your charade downstairs?"

"Oh!" Jane blushed. "A light critique on the 'accomplishments' that define our lives. But you won't give me away, surely?"

Fanny vowed discretion, and downstairs assured them only that all was well, except of course in the matter of Lydia, a confession that stirred up fresh tears.

In the afternoon, when Fanny Anne had finished consoling her aunt, she sat in the parlour knitting. It was a scarf meant for Lydia. Now there was no purpose to it, as Lydia was lost to them, but still she knitted. A round. Two. Three.

Across from her, Jane Harriet finished wrapping the cat

lovingly in a new sweater, one which ironically, might prevent the cat from its own aim of dying from pneumonia as a result of its humiliating new fashion.

The halls, which had once been filled with Lydia's shrieks and hyena giggles, were now filled with Marianne's hysteria. Mr Fussbudget had returned for town, despondent at his inability to find his daughter. After a brief conference with Mr Collins, he appeared more despondent yet, though he assured the family his brother-in-law Mr Minor-Character was continuing the search in London.

Two days after Mr Fussbudget's return, as Dilemma, Jane Harriet, and Fanny Anne were walking together in the shrubbery behind the house, they saw the housekeeper coming towards them, and concluding that she came to call them to their mother, went forward to meet her; but, instead of the expected summons, when they approached her she said to Miss Fussbudget, "I beg your pardon, madam, for interrupting you, but I was in hopes you might have got some good news from town, so I took the liberty of coming to ask, even though this means speaking to you directly, a thing altogether a great imposition."

"What do you mean, Hill? We have heard nothing from town."

"Dear madam," cried Mrs Hill, in great astonishment, "don't you know there is an express come for master from Mr Minor-Character? He has been here this half hour, and master has had a letter."

The young women stared at each other in glee. News at last! "Thank you, indeed," said Dilemma. "In fact, I am filled with such gratitude that I may overlook your interrupting our walk." The servant looked stunned for a moment, and then her face changed to the traditional whatever-you-say expression studied by all in her profession. "Yes, ma'am."

Upon this information, they instantly passed through the hall once more, and ran across the lawn after Mr Fussbudget, who was deliberately pursuing his way towards a small wood on one side of the paddock. The messenger lay nearby, dead in the road from exhaustion, his horse beside him.

Dilemma, who was not so light, nor so much in the habit of running and doing all manner of work, as Fanny, soon lagged behind, while her cousin, panting for breath, came up with him, and eagerly cried out, "Oh, Uncle, what news? what news? Have you heard from Mr Minor-Character?"

"Yes, I have had a letter from him by express."

"Well, and what news does it bring? good or bad?"

"What is there of good to be expected?" said he, taking the letter from his pocket; "but perhaps you would like to read it." Dilemma, who had just come up, impatiently caught it from his hand.

"Read it aloud," said their father, "for I hardly know myself what it is about."

"Gracechurch-street, Monday, August 2.

MY DEAR BROTHER,

At last I am able to send you some tidings of my niece, and such as, upon the whole, I hope will give you satisfaction. Soon after you left me on Saturday, I was fortunate enough to find out in what part of London they were. The particulars I reserve till we meet. It is enough to know they are discovered; I have seen them both — "

"Then it is as I always hoped," cried Jane Harriet; "they are married!"

Dilemma read on:

"I have seen them both. They are not married, nor can I find there was any intention of being so and I find their plan to join harlequin college together quite untenable; but if you are willing to perform the engagements which I have ventured to make on your side, I hope it will not be long before they are wed. All that is required of you is to assure to your daughter, by settlement, her equal share of the five pittances secured among your children after the decease of yourself and my sister; and,

moreover, to enter into an engagement of allowing her, during your life, one hundred pounds and a basket of teacakes per annum and visits every other Sunday to the family dog. These are conditions which, considering every thing, I had no hesitation in complying with, as far as I thought myself privileged, for you. I shall send this by express, that no time may be lost in bringing me your answer. You will easily comprehend, from these particulars, that Mr Wickham's circumstances are not so hopeless as they are generally believed to be. The world has been deceived in that respect; and, I am happy to say, there will be some little money, even when all his debts are discharged, to settle on my niece, in addition to a dozen sporty cuckoo clocks, several optimistically purchased pom-pom buttons, and a full shelf of naughty etchings. If, as I conclude will be the case, you send me full powers to act in your name throughout the whole of this business, I will immediately give directions to Haggerston for preparing a proper settlement. We have judged it best that my niece should be married from this house, of which I hope you will approve. She comes to us to-day. I shall write again as soon as any thing more is determined on. Yours, &c.

EDW. MINOR-CHARACTER."

"Is it possible!" cried Dilemma, when she had finished. – "Can it be possible that he will marry her?"

"Wickham is not so undeserving, then, as we have thought him!" said her sister. "My dear father, I congratulate you."

"And have you answered the letter?" said Dilemma.

"No; but it must be done soon. And you must call the servants to give that man – he nodded at the messenger's prone body – a decent burial, and start boiling the horse down for glue. If it takes them into the evening, I am willing to eat a cold supper in consequence."

Most earnestly did she then entreat him to lose no more time before he wrote.

"Oh! my dear father," she cried, "come back, and write immediately. Consider how important every moment is, in such a case. Let me write for you, if you dislike the trouble yourself. Or I could manipulate your hand with a pen in it and take charge of every thing."

"I dislike it very much," he replied; "but it must be done."

And so saying, he turned back with them, and walked towards the house.

"And they must marry! Yet he is such a man!" Fanny shivered. There were worse things indeed than being passed over or losing the embroidery scissors.

"Yes, yes, they must marry. There is nothing else to be done. But there are two things that I want very much to know: – one is, how much money your uncle has laid down to bring it about; and the other, how I am ever to pay him."

"Money! my uncle!" cried Jane Harriet, "what do you mean, Sir?"

"I mean that no man in his senses would marry Lydia on so slight a temptation as one pittance a year during my life, and half a pittance after I am gone."

"That is very true," said Dilemma; "though it had not occurred to me before. His debts to be discharged, and something still to remain! Oh! it must be my uncle's doings! Generous, good man; I am afraid he has distressed himself. A small sum could not do all this."

"No," said her father, "Wickham's a fool, if he takes her with a farthing less than ten thousand pounds and a new set of solid gold garden gnomes. I should be sorry to think so ill of him in the very beginning of our relationship."

"Ten thousand pounds! Heaven forbid! How is half such a sum to be repaid?" Dilemma tugged a scrap of paper from her pocket and began hasty calculations.

Mr Fussbudget made no answer, and each of them, deep in thought, continued silent till they reached the house. Their father then went to the library to write, the servants out to tend the bodies, and the girls into the breakfast-room.

"And they are really to be married!" cried Dilemma, as soon as they were by themselves. "How strange this is! And for this we are to be thankful. That they should marry, small as is their chance of happiness, ugly as are his poodles, and wretched as is his character, we are forced to rejoice! Oh,

Lydia! Why could you not have waited for me to find you a proper gentleman?"

It now occurred to the girls that their mother was in all likelihood, perfectly ignorant of what had happened. They went to the library, therefore, and asked their father whether he would not wish them to make it known to her. He was writing, and, without raising his head, coolly replied, "Just as you please."

"May we take my uncle's letter to read to her?"

"Take whatever you like, and get away."

Dilemma took the letter from his writing table, and they went up stairs together. Scary was with Mrs Fussbudget; one communication would, therefore, do for all. After a slight preparation for good news, the letter was read aloud. Mrs Fussbudget could hardly contain herself. As soon as Dilemma had read Mr Minor-Character's hope of Lydia's being soon married, her joy burst forth, and every following sentence added to its exuberance. She embraced the dog and half-strangled the cat, until a slash of claws reigned in her exuberance long enough for the creature to bolt. Nonetheless, she continued in an irritation as violent from delight, as she had ever been fidgety from alarm and vexation. To know that her daughter would be married was enough.

"My dear, dear Lydia!" she cried: "This is delightful indeed! – She will be married! – I shall see her again! – She will be married at barely sixteen! – My good, kind brother! – I knew how it would be – I knew he would manage every thing. How I long to see her! and to see dear Wickham too! But the clothes, the wedding clothes and matched luggage and shoe-roses, and bonnet-fastenings! I will write to my sister Minor-Character about them directly. Lizzy, my dear, run down to your father, and ask him how much he will give her. Stay, stay, I will go myself. Ring the bell, Kitty, for Hill. I will put on my things in a moment. My dear, dear Lydia! – How merry we shall be together when we meet!"

Her eldest daughter endeavoured to give some relief to the violence of these transports, by leading her thoughts to the obligations which Mr Minor-Character's behaviour laid them all under. "For we must attribute this happy conclusion," she added, "in a great measure to his kindness. We are persuaded that he has pledged himself to assist Mr Wickham with money."

"Well," cried her mother, "it is all very right; who should do it but her own uncle? If he had not had a family of his own, I and my children must have had all his money, you know, and it is the first time we have ever had any thing from him, except a few presents. Well! I am so happy. In a short time, I shall have a daughter married. Mrs Wickham! How well it sounds. And she was only sixteen last June. My dear Jane, I am in such a flutter that I am sure I can't write; so I will dictate, and you write for me. We will settle with your father about the money afterwards; but the things should be ordered immediately."

She was then proceeding to all the particulars of calico, muslin, and cambric, to say nothing of falderals, flim-flams, and fastenings, and would shortly have dictated some very plentiful orders, had not Scary, though with some difficulty, persuaded her to wait till her father was at leisure to be consulted. One day's delay, she observed, would be of small importance; and her mother was too happy to be quite so obstinate as usual. Other schemes, too, came into her head.

"I will go to Marrytown," said she, "as soon as I am dressed, and tell the good, good news to Lady Moneygrubber and Mrs Long. Jane Harriet, run down and order the carriage. An airing would do me a great deal of good, I am sure. Girls, can I do any thing for you in Marrytown? Oh! here comes Hill. My dear Hill, have you heard the good news? Miss Lydia is going to be married; and you shall all have a bowl of punch to make merry at her wedding. You shall even be allowed meat for supper."

Mrs Hill began instantly to express her joy. Fanny Anne received her congratulations amongst the rest, and then, sick of this folly, took refuge in her own room, that she might think with freedom.

NONSENSIBILITY

Poor Lydia's situation must, at best, be bad enough; but that it was no worse, she had need to be thankful. She felt it so; and though, in looking forward, neither rational happiness nor worldly prosperity could be justly expected for her poor cousin, in looking back to what they had feared, only two hours ago, she felt all the advantages of what they had gained.

Chapter 15: The Captain and the Admiral Return

The good news quickly spread through the house; and with proportionate speed through the neighbourhood. It was borne in the latter with decent philosophy. To be sure, it would have been more for the advantage of conversation, had Miss Lydia Fussbudget come upon the town; or, as the happiest alternative, been secluded from the world in some distant Yorkshire school to repent forever or perhaps die languishing of some dreadful disease. But there was much to be talked of in marrying her; and the good-natured wishes for her well-doing, which had proceeded before from all the spiteful old ladies in Marrytown, lost but little of their spirit in this change of circumstances, because with such an husband, her misery was considered certain.

It was a fortnight since Mrs Fussbudget had been down stairs, or removed her fluffy purple slippers that her girls had knitted, or returned the laudanum bottle to its customary shelf, but on this happy day she again took her seat at the head of her table, and in spirits oppressively high. No sentiment of shame gave a damp to her triumph. The marriage of a daughter, which had been the first object of her wishes since Dilemma was sixteen, was now on the point of accomplishment, and her thoughts and her words ran wholly on those attendants of elegant nuptials, fine muslins, new carriages, extra-deep bonnets, and completely silenced servants. She was busily searching through the neighbourhood for a "proper situation" for her daughter, and, without knowing or considering what their income might be, rejected many as deficient in size and importance.

"Hay-Field might do," said she, "if the Gouldings would quit it, or the great house at Croke, if the drawing-room were larger; but Worthnothin is too far off! I could not bear to have her ten miles from me; and as for Scurvy Lodge, the attics are dreadful and I hear there is an infestation of mangy pigeons."

Her husband allowed her to talk on without interruption while the servants remained. But when they had withdrawn, he said to her, "Mrs Fussbudget, before you take any or all of these houses for your son and daughter, let us come to a right understanding. Into one house in this neighbourhood, they shall never have admittance. I will not encourage the impudence, foolishness, and halitosis of either by receiving them at Longbore."

A long dispute followed this declaration, but Mr Fussbudget was firm; it soon led to another, and Mrs Fussbudget found, with amazement and horror, that her husband would not advance a guinea to buy clothes or even matching shoe-roses for his daughter. He protested that she should receive from him no mark of affection whatever on the occasion. Mrs Fussbudget could hardly comprehend it. That his anger could be carried to such a point of inconceivable resentment, as to refuse his daughter a privilege without which her marriage would scarcely seem valid, exceeded all that she could believe possible. She was more alive to the disgrace which the want of new clothes must reflect on her daughter's nuptials, than to any sense of shame at her eloping and living with Wickham a fortnight before they took place and wearing, quite likely, no clothes or shoe-roses at all.

But the spiritless condition which this event threw her into was shortly relieved, and her mind opened again to the agitation of hope, by an article of news which then began to be in circulation. The housekeeper at Netherbum had received orders to prepare for the arrival of her master, Captain Wentworth, who was coming down in a day or two, to shoot there for several weeks (ideally at the birds rather than his own remaining fingers). Mrs Fussbudget was quite in the fidgets. She looked at her eligible daughters, and smiled and shook her head by turns.

"Well, well, and so Captain Wentworth is coming down. Well, so much the better. Not that I care about it, though. He is nothing to us, you know, and I am sure *I* never want to see him again. That the man would betray such a marked preference for our poor relation, in contrast with my girls' many accomplishments." She gazed proudly at Scary, who was playing loudly, while Jane Harriet turned her pages with perfect precision. As Scary's voice rose an octave, the dog joined in, howling mournfully. Marianne lay on the couch, weeping with prostration about something – likely fallen leaves. "But, however, he is very welcome to come to Netherbum, if he likes it. And who knows what *may* happen."

Jane Harriet looked up absent-mindedly. "Fluffy needs washing. I think I'll use the soap for delicate muslins." She had sewn Mittens a pair of rabbit ears, unaware of the warm easter egg Mittens was contemplating leaving for her.

Of course, Dilemma had no particular emotions toward Captain Wentworth, whom she had foolishly prevented from wedding her cousin years before. That shame would always cloud their acquaintance – of her considering him unsuitable, who had now become such a rich and eligible gentleman who always used the correct spoon at table. Fanny Anne, however, had not been able to hear of his coming without changing colour. It was many months since she had mentioned his name. Yet now he was returning home, perhaps to see her. Or perhaps he had tired of having all the limbs he still possessed.

Fanny Anne saw nothing, thought nothing of Scary's ear-shattering song. Her happiness was from within. She was thinking only of the news. Soon, however, she began to reason with herself, and try to be feeling less. Eight years, almost eight years had passed, since all had been given up. How absurd to be resuming the agitation which such an interval had banished into distance and indistinctness! What might not eight years do? It was two American Presidential terms after all. Alas! with all her reasoning, she found, that to retentive feelings, like to her best pair of gloves, eight years may be little more than nothing.

Lydia's voice was heard in the vestibule; the door was thrown open, and she ran into the room. Her mother stepped forwards, embraced her, and welcomed her with rapture; gave her hand, with an affectionate smile, to Wickham, who followed his lady; and wished them both joy with an alacrity which shewed no doubt of their happiness.

Their reception from Mr Fussbudget, to whom they then turned, was not quite so cordial. His countenance rather gained in austerity; and he scarcely opened his lips, but punched Mr Wickham singly in the stomach, then withdrew. The easy assurance of the young couple, indeed, was enough to provoke him. Dilemma and Fanny were disgusted, and even the romantic Marianne was shocked. Lydia was Lydia still; untamed, unabashed, wild, noisy, and fearless. She turned from sister to sister, demanding their congratulations; and when at length they all sat down, looked eagerly round the room, took notice of some little alteration in it, and observed, with an annoying little laugh, that it was a great while since she had been there.

Wickham was not at all more distressed than herself, but his manners were always so pleasing, that had his character and his marriage been exactly what they ought, his smiles and his easy address, while he claimed their relationship, would have delighted them all. Fanny Anne had not before believed him quite equal to such assurance; but she sat down on the ugliest of the cushions, resolving within herself to draw no limits in future to the impudence of an impudent man. *She* blushed, and Dilemma blushed; but the cheeks of the two who caused their confusion suffered no variation of colour, though since Dilemma had a quantity of green dye and knew where they slept, this might change in future.

There was no want of discourse. The bride and her mother could neither of them talk fast enough; and Wickham, who happened to sit near Marianne, began enquiring after his acquaintance in that neighbourhood, with a good humoured ease which she felt very unable to equal in her replies. There had been a time when she had assured herself of bring Mr Wickham's favourite, and now, to chat easily with the man who had nearly ruined her sister! They seemed each of them to have the happiest memories in the world. Nothing of the past was recollected with pain; and Lydia led voluntarily to subjects which her sisters would not have alluded to for the world.

"Only think of its being three months," she cried, "since I went away; it seems but a fortnight I declare; and yet there have been things enough happened in the time. Good gracious! when I went away, I am sure I had no more idea of being married till I came back again! though I thought it would be very good fun if I was."

Her father lifted up his eyes. Dilemma was distressed. Marianne looked expressively at Lydia; but she, who never heard nor saw any thing of which she chose to be insensible, gaily continued, "Oh! mamma, do the people hereabouts know I am married to-day? I was afraid they might not; and we overtook Mr Tightly-Wound in his curricle, so I was determined he should know it, and so I let down the side-glass next to him, and took off my glove, and let my hand just rest upon the window frame, so that he might see the ring, and then I bowed and smiled like any thing."

Marianne could bear it no longer. She got up, and ran out of the room; and returned no more, till she heard them passing through the hall to the dining parlour. She then joined them soon enough to see Lydia, with anxious parade, walk up to her mother's right hand, and hear her say to her eldest sister, "Ah! Dilemma, I take your place now, and you must go lower, because I am a married woman. Also, give me your handkerchief so I may wipe my boots with it. And I trust you will not object if I borrow a few items for my trousseau? Like the cat?"

It was not to be supposed that time would give Lydia that embarrassment from which she had been so wholly free at first. Her ease and good spirits increased. She longed to see Mrs Phillips, the Lucases, and all their other neighbours, and to hear herself called "Mrs Wickham" by each of them; and in the meantime, she went after dinner to shew her ring, and boast of being married, to Mrs Hill and the two housemaids.

"Well, mamma," said she, when they were all returned to the breakfast room, "and what do you think of my husband? Is not he a charming man? I am sure my sisters must all envy me. I only hope they may have half my good luck. They must all go to Brighton. That is the place to get husbands. What a pity it is, mamma, we did not all go."

"Very true; and if I had my will, we should. But my dear Lydia, I don't at all like your going such a way off. Must it be so?"

"Oh, lord! yes; – half a dozen tradesmen in London want to shoot my husband and around here it is no better. But there is nothing in that. I shall like the North of all things. You and papa, and my sisters, must come down and see us. We shall be at Newcastle-on-time all the winter, and I dare say there will be some balls, and I will take care to get good partners for them all."

"I should like it beyond any thing!" said her mother.

"And then when you go away, you may leave one or two of my sisters behind you; and I dare say I shall get husbands for them before the winter is over."

"I thank you for my share of the favour," said Dilemma; "but I do not particularly like your way of getting husbands. I have plenty of my own prepared."

Thus stifled by the eldest, Lydia turned to the next and chirped, "Marianne, I never gave you an account of my wedding, I believe. Are not you curious to hear how it was managed?"

"No really," replied Marianne; "I think there cannot be too little said on the subject."

"La! You are so strange! But I must tell you how it went off. We were married, you know, at St. Clement's, because Wickham's lodgings were in that parish. And it was settled that we should all be there by eleven o'clock. My uncle and aunt and I were to go together; and the others were to meet us at the church. Well, Monday morning came, and I was in such a fuss! I was so afraid, you know, that something would happen to put it off, and then I should have gone quite distracted. And there was my aunt, all the time I was dressing, preaching and talking away just as if she was reading a sermon. However, I did not hear above one word in ten, for I was thinking, you may suppose, of my dear Wickham. I longed to know whether he would be married in his blue coat and his extra-tall London hat and whether his shoes would be shiny, and all the most important details and all."

"Well, and so we breakfasted at ten as usual; I thought it would never be over; for, by the bye, you are to understand, that my uncle and aunt were horrid unpleasant all the time I was with them. If you'll believe me, I did not once put my foot out of doors. Not one party, or scheme, or any thing. To be sure London was rather thin, but the foreigner-baiting and tours of the lunatic asylum were open as ever. Well, and so just as the carriage came to the door, my uncle was called away upon business. Well, I was so frightened I did not know what to do, for my uncle was to give me away; and if we were beyond the hour, we could not be married all day. But, luckily, he came back again in ten minutes' time, having told the young couple that hippopotami are no longer attainable in London, and then we all set out. However, I recollected afterwards that if he had been prevented going, the wedding need not be put off, for Admiral Haughtyton might have done as well."

"Admiral Haughtyton!" repeated Marianne, in utter amazement.

"Oh, yes! – he was to come there with Wickham, you know, But gracious me! I quite forgot! I ought not to have said a word about it. I promised them so faithfully! What will Wickham say? It was to be such a secret! The Admiral said so. Indeed, he said, 'When you talk about this day around Longbore, and I am sure you shall, you must never mention my name, particularly around your sister Miss Marianne, under no circumstances.' And from the moment he said this, I was wild to tell, as you might guess! I could not get it out of my head for a moment. I think it was his singsong way of saying, which now exists as a tune running round and round my head, so much that I can think of nothing else."

Dilemma's shared gaze with Marianne suggested eloquently that Lydia's cleverness was unlikely to be impacted any force than usual for this. "If it was to be secret," said Dilemma, "say not another word on the subject. You may depend upon our seeking no further." She fidgeted however in a manner quite opposing her words.

"Oh! certainly," said Marianne, though burning with curiosity; "we will ask you no questions."

"Thank you," said Lydia, "for if you did, I should certainly tell you all, and then Wickham would be angry."

On such encouragement to ask, Marianne was forced to put it out of her power by running away.

Later that day, Captain Wentworth arrived. Mrs Fussbudget, through the assistance of servants who sat outside Netherbum with their ears pressed to drinking glasses, contrived to have the earliest tidings of it, that the period of anxiety and fretfulness on her side might be as long as it could. She counted the days that must intervene before their invitation could be sent, the minutes until she might compliment his new selection of tall hats, the seconds until she might serve him the increasingly stale scones and toast; hopeless of seeing him before. But on this, the third morning after his arrival, she saw him, from her dressing-room window, enter the paddock and ride towards the house. This would have been more impressive had he a live horse instead of a hobby horse with a quilted head, of course. (They were all the rage in town, as it happened).

Her daughters were eagerly called to partake of her joy. Fanny, not one of them, resolutely kept her place at the table; but Marianne, to satisfy her mother, went to the window – she looked, – she saw Admiral Haughtyton with him, and sat down again by her cousin.

"There is a gentleman with him, mamma," said Scary; "who can it be?"

"Some acquaintance or other, my dear, I suppose; I am sure I do not know."

"Indeed!" replied Scary, "it looks just like that man that used to be with him before. The grandiose and yet fetchingly wealthy Admiral Haughtyton."

"Good gracious! Admiral Haughtyton! – and so it does, I vow. Well, any friend of the captain's will always be welcome here, to be sure; but else I must say that I hate the very sight of him."

Marianne Catherine had frozen. Her astonishment at his coming – at his coming to Netherbum, to Longbore, and voluntarily seeking her again, was almost equal to what she had known on first witnessing his altered behaviour in Mansfield Abbey.

The colour, which had been driven from her face, returned for half a minute with an additional glow, and a smile of delight added lustre to her eyes, as she thought for that space of time that his affection must still be unshaken. But she would not be secure, nor allow herself to be so assertive as to smile long.

"Let me first see how he behaves," said she; "it will then be early enough for expectation." She sat intently at work embroidering decorative edging on the family galoshes, striving to be composed, and without daring to lift up her eyes, till the gentlemen were announced and entered.

Captain Wentworth was looking both pleased and embarrassed. He was received by Mrs Fussbudget with a degree of civility which made her two daughters ashamed, especially when contrasted with the cold and ceremonious politeness of her curtsey and address to his friend.

"It is a long time, Captain Wentworth, since you went away," said Mrs Fussbudget.

He readily agreed to it.

"I began to be afraid you would never come back again. People *did* say you meant to quit the place entirely at Mardis Gras; but, however, I hope it is not true. A great many changes have happened in the neighbourhood, since you went away. The five Miss Moneygrubbers have settled everything with those five nice young men who live down the lane, and they have quite a large ceremony being planned, assuming they can purchase enough handkerchiefs in bulk. It is a lucky match indeed, for it seems they have been smitten with one another for some time, only the boys were too shy to act on it until their mother reminded them they might be dead of age or gangrene in only a few years."

"A great failing," noted Fanny Anne, "as women have the more tender feelings in love. Yet we cannot help ourselves or choose our own destinies. We live at home, quiet, confined, and our feelings prey upon us. You men (here she raised her eyes to the captain's if only for an instant) are forced on exertion. You have always a profession, pursuits, business of some sort or other, from harlequin college to a hotel built entirely of bananas to take you back into the world immediately, and continual occupation and change soon weaken impressions. But we women must sit endlessly in drawing rooms with nothing to occupy us, only sewing until we all go mad from it. Surely, there are true accomplishments, one of bettering others' lives, or doing good for charity, that would benefit all the world as well as the gravity of our souls." She gazed out the window at Wickham's coach. If Lydia, or Marianne, or Dilemma, had anything to do besides flirt and dream of love, surely their lives would have been fuller. "We all are devoted to love, for we have nothing else."

At this the captain looked struck to the heart, and as this

was before Kevlar vests, this seemed a near-fatal blow. He instantly turned to the desk nearby, and taking a piece of paper with a mumbled "By your leave," commenced doodling in the corner of it.

Mrs Fussbudget, paying little mention to this heartfelt speech on the frivolity of her own existence, prattled on. "And one of my own daughters is married. I suppose you have heard of it; indeed, you must have seen it in the papers. It was in the *Times* and the *Courier*, the *Onion*, and the *Turnip*, I know; though it was not put in as it ought to be. It was only said, "Lately, Willoughby Wickham, Ne'r-do-well, to Miss Lydia Fussbudget, absolute trollup," without there being a syllable said of her father, or the place where she lived, or any thing. Did you see it?"

The captain replied that he did, and made his congratulations. After the scandal, poor Marianne dared not lift up her eyes. How the admiral looked, therefore, she could not tell.

"It is a delightful thing, to be sure, to have a daughter well married," continued her mother, "but at the same time, Captain Wentworth, it is very hard to have her taken such a way from me. They are going down to Newcastle-on-time, a place quite northward, it seems, and there they are to stay I do not know how long. His regiment is there; for I suppose you have heard of his leaving the – shire for the – troops, and of his being gone into the irregulars, as the regulars are done with him. Thank Heaven! he has *some* friends, though perhaps not so many as he deserves."

Marianne, who knew this to be levelled at the admiral, was in such misery of shame, that she could hardly keep her seat. She gripped the edges hard to keep from swooning, sobbing, or worse yet, languishing. It drew from her, however, the exertion of speaking, which nothing else had so effectually done before; and she asked the captain whether he meant to make any stay in the country at present. A few weeks, he believed. And the weather? Quite fine. His health? Quite fine too. At this, sadly, all culturally-sanctioned conversational topics had been quite used up.

"When you have killed all your own birds, Captain Wentworth," said her mother, "and perhaps shot off a few fingers or toes as well, I beg you will come here, and shoot as many squirrels as you please on Mr Fussbudget's manor. I am sure he will be vastly happy to oblige you, as they are terrible pests and some of them appear to be plotting very maliciously against us."

When the gentlemen rose to go away, Mrs Fussbudget was mindful of her intended civility, and they were invited and engaged to dine at Longbore in a few days' time.

"You are quite a visit in my debt, Captain," she added, "for when you went to town last winter, you promised to take a family dinner with us, as soon as you returned. I have not forgot, you see; and I assure you, it's been warming on the back of the stove all this time and is still as fresh as it ever was."

He looked a little pained at this, and said something of his concern at having been prevented by business and by being across the country.

Mrs Fussbudget had been strongly inclined to ask them to stay and dine there that day, but she was worried because her husband had ordered quite a quantity of gruel to soothe all their nerves.

Admiral Haughtyton turned towards the door, and Captain Wentworth, too, was indeed ready, and had even a hurried, agitated air, which showed impatience to be gone. Fanny Anne knew not how to understand it. She had the kindest "Good morning" from the former, but from him not a word, nor a look. He had passed out of the room without a look!

She had only time, however, to move closer to the window, when footsteps were heard returning; the door opened; it was himself. Captain Wentworth begged their pardon, but he had forgotten his gloves, and instantly crossing the room to the writing table, and standing with his back to the other ladies, he drew out a letter from under the scattered paper, placed it before Fanny Anne with eyes of glowing entreaty fixed on her for a moment, and hastily not bothering to collect his non-existent gloves, was again out of the room, almost before Mrs Fussbudget was aware of his being in it – the work of an instant!

An instant later, the admiral was the one to re-enter the room. He too had forgotten something – his handsome peasant-beating stick in this case. While the young ladies were all fluttering about to retrieve it, he slipped a small folded missive from his waistcoat pocket and slid it atop the embroidered understockings that engaged a surprised Marianne. With a bow, he retrieved his stick and exited, Marianne's sisters none the wiser.

Just as the gentlemen had left, the servant who had accompanied the new Mr and Mrs Wickham from town brought in a letter concealed under a tea towel. This too was intended for Marianne, apparently without the knowledge of her family. On the pretext of admiring her sewing, he passed the letter to her under the towel, and departed.

"Oh," her mother said. "There's a note – "

"What!" cried Marianne and Fanny Anne together.

"– that I've written for the tradesman. Take it downstairs, Jane, do."

At this, two of the young ladies let out soft sighs of relief. Marianne was quite aquiver to discover what all this meant, but Dilemma asked her a question and her fluffy little darling head was soon diverted. Across the room, circumstances were far different.

The revolution which one instant had made in Fanny Anne was almost beyond expression. The letter, with a direction hardly legible, to "Miss F. A. C., Unattached Spinster Fated to be a Burden unless Someone Snatches her" (the correct mode of address in fashionable circles) appeared before her. On the contents of that letter depended all which this world could do for her. Any thing was possible, any thing might be defied rather than suspense. It might be a treasure map, a frivolous riddle, a lifechanging pronouncement. She hoped of course for the last of these, though treasure would also be nice. Mrs Fussbudget had little arrangements of her own at her own table; to their protection she must trust, and sinking into the chair which he had occupied, her eyes devoured the following words:

I can listen no longer in silence. I must speak to you by such means as are within my reach. You pierce my soul. I am half agony, half hope, and half gastric troubles brought on by an undercooked shepherd's pie. For no less reason, I leave you. Tell me not that I am too late, that such precious feelings are gone for ever. I offer myself to you again with a heart even more your own than when you almost broke it eight years and a half ago. Dare not say that man forgets sooner than woman, that his love has an earlier death, that he cares more for hotels built of bananas (expanding now to one built of monkeys right next door). I have loved none but you. Unjust I may have been, weak and resentful I have been, occasionally flatulent, but never inconstant. You alone have brought me to Marrytown. For you alone I think and plan. – Have you not seen this? Can you fail to have understood my wishes? – I had not waited even these three days, could I have read your feelings, as I think you must have penetrated mine. I can hardly write because of my overpowering feelings and also this cursed hook hand. I am every instant hearing something which overpowers me. You sink your voice, but I can distinguish the tones of that voice, when they would be lost on others beneath the yowling of the cat in her bonnet and the dog in his cravat where you shut them upstairs. – Too good, too excellent creature! Believe true attachment and constancy to be most fervent, most undeviating, until my death from scurvy a few years hence, in

F. W.

I must go, uncertain of my fate; but I shall return hither, or follow your party, as soon as possible if you go walking out. A word, a look, a vigorous sneeze will be enough to decide whether I enter your uncle's house this evening, or never. I really really hope it's the first one though.

Such a letter was not to be soon recovered from. Half an hour's solitude and reflection might have tranquillized her; but the ten minutes only, which now passed before she was interrupted, with all the restraints of her situation, could do nothing towards tranquillity. Every moment rather brought fresh agitation. It was overpowering happiness.

The absolute necessity of seeming like herself produced in Fanny Anne an immediate struggle; but after a while she could do no more. She began not to understand a word the ladies said, and was obliged to plead her own terrible gastric troubles and excuse herself. They could then see that she looked very ill – were shocked and concerned – and would not stir without her for the world. This was dreadful! Would they only have gone away, and left her in the quiet possession of that room, it would have been her cure; but to have them all standing or waiting around her was distracting, and, in desperation, she said she would go for a walk. Dilemma eagerly volunteered to come along and bring Jane Harriet; there was no preventing her. This was almost cruel!

They were on Bunion Street, when a quicker step behind, a something of familiar sound, gave her two moments preparation for the sight of Captain Wentworth. He joined them; but, as if irresolute whether to join or to pass on, said nothing – only looked. Fanny Anne could command herself enough to receive that look, and gaze at him with a little veiled admiration though to meet his eyes on the cusp of a deeper attachment still seemed remarkably immodest. The cheeks which had been pale now glowed, and the movements which had hesitated were decided. He walked by her side. He mentioned the weather and inquired if their healths had changed in the last quarter hour and expressed relief they had not.

Presently, as if struck by a sudden thought, Dilemma said, "Captain Wentworth, which way are you going? Only to Filth-street, or farther up the town?"

"I hardly know," replied Captain Wentworth, surprised.

"Are you going as high as High Street? Are you going near Near Lane? Because if you are, I shall have no scruple in asking you to take my place, and give Fanny Anne your arm. She is rather done for this morning, and must not go so far without help. And I ought to be calling on my dear friend, whom I hear has taken ill with a severe infection from a splinter and will shortly die."

There could not be an objection. There could be only the most proper alacrity, a most obliging compliance for public view; and smiles reined in and spirits dancing in private rapture. In half a minute, Dilemma, Jane Harriet's hand in hers, was racing around the corner, gloating at her own cleverness, and the other two proceeding together; and soon words enough had passed between them to decide their direction towards the comparatively quiet and retired graveyard, where the power of conversation would make the present hour a blessing indeed; and prepare for it all the immortality which the happiest recollections of their own future lives could bestow until they should find themselves permanent residents there. There they exchanged again those feelings and those promises which had once before seemed to secure every thing, but which had been followed by so many, many years of division and estrangement. There they returned again into the past, more exquisitely happy, perhaps, in their re-union, than when it had been first projected; more tender, more tried, more fixed in a knowledge of each other's character, truth, and attachment; more equal to act, more justified in acting. Bluebirds spontaneously fluttered in circles around them, joyfully devouring the butterflies who had arrived for the same task.

At last Fanny Anne was at home again, and happier than any one in that house could have conceived. All the surprise and suspense, sensibility, and persuasion, and every other painful part of the morning dissipated by this conversation, she re-entered the house so happy as to be obliged to find an alloy in some momentary apprehensions of its being impossible to last. An interval of meditation, serious and grateful, was the best corrective of every thing dangerous in such high-wrought felicity; and she went to her room, and grew steadfast and fearless in the thankfulness of her enjoyment. For indeed, the feeling of emotions, even on one's engagement day, was a heady and self-indulgent practice; Fanny must calm herself and prepare to enter into domestic bliss with a reverent, even mouselike unassuming modesty. Her brother would surely be overjoyed, and even more surely, would talk enough for the both of them.

NONSENSIBILITY

Chapter 16: Further Correspondence

Meanwhile, Marianne, crouched behind a hedge with her skirts all in the mud, took advantage of the momentary quiet to unwrap her letters. She began with the servant's as this might be a more immediate matter. However, as she discovered, it was not a report of Lydia's latest behaviour, but a note from Mrs Minor-Character in town.

My Dear Niece,

I can be silent no longer – though I was sworn to silence and kept it up for nearly a full week, I must tell you the particulars of Lydia's wedding, and how it all came to pass. On the very day of my coming home from Longbore, your uncle had a most unexpected visitor. Admiral Haughtyton called, and was shut up with him several hours. It was all over before I arrived; so my curiosity was not so dreadfully racked as your's seems to have been, thanks to my handy drinking glass, sent over by your mother expressly for evesdropping purposes some years ago. He came to tell Mr Minor-Character that he had found out where your sister and Mr Wickham were, and that he had seen and talked with them both; Wickham repeatedly, Lydia once. He also took them to see street theatre and bought them sausages, but that is of no matter. From what I can collect, he came to town with the resolution of hunting for them. The motive professed was his conviction of its being owing to himself that Wickham's worthlessness had been a closely-guarded secret for some truly stuffy reason, thus allowing every young woman in Marrytown to fall prey to his advances. Indeed, three are in a delicate and terribly scandalous condition, but as long as your sister is safely packed off, we need say no more about that.

He saw Wickham, and afterwards insisted on seeing Lydia. After all this visiting and seeing, he began talking. Indeed, he talked so long that I heard it reported they both fell asleep, only to be kicked awake so he continued continue blasting their ears with his diatribes.

Our visitor was very obstinate. Nothing was to be done that he did not do himself. Indeed, the admiral arranged the periwinkle coloured tablecloths with little matching place cards, the four-tiered cake, the orchestra, the little baggies of almonds. He took Lydia dress shopping and lectured her on shoes for not less than two hours. And he attended, shotgun at the ready, to see their nuptials take place.

But, Marianne, this must go no farther than yourself, or Dilemma at most. You know pretty well, I suppose, what has been done for the young people. His debts are to be paid, amounting, I believe, to considerably more than a thousand pounds, another thousand in addition to her own settled upon her, and his commission purchased. The admiral bought them his and hers slippers, matched luggage, monogrammed handkerchiefs, and all the requirements of a settled marriage according to British law.

Will you be very angry with me, my dear Marianne, if I take this opportunity of saying (what I was never bold enough to say before) how much I like him. His understanding and opinions all please me; he wants nothing but a little more liveliness, to hop and skip and enjoy his many decades of life to their fullness. I thought him very sly; – he hardly ever mentioned your name. But slyness seems the fashion. But I must write no more. The children have been playing in the street this half hour, all the while in danger of being run over by a hackney cab.

Your's, very sincerely,
M. Minor-Character.

The contents of this letter threw Marianne into a flutter of spirits, in which it was difficult to determine whether pleasure or pain bore the greatest share. The vague and unsettled suspicions of how this match could have come about were proved beyond their greatest extent to be true!

Admiral Haughtyton had followed them purposely to town, he had taken on himself all the trouble and mortification attendant on such a research; in which supplication had been necessary to a woman whom he must abominate and despise, and where he was reduced to meet, frequently meet, reason with, persuade, bribe, and likely kick in the teeth of the man whom he always most wished to avoid, and whose very name it was punishment to him to pronounce thanks to his own bad teeth. He had done all this for a girl whom he could neither regard nor esteem. Her heart did whisper that he had done it for her. But it was a hope shortly checked by other considerations, and she soon felt that even her vanity was insufficient, when required to depend on his affection for her – for a woman who had already refused him – as able to overcome a sentiment so natural as abhorrence against relationship with Wickham. Brother-in-law of Wickham! Every kind of pride must revolt from the connexion. Even her own relation with the man left her prepared to vomit.

With a sob of self-indulgent shame, she then opened the second letter. This one was much briefer, the shortest letter any of the sisters had ever received, without pages of family history or scandal at all – with many compliments and apologies for the impropriety, he hoped he might have the pleasure of speaking with her, if she were to walk out.

She stood from her crouch only to find herself nearly bumping heads with the admiral himself. He bowed, imperilling her right eye with his monumentally pointy three-quarter hat, then giving her a moment to straighten and compose herself before he greeted her with polite civility. She responded to his obligatory concerns for her health and her family's, and they passed a few minutes in ordinary compliments before she suddenly burst out, "Admiral, I am a very selfish creature; and, for the sake of giving relief to my own feelings, care not how much I may be wounding yours. I can no longer help thanking you for your unexampled kindness to my poor sister. Were it known to the rest of my family, I should not have merely my own gratitude to express.

They would fall at your feet, grip your ankles, and fawn all over you, even more than they have already. Let me thank you again and again, with sobs and torrents of guilt and gratitude in the name of all my family, for that generous compassion which induced you to take so much trouble, and bear so many painful, terrible mortifications, for the sake of discovering them. Oh, how I must sob and gesticulate at the terribleness of it all!"

"If you will thank me," he replied quietly, "let it be for yourself alone. Your family owe me nothing. Much as I respect them (and here the admiral seemed to choke a little on the word), I believe I thought only of you."

For the first time in her life, Marianne was too much embarrassed to say a word. After a short pause, her companion added, "I have every hope that your friend Miss Collins will soon have some happy news to share with you all!"

"Miss Collins? Oh, how gratifying." For she and all her sisters had an inclination what this might be, though the change in topic was rather confounding.

"And this joyous circumstance gives me the opportunity – frees me to relate – oh! There is so much to say!"

"On what matter?" Marianne asked a bit timidly. Within her all was a terrible jumble, her thoughts and feelings all colliding. She scarcely knew whether to sing or sob.

"A matter of great delicacy, but one I feel – I insist to myself – you must know. This is a personal story, of great scandal."

"Ooh, that is more like it," Marianne said eagerly. She seated herself on a nearby hedge, which promptly gave way under her, and prepared for a lengthy tale. He obliged:

"I grew up in the country, where I became much attached to my father's only ward. This lady was one of my nearest relations, an orphan from her infancy. Our ages were nearly the same, and from our earliest years we were playfellows and friends, romping unsupervised in the nearby fields. I cannot remember the time when I did not love Eliza; and my affection for her, as we grew up, was such, as, perhaps, judging from my present stately and cheerless gravity, you might think me incapable of having ever felt. We tripped through tulips, frolicked in the fields, and romped in the roses – though owing to the thorns, this was a dreadful mistake indeed. Hers, for me, was, I believe, fervent as the attachment of your sister to Mr Wickham, and it was, though from a different cause, no less unfortunate. At seventeen she was lost to me for ever. She was married – married against her inclination to my brother, a terribly wicked soul. My brother did not deserve her; he did not even love her.

"I had hoped that her star-crossed love for me would somehow comfort her under any difficulty, even marriage to a terrible man, and for some time it did; but at last the misery of her situation, for she experienced great unkindness as he ridiculed her oversensitive, weepy poetry and ate her pet parrot, overcame all her resolution, and though she had promised me that nothing – but how blindly I relate and with how many dependent clauses! I have never told you how this was brought on. We were within a few hours of eloping together for Scotland. The treachery, or the folly, of my cousin's maid whom I had unwisely seduced then abandoned betrayed us.

"I was banished to the house of a relation far distant, and she was allowed no liberty, no society, no amusement, not even a hair ribbon to practice tying, till my brother's point was gained. My father locked her up on artichokes in aspic and made her days a torment in that very gothic room that I showed you upon your arrival; had her marriage been happy, so young as I then was, a few months must have reconciled me to it, or at least I should have taken consolation with the many nubile maidservants serving me. This, however, was not the case. My brother had no regard for her; his pleasures were not what they ought to have been, as he graduated from devouring her parrot to preying on her beloved pony, which was also cooked and served to him. The consequence of this, upon a mind so young, so lively, so preciously inexperienced as her's, was but too natural.

"The shock which her marriage had given me," he continued, in a voice of great agitation, "was of trifling weight to what I felt when I heard, about two years afterwards, of her divorce – a far greater scandal in a proper society family than any stewing of ponies into a ragout or midnight snacking on parrot custard. This may indeed have been precipitated by a late night visit I made while my brother was away, a single night of such passion – but then stolen away forever. It was that which threw this haughty gloom, – even now the recollection of what I suffered – "

He could say no more, and, rising hastily, walked for a few minutes about the lane. Marianne Catherine's bosom heaved. A proposed elopement, a passion for a brother's wife, an affair, a divorce – here indeed was more scandals that she had ever heard described, all crowded into a single conversation. Without doubt, this was the most thrilling moment of her young life. And yet her heart turned over at the elderly gentleman's distress. He saw her concern, and coming to her, took her hand, pressed it, and kissed it with grateful respect and gnarled lips. A few minutes more of silent exertion as he tugged at his nearly non-existent hair enabled him to proceed with composure.

"It was nearly three years after this unhappy period before I returned to England. My first care, when I did arrive, was of course to seek for her; but the search was as fruitless as it was melancholy. Without a man to fill her life, she had lost her mind and wandered London half-dressed, allowing men to treat her as they would, if only at the end they would let her darn their socks and admonish them to wear a warm scarf. I could not trace her beyond her first seducer, and there was every reason to fear that she had removed from him only to sink deeper in a life of sin. Though she had written me, I later discovered, dozens of letters, propriety would not allow me to accept such things from my brother's divorced wife, so I had rejected them all. At last, however, and after I had been six months in England, I did find her. Regard for a former servant of my own, who had since fallen into misfortune, carried me to visit him in a cruel sausage factory, where they worked their prisoners day and night; and there was my unfortunate lover. To my servant I gave a lump of sugar and bade him luck with his struggle to pay back the two pounds he owed. I then turned to my poor love. So altered – so faded – worn down by acute suffering of every kind! hardly could I believe the melancholy and sickly figure before me, to be the remains of the lovely, blooming, overly attractive girl, on whom I had once doted. What I endured in so beholding her – but I have no right to wound your feelings by attempting to describe it – I have pained you too much already."

"Oh, pray continue!" Marianne breathed faintly. As she gasped for air and didn't receive it, she quickly began fanning her flushed face. She gasped for air until this suddenly brought on hiccoughs.

"That she was, to all appearance, in the last stage of dying of terrible incurable languishing, was – yes, in such a situation, it was my greatest comfort. Life could do nothing for her, beyond giving time for a better preparation for death; and that was given. I saw her placed in comfortable lodgings, and under proper attendants; a doctor offered to cure her, but it would have cost the same as my argyle socks allowance for the year and could not be thought of. Still, I hired a string quartet to play her sad airs that recalled the tragedy of our attachment; I visited her every day during the rest of her short life: I was with her in her last moments."

"Oh my poor dear! But to what does all this lead?"

"Ah! Miss Marianne – a subject such as this – untouched for twenty years – it is dangerous to handle it at all! I fear so for your poor delicate ears, which may snap under the strain. I will be more collected – more concise. She left to my care her only children, a pair of twins, the offspring of her first connexion (or so she claimed, but the date of my midnight visit to her suggests something far more), who were then about three years old. She loved the children, and had always kept them with her, even in the horrible sausage factory where everyone was dying of contagious diseases. It was a valued, a precious trust to me; and gladly would I have discharged it in the strictest sense, by watching over their education myself, had the nature of our situations allowed it; but I had no family, no home, and they both appeared more than a little dribbly."

"So you split up the identical twins, leaving each with only half a ring, and today they have found each other, quite by accident?"

He blinked, jarred momentarily form his melancholy tale. "No, indeed. The boy and girl, for so they were, I kept together. I found a worthy woman in the country and bade her pretend that the children were her own as so many of our class seem to do with such regularity. In doing so, however, I may have inadvertently complicated your family's situation exceedingly."

"Are you saying – ? No! It cannot be!"

"Indeed, William and Fanny Collins are my natural children."

"But Fanny has been washing all our unmentionables!" Marianne burst out, quite indecorously. "We have all been smiling at her lack of refinement, and now to discover her father is the wealthiest man in England! All this time she has been the most refined of all. Why have you not told her?"

His voice returned to the grave melancholy drone from his prior telling. "At sea I fell in much with Captain Wentworth. Imagine my surprise when he described his disappointment in love and I realized he had an attachment to my own natural daughter! As I discovered the gentleman's worthiness, I put him in the path to make his fortune in bananas and hotel management (though I daresay he would have succeeded without assistance) and finally escorted him to Marrytown under the pretext of building a new hotel, this one out of good English geese, so he might renew his long-delayed courtship. When all is settled without interference from me, I shall then call them into a room and dramatically relate the circumstances of her birth."

"So she is not our cousin at all," Marianne wondered. "And neither is her brother. What a pleasant – I mean, that is, oh! The entail! I had forgot! Is the house now ours, forever?"

He shook his head. "I must tell you, dear simple sweet little precious one, that entails, which pass to the nearest male relative, do not vanish because of the ineligibility of the next heir. I fear you must consult with your father for the knowledge of who lies next in line. Certainly, the truth will be a blow to Mr Collins, but I content myself in knowing I can provide for him, at least at a distance."

"You will not adopt him formally as your heir?"

He shuddered slightly. "My legitimate daughter, born to my worthy and adventurous wife, daughter of a marquis, stands ready to inherit. Unless, of course, I should marry and be so fortunate as to produce a proper son, in which case, she shall have nothing. However, I am sure something may be done for Mr Collins, in the line of a small bequest or gifts of fruit and game in season. However, with the affairs of my children settled at last, I may concentrate on my own happiness, which I daresay might finally come. If, that is – "

"Poor Mr Collins! And yet, such a romantic tale. A foundling, placed in the way of a fortune, and then suddenly deprived of it. Oh my!" Marianne turned so pale, that the admiral was obligated to help her back to the house, and his motive for telling her this must be abandoned for another occasion.

The evening came, the drawing-rooms were lighted up, the company assembled. It was but a card-party, it was but a mixture of those who had never met before, and those who met too often – those who enjoyed coffee and those who enjoyed tea with a spritz of opium; but Fanny Anne had never found an evening shorter. Glowing and lovely in sensibility and happiness, and more generally admired than she thought about or cared for, she had cheerful or forbearing feelings for every creature around her. She nearly ventured a shining smile. Lydia and Mr Wickham were out visiting, and her brother triumphant at the family's vindication, as well as his escaping a nearer connexion. Mr and Mrs Fussbudget were all smiles. Dilemma had resumed matchmaking, Scary, playing her music, and Jane Harriet, walking about – and with Captain Wentworth, some moments of communications continually occurring, and always the hope of more, and always the knowledge of his being there!

It was in one of these short meetings, each apparently occupied in admiring a fine display of green-house plants, that she boldly stole a kiss from her intended.

After they had thus reunited, she said rather priggishly – "Now that we have each other at last, I must make a pompous speech, so do settle in."

Accordingly, he seated himself on the edge of the planter, though this upturned it and got potting soil positively everywhere. After she had industriously cleaned up the mess with the embroidered dustclothes she always carried, they both resumed their places and she continued:

"I have been thinking over the past, and trying impartially to judge of the right and wrong, I mean with regard to myself; and I must believe that I was right, much as I suffered from it, that I was perfectly right in being guided by Dilemma, the friend whom you will love better than you do now. To me, she was in the place of a terribly bossy parent. Do not mistake me, however. I am not saying that she did not err in her advice. It was, perhaps, one of those cases in which advice is good or bad only as the event decides; and for myself, I certainly never should, in any circumstance of tolerable similarity, give such advice. All right, I admit, it was flat out bad. But I mean, that I was right in submitting to her, and that if I had done otherwise, I should have suffered more in continuing the engagement than I did even in giving it up, because I should have suffered in my conscience. That is far too great a punishment to bear that would forever spoil a lifetime of happiness. I have now, as far as such a sentiment is allowable in human nature, nothing to reproach myself with; and if I mistake not, a strong sense of duty far surpasses any woman's claim to happiness."

He looked at her, looked over at Dilemma, and looking again at her, replied, as if in cool deliberation, "I too have been thinking over the past, and a question has suggested itself, whether there may not have been one person more my enemy even than that lady? My own self."

She gasped at this twist, and he continued:

"Tell me if, when I returned to England in the year eight, with a few thousand pounds and as captain of the HMS Take That, Frenchies! – if I had then written to you, would you have answered my letter? Would you, in short, have renewed the engagement then and finally joined me on the high seas as my wife, to possibly be blown to bits and eat plum duff and weevily biscuit each day?"

"Would I!"

"I don't know – that's why I asked."

"Well, yes!"

"Good God!" he cried, "you would! It is not that I did not think of it, or desire it, as what could alone crown all my other success. But I was proud, too proud to ask again. I did not understand you and feared you were too prejudiced but no, it was Dilemma. I shut my eyes, and would not understand you, or do you justice. I have been such a doofus!" And with this he beat himself about the head and shoulders with his sheathed sword until Fanny Anne made him stop.

Who can be in doubt of what followed? When any two young people take it into their heads to marry, they are pretty sure by perseverance to carry their point, be they ever so poor, or ever so imprudent, or ever so hideously ugly, even. If such parties succeed, how should a Captain Wentworth and a Fanny Anne, with the advantage of pontificating maturity of mind, stuffy consciousness of right, and one successful line of banana-walled hotels with another fashioned of monkeys quite nearby and a grand estate of eighty rooms besides, fail of bearing down every opposition? They might in fact have borne down a great deal more than they met with, for there was little to distress them beyond the want of graciousness and warmth. – Mr Fussbudget made no objection, in fact, expressing his eagerness to have her off his hands straightaway, and Mrs Fussbudget did nothing worse than look bluntly disappointed and suddenly become ill in an antique vase.

The only one among them whose opposition of feeling could excite any serious anxiety was Dilemma. Fanny Anne knew that Dilemma must be making some struggles to become truly acquainted with, and do justice to Captain Wentworth despite his wealth, gentility, and success. This however was what Dilemma had now to do. She must discover that she had been a meddlesome bossypants; that because Captain Wentworth's manners had not suited her own ideas, she had been too quick in suspecting them to indicate a character of dangerous impetuosity. There was nothing less for Dilemma to do, than to admit that she had been pretty completely wrong, and to find other couples to browbeat in and out of marriage.

As the family celebrated this engagement, and Mrs Fussbudget put her best face on a set on disappointed hopes, and concluded aloud that perhaps Fanny Anne would feel indebted to the family and make generous presents to her cousins, only Marianne dwelt in unhappiness. As she sat in the garden the next day, thoughts turned round and round in her head. Admiral Haughtyton's behaviour astonished and vexed her.

"Why, if he came only to be silent, grave, and indifferent," said she, "and impart terrible confidences to me and then convey me home, did he come at all?"

She could settle it in no way that gave her pleasure. "A man who has once been accused of murdering his first wife, by one he might be considering for his second! And then to have her become in-laws to his most hated foe! And then to have her have a fit of indecorous hiccoughs! How could I ever be foolish enough to expect a confession of his love? Is there one among the sex, who would not protest? If he fears me, why come hither? If he no longer cares for me, why silent? Teazing, teazing, man! I will think no more about him. I will turn my attention to another, worthier suitor."

When Marianne Catherine had discovered that Mr Collins was in fact a foundling, her feelings toward him began to warm, however, these sentiments vanished as soon as she met him in person again.

Of course, her resolution to think elsewhere could not be kept, and she tossed far into the night, heaving and groaning with terrible passion.

NONSENSIBILITY

Chapter 17: Mr Wickham Departs

Dilemma sat outside Longbore feeling quite wretched. Her attempts to match Fanny Anne with the admiral, to pair Scary with Mr Collins, all had come to naught. Her own conduct, as well as her own heart, was before her in the same few minutes. She saw it all with a clearness which had never blessed her before. How improperly had she been acting by them all! How inconsiderate, how indelicate, how irrational, how unfeeling had been her conduct! What blindness, what madness, had led her on! It struck her with dreadful force, and she was ready to give it every bad name in the world, even a few from her naughtiest novels.

She was roused from her seat, and her reflections, by someone's approach; and before she could strike into another path, she was overtaken by Wickham.

"I am afraid I interrupt your solitary ramble, my dear sister?" said he, as he joined her.

"You certainly do," she replied with a smile; "but it does not follow that the interruption must be unwelcome."

"I should be sorry indeed, if it were. We were always good friends; and now we are better."

"True. Are the others coming out?"

"I do not know. Mrs Fussbudget and Lydia are going in the carriage to Marrytown. I was surprised to see Haughtyton in town last month. We passed each other several times. I wonder what he can be doing there."

"Perhaps preparing for his marriage with some society lady," said Dilemma. "It must be something particular, to take him there at this time of year." For Marianne had already acquainted her with the particulars of the admiral's grand gesture. "I did hear, too, that there was a time, when harlequin college was not so palatable to you as it seems to be at present; that you actually declared your resolution of never taking a position in the circus, and that the business had been compromised accordingly."

"You did! and it was not wholly without foundation. You may remember what I told you on that point, when first we talked of it. I chose my words of complaint very carefully indeed."

Unwilling, for her sister's sake, to provoke him, she only said in reply, with a good-humoured smile, "Come, Mr Wickham, we are brother and sister, you know. Do not let us quarrel about the past. In future, I hope we shall be always of one mind."

She held out her hand; he kissed it with affectionate gallantry, though he hardly knew how to look, and they turned toward the house. Then Dilemma paused. "Mr Wickham, I must speak with you further."

"Oh yes?"

"Yes indeed. What you did to my sister was reprehensible. I admit, I encouraged my sisters to pursue you, and was friendly and welcoming myself, but you are a rake, a scoundrel, and the foulest cad. Our family will never forgive you for ruining her."

"Oh come now, we only had a bit of fun, a bit of adventure." Wickham smiled the disarming smile that had charmed his way out of so many disasters in the past. "Lydia was bored in an endless schedule of embroidery and frivolous accomplishments."

"Frivolous accomplishments." The fact that Dilemma agreed with this assessment was not of immediate importance. Far more interesting was that they were rounding the archery shed. She lifted a perfectly-strung bow from the table where one of her sisters had abandoned it earlier that day, fitted an arrow to it, and aimed it straight between Wickham's eyes.

"Indeed, you are right," she said. "I find myself terribly bored with learning accomplishments all day. Indeed, so bored am I that I might perhaps let go of this tense string, which is wearying my fingers, and see what may occur."

Wickham backed away in terror. "I assure you, your point is made. Do remember, dear sister, that I have made amends to your family, all indeed, that it is possible to do."

"Have you?" Dilemma asked, gazing thoughtfully into space and swinging the bow down toward a part of Wickham's anatomy that made him flinch all over again, "I do not think that is true. For, look, you have not apologized to any of us, or assured us you have changed, or asked how you night be of service to us after your 'little adventure.' Indeed, if my sister has found herself so uncivilized a husband, I think it my duty to impart a few lessons."

Wickham hastily began to stammer all that she might wish to this effect, but then two more of the sisters came upon this juicy tableaux.

"I say," said Marianne Catherine. "Is Wickham obliging you with an archery target? For that seems a more useful skill than I had dreamed he could supply. Tell me, dear sister, is there another bow?"

"No need," said Scary, "when I've my knitting needles and scissors in my housewife here." And she drew the terribly glittery and offensive objects for her sister to see. "Would you care for one or the other?"

"With all my heart," Marianne Catherine said. As Wickham gulped and backed away, arrow still trained on him, we must close the curtain of discretion over the scene, for the young Fussbudget ladies may be less than ladylike as they try their accomplishments in new directions.

"Has anyone seen my dear Wickham?" Lydia inquired at dinner.

"Indeed, yes," Dilemma said. "He has removed himself from the house at present, but he offers you a choice. He will be delighted to accompany you to his regiment, with the understanding that if he ever strays or makes you unhappy, a bevy of your sisters will arriving with knitting needles and suchlike to permanently incapacitate him. Or he offers you this." She held out a will, carefully witnessed and notarized in town, offering Lydia all the money on the event of Wickham's death. "You may have everything that Admiral Haughtyton offered Wickham and the identity of a widow, if you choose. Wickham will disappear and change his name, continuing his profligate life where it can no longer offend you. Do consider, sister – total independence and freedom to do as you will, or a life of indignities and sorrow, chained to the cheating filth who meant to ruin you for his own amusement."

"Oh I am," Lydia said readily. She plucked the will from her sister's hand. "A life of true independence, with enough money to have some real fun with and no family nattering on about propriety. At last I can do what I like!"

"But your reputation – " her mother protested.

"Hang my reputation. You know propriety has never appealed for me. I want to go to France, have a string of affairs, perhaps turn actress or somesuch. But I will be choosing the affairs, not some weak-willed man upon whom I must base my entire identity." She perceived the looks of horror round the table and gave a pretty shrug. "Fear not, it will be Wickham's name I shall drag through the mud, not yours. And when he hears of my success, ooh how he shall squirm!"

Her parents exchanged uneasy glances, but Lydia had always been determinedly headstrong. And as a widow doing what she pleased in Europe, far away and under a new name, she would bring less scandal to the family, or so they could hope. At any rate, she would be far happier there than as Mrs Wickham, slave to an undeserving and profligate husband.

"Remember that a woman's reputation once lost – "

"Oh, stuff it, Scary, you've never had fun in your whole life."

"Ah but I intend to." Everyone jumped. This was more surprising than Lydia's announcement. "A very worthy gentleman has asked me to be his wife, and I believe we shall suit admirably."

"Mr Collins?" Dilemma asked before she could help it.

"No indeed. Though his moralizing does not grate on me as it does on the rest of you, I must condemn him as a rather silly and self-serving individual. No, Mr Tightly-Wound has made me an offer, and I plan to accept it, as his grave demeanour, firm character, and stuffy boringness seem to me the epitome of a gentleman. I must inform you I shall now have finances greater than all of my sisters. For indeed, he is very well off, and he says that his slight deafness need not prevent him from enjoying my musical offerings."

Mrs Fussbudget beamed. "My dear middle girl married. And my Lydia..." here she paused, and then resigned herself to the most positive light of the situation. "Rich and happy. I tell you, dearest, if I was not so well-settled here in Marrytown, I might be tempted to join you."

"My dear!" her husband erupted in horror. And so we shall leave the Fussbudgets with the newly widowed Mrs Wickham, ready to depart on more adventures.

NONSENSIBILITY

Epilogue

Dilemma was one of those born to be a matchmaking widow, unfettered by a husband and wholly in command of her own property. As such, Mr Tightly-Wound might have been a well-reasoned choice as a match notably older than herself. But Dilemma found herself seeking a helpmate her own age – one who could be controlled, dominated, and quelled into submission as her mother had her father.

As in so many romantic novels, as Dilemma gazed about herself, this affectionate object appeared. Edward Edmunds, the polite, aimless lad whom she had rescued at Netherbum, was the proper degree of near-incestuousness popular among the aristocracy and now destined to inherit Longbore now that Mr Collins was ineligible. All his life he had looked toward the clergy, but could not be counted on to commit to it or anything else. His speech was so deferential and milksoppish that no one was in any danger of understanding his desires and thus had no need to heed them. He had until recently been under the thumb of a domineering mother, but happily the lady had just gone to her just rewards, leaving a place in Edward's life for a lady to quite take it over. This Dilemma did with a ready will, almost from the moment she had heard he was to inherit, and before the young man knew what had happened, he was established in the county parish, with Dilemma only waiting an auspicious day for them to say their vows.

Happy for all her maternal feelings was the day on which Mrs Fussbudget got rid of her two most deserving daughters, Dilemma and Scary. With what delighted pride she afterwards visited Mrs Edmunds and Mrs Tightly-Wound, may be guessed. I wish I could say, for the sake of her family, that the accomplishment of her earnest desire in the establishment of so many of her children produced so happy an effect as to make her a sensible, amiable, well-informed woman for the rest of her life; though perhaps it was lucky for her husband, who might not have relished domestic felicity in so unusual a form, that she still was occasionally nervous and invariably silly, declaring her life was at an end if the cook so much as burned the trifle.

As a married woman, Scary was obliged to mix more with the world, but she could still moralize over every morning visit; and as she was no longer mortified by comparisons between her sisters' beauty and her own, it was suspected by her husband that she submitted to the change without much reluctance. She and Mr Tightly-Wound could be heard criticizing each change of fashion, each article of the newspaper, each of their neighbours, and they were never happier than in doing so.

Mr Fussbudget missed his eldest daughter exceedingly; his affection for her drew him oftener from home than any thing else could do. He delighted in going to the parsonage, especially when he was least expected. His daughter's voice, booming commands at her henpecked husband, reminded him greatly of home, and many were the hours he would spend on Dilemma's porch, avoiding his wife, and celebrating that he need not follow Dilemma's commands in his station in life.

Jane Harriet, to her very material advantage, spent the chief of her time with her two elder sisters. In society so superior to what she had generally known, her improvement was great. Removed from the chore of being the confidante of four livelier spinster sisters at once, she became, by proper attention and management, less ignorant and less insipid.

From the farther disadvantage of Lydia's society she was of course carefully kept, and though "Mrs Wickham" frequently invited her to come and stay with her, with the promise of balls and young men, her father would never consent to her going. She married a clerk of her uncle's, who was eager to help her achieve her literary dreams and become useful to the world and though her eldest sister was quite in shock of her sister's committing to a man "in trade" and even taking on a profession herself, she was finally forced to get over her snobbishness as her sisters reminded her that this man too might be a secretly illegitimate child to someone of significance.

"I will not say that I am disappointed, my dear sister," said Mr Collins, as they were walking together one morning near her new home at Netherbum and watching the geese struggle and flap in their new arrangement as a two-story hotel, "*that* would be saying too much, for certainly you have been one of the most fortunate young women in the world, as it is. Though he was born a commoner, your captain has acquitted himself well. But, I confess, it would give me great pleasure to call Admiral Haughtyton adoptive cousin-in-law as well as father – though this should be a tangle quite perplexing, he must then be forced to invite me now and then, as he somehow has not yet managed to do. His property near Bath, his place, his house, every thing is in such respectable and excellent condition! – and his woods! – I have not seen such timber any where, though it might be used to build hotels of something superior even to geese! – And though, perhaps, Marianne may not seem exactly the person to attract him – yet I think it would altogether be advisable for you to have them now frequently staying with you, for, nobody can tell what may happen – for, when people are much thrown together, and see little of anybody else, and are browbeaten by every one around them – and it will always be in your power to set her off to advantage, and so forth; – in short, you may as well give her a chance – You understand me."

Fanny Anne's marriage divided her as little from her many cousins as could well be contrived, without rendering the cottage at Longbore entirely useless, for her aunt and cousins spent much more than half their time with her. (Her new estate was by far grander than theirs, after all, and had entire walls in need of watercolours and embroidered panels.) Mrs Fussbudget was acting on motives of policy as well as pleasure in the frequency of her visits at Netherbum; for her wish of bringing Marianne and Admiral Haughtyton together was hardly less earnest than what Mr Collins had expressed. It was now her darling object. Precious as was the company of her daughter to her, she desired nothing so much as to fling her at their wealthiest acquaintance; and to see Marianne settled was equally the wish of Fanny Anne and Captain Wentworth. Mr Collins could barely contain himself at the prospect. Lydia, too, aware of all Admiral Haughtyton had done for her, wrote frequently to Marianne enumerating his good qualities. They each felt his sorrows, and their own obligations, and Marianne, by general consent, was to be the reward of all.

With such a confederacy badgering her night and day – with a knowledge so intimate of his tragic and checkered past – with a conviction of his fond attachment to herself, which at last, though long after it was observable to everybody else – burst on her – what could she do?

Marianne Fussbudget was born to an extraordinary fate. She was born to discover the falsehood of her own opinions, and to counteract, by her conduct, her most favourite maxims. She was born to overcome an affection formed so late in life as at seventeen, and with no sentiment superior to strong esteem and lively friendship, voluntarily to give her hand to another! – and *that* other, a man who had suffered no less than herself under the event of a former attachment, whom, a few months before, she had considered too old to be married at only three and eighty, – and who still sought the constitutional safeguard of a flannel waistcoat! She was even born to conclude this story.

While this may seem an inopportune match for such a romantic young lady, Marianne was won over by her suitor's former wickedness, with a tragic past that should comfort even the most sentimental of heroines (which Marianne so clearly was). Even more than his great fortune and majestic house was the knowledge that scandal and whispers had once followed him, that his handsome face had once tempted a girl to ruin, and that he would tend to brood over such things in a melancholy manner. This to Marianne was irresistible. (Nonetheless, she remained oblivious to any theft, counterfeiting, or scandals of a more prosaic nature. She was, after all, a fluffhead.)

Admiral Haughtyton was now as happy, as all those who best loved him, believed he deserved to be; – in Marianne he was consoled for every past affliction; – her regard and her society restored his mind to animation, and his spirits to cheerfulness; and that Marianne found her own happiness in forming his, was equally the persuasion and delight of each observing friend. Though Marianne liked him not so well happy as unhappy, she resigned herself to this too, contenting herself that she might moon over her romantic novels in the finest house in the county. With their wedding, society deemed her as fully actualized as a woman – fulfilling the role she was born for by taking care of a man for the rest of her days (or at least his). Marianne could never love by halves; and her whole heart became, in time, as much devoted to her husband and his gothic halls, as it had once been to the abstract world of gushy romance.

Willoughby Wickham could not hear of her marriage without a pang; and his punishment was soon afterwards complete in his isolated life on the continent, living under a false name. But that he was for ever inconsolable, that he fled from society, or contracted an habitual gloom of temper, or died of a broken heart, or even died of unspeakable diseases must not be depended on – for he disobligingly did none. He lived to exert, and frequently to enjoy himself. For all the Fussbudget women, however – in spite of his incivility in surviving their loss – he always retained that decided regard which interested him in every thing that befell them, and made them his secret standard of perfection in woman; – and many a rising beauty would be slighted by him in after-days as bearing no comparison with the former Miss Fussbudgets. His wife, Lydia Wickham, found this a revolting practice, but as she was busy trodding the boards in gay Paris, she pretended to give it no notice.

About the Author

Valerie Estelle Frankel is the author of many books on pop culture, including *Doctor Who – The What, Where, and How*, *Sherlock: Every Canon Reference You May Have Missed in BBC's Series 1-3*, *History, Homages and the Highlands: An Outlander Guide*, and *How Game of Thrones Will End*. Many of her books focus on women's roles in fiction, from her heroine's journey guides *From Girl to Goddess* and *Buffy and the Heroine's Journey* to books like *Women in Game of Thrones* and *The Many Faces of Katniss Everdeen*. Once a lecturer at San Jose State University, she's a frequent speaker at conferences. Come explore her research at www.vefrankel.com.